"Kansas bursts from the pages of this ingenious, dazzling collection. Andrew Malan Milward turns his home state into an enthralling main character, escorting us through corridors of history and mythology into the very core of the country."

—Shawn Vestal, author of *Daredevils* and *Godforsaken Idaho*

"'The Burning of Lawrence,' the masterful first story in Andrew Malan Milward's *I Was a Revolutionary*, is reason enough to read this remarkable collection. In that story, the narrator's guitar-playing friend says, 'I don't do political stuff. I write love songs, girl.' But Milward's collection is both political and a love song. Milward's aching ballads are about Kansas, in particular, but in their brilliant, expansive view of history, they offer penetrating insight about America as a whole. Read this book."

—Elliott Holt, author of *You Are One of Them*

"Here is history with kinetic energy. The writing is always bold, the stakes are always high. *I Was a Revolutionary* recalls W. G. Sebald in its interweaving of historical memory and present concerns, and Aleksandar Hemon in its understanding that fragments can set off adventures."

—Will Chancellor, author of *A Brave Man Seven Storeys Tall*

"I've never read anything quite like *I Was a Revolutionary*. I was stunned by how moving I found these stories. Although they center on the state of Kansas, they were deeply relevant to me as an American and a red-blooded member of the human race, in all our grief and fury and bravery and hopefulness. Andrew Malan Milward's achievement is—dare I say it?—revolutionary."

—Alan Heathcock, author of *Volt*

I

WAS A

REVOLUTIONARY

ALSO BY ANDREW MALAN MILWARD

The Agriculture Hall of Fame

I

WAS A

REVOLUTIONARY

STORIES

ANDREW

MALAN

MILWARD

HARPER ● PERENNIAL

NEW YORK ● LONDON ● TORONTO ● SYDNEY ● NEW DELHI ● AUCKLAND

HARPER ● PERENNIAL

A hardcover edition of this book was published in 2015 by HarperCollins Publishers.

I WAS A REVOLUTIONARY. Copyright © 2015, 2016 by Andrew Malan Milward. All rights reserved. Printed in the United States of America. No part of this book may be used or reproduced in any manner whatsoever without written permission except in the case of brief quotations embodied in critical articles and reviews. For information, address HarperCollins Publishers, 195 Broadway, New York, NY 10007.

HarperCollins books may be purchased for educational, business, or sales promotional use. For information, please e-mail the Special Markets Department at SPsales@harpercollins.com.

FIRST HARPER PERENNIAL EDITION PUBLISHED 2016.

Design by Fritz Metsch
Photograph on title page by GeriDagys Photography/iStock Photos

Library of Congress Cataloging-in-Publication Data has been applied for.

ISBN 978-0-06-237732-6 (pbk.)

16 17 18 19 20   OV/RRD   10 9 8 7 6 5 4 3 2 1

AUTHOR'S NOTE

"The Burning of Lawrence" appeared in *Zoetrope All-Story*, fall 2007. It was a finalist for the 2008 National Magazine Award and included in *Best New American Voices 2010*, edited by Dani Shapiro.

"O Death" appeared in *FiveChapters*, August 2012.

"Hard Feelings" appeared in *Story*, winter 2014.

"Good Men a Long Time Gone" appeared in *American Short Fiction*, spring 2015.

"What Is to Be Done?" appeared in *Ninth Letter*, winter 2015.

"I Was a Revolutionary" appeared in *Virginia Quarterly Review*, spring 2015.

For Renée and Cal,
Believers

It is impossible to play with history. Here the punishment follows immediately upon the crime.

—LEON TROTSKY, *Literature and Revolution*

Remarkable things went on, certainly, but there's been so much trouble in the world since then it's hard to find time to think about Kansas.

—MARILYNNE ROBINSON, *Gilead*

CONTENTS

I
WAS A
REVOLUTIONARY

THE BURNING OF LAWRENCE

(1) Photograph

In the photograph from 1912, taken forty-nine years after the raid, the remaining men kneel, sit, and stand in wide rows three deep. As I count it, there are nearly fifty in all. The photographer had to move the camera so far back that their expressions are only the ghosts of expressions. You can tell they are hardened, though—gaunt and weathered; these are faces upon which to break firewood. Some look as though they might be smiling, others grimacing. By virtue of their posture and the positioning of their heads, one gives off an air of pride while his neighbor communicates shame. By this time they were old men in suits with canes and prickly gray beards. Before the raid they had been farmers, had survived the bitter fighting of the Civil War, and now they found themselves in a new world, with Europe fixing to blow like a powder keg. These men survived the raid, but they weren't *survivors* of the raid. They were who was left of Quantrill's band of 450 men who rode through Lawrence, Kansas, in August of 1863 and murdered most of the men and boys in town.

So I return to the photo: How long had it been since they'd seen each other? Whose idea was it to have this strange reunion? Did they speak of the raid? What on earth did they talk about? I think of myself and wonder: Where are all the women?

(2) The Secret Bride

On the eve of the raid, Quantrill is sullen, stalking, brood-
ing—in love. He has left his men at the camp, hidden in the
covering brush and mouthlike gorges of Sni-A-Bar, and snuck
away to see his young mystery bride. The men whisper about
her; there are rumors, but few have ever actually seen her. She
is young, just thirteen, and he wants her unsullied, protected
from the glower of his men. Tonight he and Kate walk through
the spinney of oak trees near her parents' home, fingers laced,
and he builds a fire along the banks of the creek. Like others,
she pronounces his name *Quantr-elle* after a misspelling in the
newspaper, and he hasn't corrected her, thinking the sound
sweet and exotic. For a time she lets his hand inch up her naked
thigh, beneath the thinning brown dress she's worn all summer, and he knows he should take her right there and make
love to her, but he can't. His mind's awash, thinking about tomorrow, the ride into Lawrence. He knows he very well might
not return, knows the chances are quite good in fact, but this
is a war after all, even if he and his men are uncommissioned,
unofficered, and unacknowledged by Southern leadership. A
few nights ago, prior to taking the vote, he announced his
intentions by yelling, "We need to burn that gal-boy to the
ground," and his men thundered their approval, stamping their
boots and rifle butts in the dirt, and then passed the vote unan-
imously. But as he worked to finalize the plans over the next
few days, he walked through camp and heard rumblings of
suicide, impossible, tyrannical.

"I'm going to Lawrence tomorrow," he says now, and Kate
smiles, taking his hand. She wants to ask why but thinks better
of it, knowing well enough the answer is simply that he must
go. Like every other time he's left, she fears he won't return, that
she'll never see him again. She wants to seize his hand quickly

and say something—*Don't go* or *Put yourself on me and give me a baby*—but can't bring herself to speak, her young body fit to explode in a burst of light and heat. For some time they sit silent, watching the play of fire against shadow until she grabs his hand and says coyly, "How many men have you killed?" This is a joke they have, a game, something she asks often in jest, though in truth the thought excites her. He is, after all, famous. And Quantrill, being a gentleman and a liar, responds, "None, my dear. I've never harmed a soul." Before leaving he leans forward and, as her father does every night, kisses her forehead.

(3) Book, Monument

Written during the Depression, the WPA guide to Kansas describes a Lawrence with three hotels, twenty-five-cent movie houses, and a population of 13,726. It tells the origin of the University of Kansas and of the other institute of higher learning: Haskell Indian Junior College, where "smartly clad Indian coeds and white-collared braves seek to adjust themselves to a new culture, replacing lacrosse and old war cries with football and 'Rah! Rah! Haskell.'" There is mention of the town's historical importance as the center of the abolitionist movement in Kansas, noting John Brown and other Jayhawkers who fought to keep Kansas a free state after the Kansas–Nebraska Act of 1854 allowed the citizens of the territory to decide for themselves. Northerners, many from Massachusetts, flooded into the territory, armed to the teeth, as did pro-slavery Missourians like Quantrill and his raiders, and what followed were years of atrocities on both sides. In the history section of the guide there is a brief reference to the raid: "At daybreak on August 21, 1863, Lawrence citizens were aroused by the sound of firing and the shouts of guerrilla raiders who swept down on the town from the east, led by the notorious irregular, William

Clarke Quantrill. . . . After four hours they withdrew, leaving 150 dead and the major portion of the town in ruins. So futile was the resistance offered by the surprised and terror-stricken citizens that the Quantrill band retired with the loss of only one man."

By the time I enrolled at KU in the mid-nineties, the town's population had swelled to nearly one hundred thousand, and movie tickets were seven dollars. Haskell had grown to become one of the largest Native American universities in the country, and, needless to say, there were many more hotels. Having grown up in Lawrence, I'd learned about the raid as a young girl, probably in school, and promptly forgotten about it. However, the name *Quantrill* floated in my unconscious, something, like so many occupants of that dream space, at once intensely familiar and foreign. It wasn't until my sophomore year of college, when I went on a dark walk with a boy, that Quantrill returned to me permanently.

This boy and I shared a row in the huge auditorium that held our 8:00 a.m. American history survey. There, as we sat amidst the pajama'd and unwashed masses, our eyes met. A quizzical half smile was exchanged, and afterward he told me he thought the band on my T-shirt was all right. He liked music too—he played, he said, asking if I wanted to hear some songs he'd written. This was years before he'd given up on music and shipped off to fight in the wars, to die so far away. That night he led me—guitar over his shoulder, bottle of red wine in hand—to Oak Hill Cemetery. I followed, curious. I expected something dramatic, recitations of Baudelaire and running naked past gravestones, but we just drank wine while he played a few songs. I made a joke about him trying to seduce me and he laughed and then got serious, asking what I thought of his songs. I said they were beautiful, and I said they were sad.

He smiled at that. But later, when we had finished the bottle of wine, I moved closer to him, setting my hand on his knee, and he shook his leg so that my hand fell from him. And as if nothing had happened, as if I'd only just asked him a question, he told me so earnestly that he wanted his songs to be good, that he'd written them for his girlfriend. I felt embarrassed and walked away as he bent over the body of the guitar, picking at the strings.

Then, with those notes traveling in the air between us, I came upon the large granite monument and, aided by the soft light from the moon and stars, made out the engraved tribute to the victims of the raid. I had seen it once before, I realized, on a class field trip many years ago but had forgotten. In that moment, the parallax of memory upon me, time and distance disappeared and I was a young girl again, raising my hand to ask why this had happened.

(4) The Calming

Second-in-command George Todd, handsomely dressed and devilishly sharp with a pistol, makes one final stop before meeting up with Quantrill. Thinking it better to travel in smaller numbers, Quantrill had sent him to the Northland for a few days, dispatching a rider to give word of his plan to attack Lawrence. Never one to back away from a fight, Todd is excited, but he has some unfinished business to attend to before joining the others. There is a man, supposedly sympathetic to the abolitionist cause, living in S—— and for Todd his presence is unacceptable. This is Missouri after all, not Kansas. So he and his crew of twenty pay a visit to S——. When they arrive, Todd has fifteen of his men circle the house, rifles shouldered, pistols cocked, and with the others he dismounts and stalks to the front door, calmly tapping on the smooth oak as if only a neighbor wanting to draw from the well. Todd hears footsteps inside and feels the blood course through his body. When an older woman answers the door, she doesn't notice the bulging growth below his midsection because she's admiring his blue eyes, the way he stands out—with his short, well-kept brown hair and fancy attire—from the others beside him, who are shaggy, slouched, stinking. He politely inquires whether Mr. W—— is at home. But when she says he's in Kansas City and not to return for another three days, he pushes the door open. "Where is he?" he says, all rotten teeth and sneer now, as she backs away. But she's telling the truth, she swears, and so he and the men start tearing the place apart, looking for her husband. A bit of the dandy in him, Todd opens the lid of a large wooden chest in the bedroom, thinking at least he might find some nice garments worthy of expropriation. But these people are farmers and there is nothing for him but a pair of plain brown trousers worn through at the knee. A rage fills him that sends the chest flying through the air toward the bedroom wall.

After searching the house, Todd is satisfied with her answer, but not satisfied. No, he wants to prove a point—that there will be no quarter for abolitionists in Missouri—and this woman has undermined him. His blood has cooled, settling like the thick lip on curdled milk. He looks around the room, his men's eyes expectant as puppies', waiting for the order to torch the place. But what Todd spies by the window, overlooking the stretch of poorly tended wheat fields starved with drought, is an organ.

"Why do you have this?" he says.

"My husband—"

"Shut up."

He moves over to the bench and sits. His foot begins to pump the organ, slowly at first and then quicker as he feels the great suck of air fill the machine. He lets a mischievous pinkie ease down a key. The sound is loud, booming. The woman startles. Now he lays both hands on the keyboard, the old lessons coming back. His foot has found the rhythm and continues to pump as his fingers move with a long-dormant familiarity, and the sound is calming. He looks at the others in the room as he plays—outside, the horses shudder and twitch to the arresting sound, his men wondering what the hell is going on in there—and what he wants to say is: *I'm trying to tell you all something. This is how I feel.*

(5) Song

Though its invention certainly came years before, the first documentation of a traditional ballad called "Quantrill" can be traced back to the 1920s. In his book *Frontier Ballads*, Charles J. Finger recalls having heard it in Devils River, Texas. John and Alan Lomax came across it in their American wanderings as well. The lyrics imagine Quantrill as a hero.

> *Come all you bold robbers and open your ears,*
> *Of Quantrill the lion-heart you quickly shall hear.*
> *With his band of bold raiders in double-quick time*
> *He came to lay Lawrence low, over the line.*
>
> *Oh Quantrill's a fighter, a bold-hearted boy,*
> *A brave man or woman he'd never annoy.*
> *He'd take from the wealthy and give to the poor*
> *For brave men there's never a bolt to his door.*

In school I was surprised to find that the subject that most interested me was Kansas history. While the record of my home state's past had never meant much to me before, I'd taken a class that made the history come alive, made it seem relevant to the present, and it made me abandon the regular pathways to steady future employment, much to my parents' dismay. In particular, Quantrill's Raid fascinated me. Senior year, I was working on my thesis about the raid and I had a hard time finding a recording of the song. Eventually I found one by Joan O'Bryant on an old Folkways record, but before that I took the lyrics to that friend who played guitar. We still hung out now and again. By this point he'd withdrawn from school and was tending bar downtown, trying to finish songs for his album. His girlfriend was there and said she was running out for cigarettes. We smiled at each other as I entered and she left. He was sitting on the couch, and I sat across from him in a chair, the two of us talking a while. He lit a joint and took a few drags as I told him about the raid. Born out of state, he'd never heard of it. "Before Oklahoma City it was the deadliest act of domestic terrorism in our history," I said. "Right here in Lawrence."

He nodded, his eyes shot bloody, and passed me the joint. "Why don't we remember this kind of shit?"

I asked him if he could put music to the lyrics, and he took the paper from my hands and looked at it a minute. He sipped his whiskey, picked up his acoustic, and strummed a couple chords, humming a little. Then he put the guitar down and said, "Is this political? I don't do political stuff." I told him it was historical, and he dropped his pick and reached for the joint. "I write love songs, girl."

(6) Pelathe

When Quantrill's men storm into Kansas unscathed, blowing right past a number of federal checkpoints that line the border, Union leadership in Kansas City know the raiders are heading for Lawrence. It's the Free State citadel, Yankee Town, the center of militant abolitionist and Jayhawker activity, the home of despised Governor Charles Robinson and Senator Jim Lane. They know they must get word to the townsfolk of the hellfire headed their way. But Lawrence is fifty miles from the city yet, and who could beat Quantrill's men on their superior steeds?

Pelathe, a Shawnee Indian scout, happens to be accompanying one of the Union leaders when the news arrives, and asks to go, to try to beat the raiders to Lawrence. So they saddle him up with their best horse and tell him to fly. Known to other scouts as the Eagle, Pelathe does feel like a bird as he burns a trail through the brambled scrub. He rides full speed for one hour, and then two, through the night until the horse begins to fail, coming to a dead halt in the pitch-black early morning, no water in sight. There are still miles to go. He considers the beautiful animal a minute, runs a slow hand through her mane, then imagines the people in Lawrence, and so he pats her head, whispering a few final words in her ear, before unsheathing his bowie knife and pricking her shoulder with it. The horse whinnies and rears as Pelathe rubs gunpowder into the wounds, and before he can get his feet back in the irons, the sorrel mare takes off again. By means of this sacrifice he's able to get a few more miles out of her before she expires, collapsing, Pelathe tumbling forward over her. He must keep going, though, he tells himself, and begins to run until his own legs give out at the Delaware Indian tribe's camp near the outskirts of Lawrence. He tells them what is happening, of the urgency, that they must rush to town, and with fresh horses they head out, thundering through the purple of early morning. But when they get to the ferry landing on the Kaw River they see it is too late, the horror has already begun. Quantrill has beaten them to town.

(7) Seeds

A few points of interest:

- A previous raid on Lawrence occurred May 21, 1856, nearly five years before Kansas became the thirty-fourth star on the flag, and seven before Quantrill's Raid. Led by former Senate president David Atchison, a large group of Missourians stormed into town, firing cannons at the Free State Hotel and printing press and looting most of the stores.

- Following Atchison's raid, Senator Charles Sumner of Massachusetts delivered an impassioned speech on the Senate floor, lasting two entire days, called "The Crime Against Kansas." A few days later, so upset by the rhetoric of the speech and the blame assigned to Southern states, Congressman Preston Brooks of South Carolina calmly walked up to Sumner and began clubbing him with his golden-knobbed cane for several uninterrupted minutes, until the cane broke, upon which time he attempted to stab Sumner with the splintered end, giving the senator a beating from which he would not recover for three years.

- When news of the caning reached Kansas, John Brown demanded retribution. With his company of Free State Volunteers, he set out for Pottawatomie Creek, calling for the lives of five pro-slavery men. This, he said, was what God had told him he must do. First he directed the group to the Doyle family's cabin and led two of Mr. Doyle's sons outside, where they were stabbed, dismembered, and pierced in their sides in front of their father and mother. Then Brown produced a pistol and shot Mr. Doyle in the head. After two more stops of a similar fashion, Brown had his five.

- And so it went, back and forth like this for the next several years, raids perpetrated by both sides with the innocent often paying the price. Like the women who were rounded up in Missouri by federal soldiers and taken to Kansas City and placed in a dilapidated jail cell on suspicion of aiding the rebel bushwhackers. Some of these women were in fact the wives, mothers, and sisters of Quantrill's men. So when the jail collapsed, killing a number of them, one knew there would be consequences. Eight days later, Quantrill was leading his men into Lawrence.

(8) Forever the South

The first to die are the young boys from the Fourteenth Kansas Regiment, encamped on the edge of town, training to join up with the Union Army. Quantrill's men cut right through them, picking the thirteen- and fourteen-year-olds off as they sleep, or as they wander out of their tents, scratching their heads and balls, rubbing their eyes, wondering what the hell all the racket is, then *boom*: they're dead. They are unarmed and defenseless thanks to a recent city ordinance forwarded by Mayor Collamore decreeing all weapons in Lawrence be kept locked inside the armory as a safety measure—all those reliably accurate Sharps rifles sent by train to Lawrence from eastern abolitionists in boxes labeled BIBLES so as to go unsearched.

Two blocks away, the Second Colored Regiment, a camp of black troops, reach for pistols that aren't on their hips, rifles that aren't slung over their shoulders, and must make a tough decision. Twenty or so stay long enough to be slaughtered while others flee for the river, away from Quantrill's men, wading across, silently cursing their lack of weapons, then themselves, their unwillingness to martyr.

At five-thirty in the morning, Massachusetts Street is bedlam, horses thundering every which way, raiders making easy work of scurrying storeowners—targets hardly more difficult than lone whiskey bottles atop fence posts. Quantrill watches with an unsettled, pensive look: things are going too well; any minute, surely, the federals will sweep through and send his men hightailing back toward the border. He is supposed to die today. But the army never comes and soon his stony look gives way to amusement as cries of his name, audible over pistol shots and whinnies, sound all around him: *Long live Quantrill! Long live Jefferson Davis! Forever the South!* Sure that this raid will win him the respect and recognition of the Confederate army, he is already savoring the sweet euphony of: *General Quantrill.*

Some years ago, before the war, Quantrill had lived in Lawrence for a time, and now he notes the unexpected pleasures of destroying the familiar. He visits Eldridge House, a hotel, the largest building in town, taking a seat in the lobby after his men have cleared the rooms and rounded up the guests. "How about some breakfast," Quantrill says to the proprietor, who hurries to the kitchen to prepare the food himself. Upstairs, Quantrill's men loot the rooms, stuffing into their pockets watches, jewelry, and women's silken undergarments of amethyst, rouge, and Nile green. Downstairs, the collected guests consider their impending execution, silently mouthing prayers, smatterings of whispered mercies, watching the back of the man who will issue the order, if it is to be. Quantrill sits down at a table by the window, watching the theater in the street, waiting for his biscuits and eggs, listening to the anxious shifting of bodies behind him. Yet his mind is elsewhere, away, thinking of Kate, humming a ballad: "*I don't know when I'll see you again, my dear . . .*" He closes his eyes and sees her face, beautiful, but then her mouth is asking why he's left her and gone to Lawrence.

"What do you want to do?" George Todd asks. "Leave them or kill them?"

One of the ladies shifts her weight to the other foot, nudging a chair, which squeaks, as Quantrill thinks, relishing the privilege of mercy. He tells Todd to take them over to City Hall as prisoners of war. As Todd is about to lead the prisoners into the street, he notices one man wearing a Union uniform: Captain Banks, provost marshal of Kansas. He inspects the man's clothing, examining the pretty blue coloring and careful stitching. He moves over to Banks, hand on his gun, leaning close to his face, and says, "Gimme your clothes," making the captain undress right there in front of him.

(9) Film

In Ang Lee's 1999 film *Ride with the Devil*, Tobey Maguire plays a Dutch emigrant, now living in Missouri, who takes up the Southern cause, joining the irregulars waging guerrilla warfare on the Kansas-Missouri border. It's a fictionalized account, based on a novel called *Woe to Live On*, though, interestingly, the movie's title is borrowed from an earlier biography of Quantrill. It's mostly a buddy movie and a love story, but Quantrill does make an appearance, a kind of historical cameo almost no one would recognize. Lee attempts to re-create the raid on Lawrence, devoting roughly ten minutes to it, and most of the sequences carry the bogus verisimilitude of Wild West reenactments at Boot Hill in Dodge City. The best part of the movie is before the raid, when Quantrill and his men gather atop Mount Oread, from which they look down at the sleeping, unsuspecting town. Quantrill, played by John Ales, passes out death lists bearing the names, ranked by importance, of the men to kill. He offers a few brief remarks, which elicit a cacophonous hodgepodge of syllables belonging to words like *abolitionistfuckerswhoresniggersfreesoilers*, and the men raise their hats and scarves and head down the mountain in a thunderous swirl of dust, pounding hooves, and rebel yells.

It's not the first film to feature Quantrill. The earliest dates back to 1914, a two-reeler called *Quantrell's Son*, and there was a slew of B westerns in the forties and fifties in which Quantrill, or some incarnation of Quantrill, appears. In *Dark Command*, from 1940, he is Will Cantrell, played by Walter Pidgeon, a Lawrence schoolteacher who loses a local sheriff's election and his girlfriend to John Wayne, which combine to become the impetus for his raid. In this movie, however, the raid fails, and it ends with Wayne killing Pidgeon. The film's not alone in playing fast and loose with history, and it's certainly not the only one to change the outcome of the raid. But even the ones that don't do so—and I've seen them all—approach the raid timidly, presenting a toothless version of the event.

I tried to tell this to the guitar player when he accompanied me to a matinee showing of *Ride with the Devil*. The movie had come out soon after I graduated, and I was working odd jobs around Lawrence, thanks to my history degree. I saw it eight times before it left Liberty Hall, and on the occasion I took him with me I spent most of the movie leaning over to explain the historical references and inaccuracies. God, how annoying I must have been, but he listened politely, eyes moving between the screen and me. When it was over, he said he was glad I'd brought him, and we smiled at each other. It seemed like something might happen. But when I told him that just once I wished I could see the movie the way he had, without any background knowledge, he grew defensive, distant, and said it seemed like I had enjoyed it pretty well anyway. This was around the time he was starting to get local gigs, playing that night at the Bottleneck, a big deal. He was stuck on some new girl, he said, and was writing great songs about the one who'd just left. I told him I wouldn't be able to come but showed up later, halfway through his set, and stood in the back of the bar, nursing a beer, watching him sing songs about girls he'd left and been left by.

(10) Three Ghosts

A/ GETTA DIX

Proprietor of a boardinghouse for local workers, Getta draws a hand to her chest when she realizes what's happening. Her husband, her love, is over at the Johnson House with his brother. She leaves her children with a nurse and rushes into the street, knowing the raiders won't harm her. When she reaches the house, she sees her brother-in-law stumble down the back steps, falling to the ground before her. She cups his head with her hands. He looks at her with the eyes of one who has seen God—with unflinching terror—and then his lids slide closed. She tries to remove her hands, but part of his brain has fallen out the back of his head and now rests in her palms. What she yells then, looking at her hands, is not his name but her husband's, and she drops the bits of jellied brain into the dust and scrambles up the steps of the house, where she finds a trio of bushwhackers holding several local men at gunpoint. Her husband stands near them, and she hurries to his side, pleading for his life. She's convincing, talking two of them out of killing her husband, but the third, the leader, is too soused to abide any talk of mercy and pushes all seven men outside to the street, where he and his compatriots unload multiple rounds into their chests. Getta watches her husband's body fall; it happens so quickly—*crack, thump*—that it's not until he's on the ground that everything slows down. She sits on the bottom step of a storefront near his body, exhaling hard until her breath slows and all that's left is the absence of feeling. She watches the world pass before her, the horror it has so quickly become. A straw hat belonging to one of the dead blows along the street like tumbleweed and she reaches for it, places it over her husband's placid face. She walks away slowly, desultorily, between the bustle of jigging horses, the giggle and snarl of drunks, and the mangle of the quiet, lonesome dead.

B/ KASPER KASPAR

Seventeen-year-old apprentice newspaperman Kasper Kaspar is at the press early on the morning of the raid. He doesn't know it yet, but his father is already dead, killed while asleep in bed, and his mother is in shock, still shaking the body, expecting it to wake at any moment. What brings young Kasper to the office so early, however, has nothing to do with newspapering. He's locked in an embrace with the office printer, an older man affectionately known as Rooster. It is as Kasper finally works up the nerve to take the tip of Rooster's penis in his mouth that he first feels the heat closing in, a warmth more than their own bodies' doing. The raiders have set fire to the building, which goes up instantly, like tinder, thanks to the paper, ink, and kerosene. There's a moment as the two men huddle amid the flames, watching smoke funnel under and over closed doors, when they have a decision to make. A future as outcasts awaits them if they run out into the street as they are, flushed, shivering, womanly. Their decision is communicated through look and gesture as they embrace, kiss, and then whisper in each other's ears only as the fire overtakes them. Barely audible over the hiss of burning wood and the sizzle of steaming printer blocks are their oaths and cries:

"Come closer."

"What?"

"Hold me."

"I'll follow you to the other side."

When the flames consume them, the heat is so intense that their bodies dissolve, later to scatter in the wind and disappear. For this reason, Kasper's mother will, for the rest of her life, believe he is still alive, setting a place for him every night at the dinner table.

C/ MAYOR COLLAMORE

Mayor George Washington Collamore, he of the infamous and untimely gun seizure that leaves his town unarmed, wakes to find his house surrounded by raiders. With his hired hand, Patrick, he dashes out of the kitchen, through the swaths of wheat, and into his well house. Patrick lowers the mayor down the shaft first before joining him at the bottom of the stone well. There, the proximity of quarters forces them to press close together, from which vantage they look up at the circle of light above them, waiting either for the mayor's wife to appear and tell them it is okay to come out or for a man in a slouch hat to fire his Colt blindly into their hiding spot.

But history has something else in store. The raiders press the mayor's wife, but she won't give up her husband. Somehow the men at the top of the death list—Governor Robinson, Senator Lane, and Mayor Collamore—have all managed to escape. Frustrated and drunk, the bushwhackers loot the place of all its worth and then set it on fire. They wait out front, figuring that if the mayor is hiding in the house he will come running. There's the transfixing beauty of the fire, too. They've been lighting them all morning, yet none like this. Something inside, perhaps the canisters of furniture wax and shoe polish, feeds the blaze, a tongue of fire shooting dragon-like out the chimney top. The smells of burning linens and flowers in the garden mix in the air and the conflagration roars until the walls come crashing down and finally the house collapses. Only then does this audience disperse.

As the mayor's wife rushes to the well house, she doesn't realize that smoke from the fire has funneled all the oxygen out of the shaft like a whirring gust of wind on the open prairie, leaving the mayor and Patrick to a much slower and more horrifying death than if a gun had just been put to their heads and unloaded into their brains. Inherent in those last moments, in the groping push and pull of their hands as they slowly run out of air, is nothing amorous, but a simple prayer of human touch, an instinctive hope: *You can get me out of here, can't you?*

(11) *Correspondence*

Date: 08/21/2003
From: Janice_Stallings@missouri.edu
To: jayhawkergirl@hotmail.com
Subject: re: Inquiries?
Thank you for your interest in the State Historical Society here at MU. Excuse the formality, but I'll answer your questions in turn:

1) Yes, we have a good deal of material on Quantrill, specifically, and rooms full of general Civil War–era Kansas/ Missouri material: letters, newspapers, books, pictures, paintings, etc. You should come visit—Columbia's only a three-hour drive from Lawrence.

2) There is certainly a small but avid group of enthusiasts interested in—some would say obsessed with—that Border War period. There are a number of Civil War battle reenactments across Missouri that attract good-size crowds. More than the reenactments, however, there is a culture that goes along with it, some of it truly bizarre. I've heard of small-town bars where patrons dress as Confederate soldiers or bushwhackers. I once even came across a woman-seeking-man ad in the *Weekly* in which a woman was looking to marry anyone who could prove a family connection to Quantrill.

3) I don't know if I can offer a definitive answer on how people here today look back on those times or how they feel about men like Quantrill and George Todd. I think a lot of people in Missouri feel that even though we look at what these men were trying to preserve—the institution of slavery—as abhorrent, they were not simply bloodthirsty monsters. I think some people feel, as the historian Donald Gilmore writes, that "the Missouri guerrillas were legitimate partisan warriors who fought bravely for their cause against insurmountable odds." When you're on the wrong moral side of history and constantly reminded of it, you get defensive. I'm not saying that's how I feel. It's complicated.

4) I mean, can anyone in Kansas or Missouri understand the horrors of the past any better than they can what's happening in Afghanistan or Iraq? Distance, temporal or otherwise, is a leveling force. There have been countless books written about awful events like the raid on Lawrence, but they're at best approximations, in my opinion. We'll never truly understand. That's the thing about history, right? It's not graven—it's points of view.

Thank you for your interest and please don't hesitate to contact me again. I hope you do decide to come visit, even if you are a KU alum . . . just kidding.

Best,
Janice Stallings

(12) Poor Kansas, Poor Bleeding Kansas

As the raid wears on, the bushwhackers anticipate the out-the-back-door-and-into-the-potato-vines escape, and now they simply set the fields aflame and wait for the men to stream out. The raiders make sport of it, a lively sort of target practice.

But as the hours pass, the guerrillas also get sloppy. Drinking and looting take priority, and this affords a few hard-won victories for the townsfolk. There is the incident in which an elderly man quickly shaves and dresses as a sickly old woman. When the raiders arrive, they carry him out of the house in his bed, Cleopatra-style, before torching the place. Some townsfolk, emboldened by the imminence of their own deaths, start fighting back. Lacking guns, a few men challenge the bushwhackers with pitchforks and knives. Surprisingly, many of Quantrill's men simply leave when confronted, seeming to respect the suicidal gumption of the defenseless.

When the raiders open fire on a crowd of local men gathered on Massachusetts Street, Josiah Simeon falls to the ground, feigning death, and pulls the bodies of the dead atop him. The blood trickles down, the pleas for help worm through the pile, through crevices and openings between skin, until all is still, dead. Sometime later he hears a noise, footsteps nearby, bodies being turned over, rummaged through. When the body above him is removed, he opens his eyes reluctantly, expecting to be staring straight into the barrel of a Colt. But what he sees instead are the vacant, soul-deadened eyes of a woman trying to find her son. And at last, here, she has found him, this body that has thus far saved Josiah's life. Josiah looks at her, into those eyes, and says, "Leave him be—he's my only chance," pulling the woman's son out of her hands to cover himself.

(13) Painting, Drawing, Newspaper

Lauretta Louise Fox Fisk depicts nearly all of Lawrence aflame in her painting *The Lawrence Massacre*. You likely wouldn't recognize the subject on initial viewing, however, which is one of the painting's interesting effects. In the foreground, raiders ride their horses down the main thoroughfare, Massachusetts

Street, toward the viewer. Their guns are drawn, but their numbers are not great, nor do they seem particularly menacing. The tone of the scene is oddly calm. In the background, the burning town is easily mistakable for a tawny sunrise to the casual eye. This contrasts greatly with the pencil drawing that ran a month after the raid in *Harper's Weekly* titled *The Ruins of Lawrence*, which today looks anachronistic, more like a postwar bombed-out Berlin than a torched Old West prairie town.

A curious thing about the burning of Lawrence is the lack of a definitive death count. Most references cite "nearly 150," while other estimates range from 132 to more than 200. The August 23, 1863, edition of the *New York Times* reported "about 180 murdered" under the heading "The Invasion of Kansas." The granite monument in the cemetery abides by the general estimate of 150 victims, but the surrounding gravestones all etched with the same date make estimates inadequate.

His grave is in another cemetery, far from the monument. The wars didn't mean anything to him. He'd never voted, didn't know Sunni from Shia. He was in debt and depressed, having banked everything on a music career that hadn't panned out. He enlisted for the money, for the experience. He enlisted, he said, because he needed to fucking grow up.

(14) The Living and the Dead

After four hours Quantrill's men leave town, and the people of Lawrence abandon their hiding spots to survey the destruction and to search for husbands and fathers, sons and lovers, usually to sadness and horror. At first it seems the majority of the dead are colored, but they're mostly charred white men. All over town, long wailing cries trouble the air like the caterwauling of animals in the rut. A makeshift hospital is raised in the only church that survived the onslaught, but the remaining doctor is little more than mortician and bartender, dispensing whiskey to the newly amputated or slowly dying.

Massachusetts Street is completely devastated. People hurry pails of water from nearby wells and the Kaw River to the burning buildings, continuing on that first morning, mostly in silence now, mostly in vain, to salvage what they can of Lawrence. And then a strange thing happens: one of Quantrill's men appears. Slowly he makes his way up the thoroughfare. People turn to watch him, wondering why he is still here. Having drawn from hiding the few surviving men, perhaps the raiders' exit was a trick and a second attack is imminent. But in actuality this raider, Larkin Skaggs, has been left behind, separated from the group while indulging in drunken plunder. Why he doesn't hurry to catch up with the others is part of the mystery of this moment. Full daylight now, he seems appreciative, pensive in his appraisal of the destruction, a prince surveying his grounds. No trot, no canter, no gallop—the dapple colt simply walks the street, dragging the Union flag tied to its tail in the dirt.

No one sees where it comes from, but the first shot hits Skaggs in the shoulder and knocks him off his horse. For a few moments everyone just watches him squirm around, silently clutching his shoulder, before White Turkey, a Delaware Indian, approaches and fires a single shot directly into his heart. If Skaggs, a former Baptist minister, desires a martyr's death, the survivors of the raid are prepared to grant it. They descend on Skaggs, still alive, and tie a rope around his neck. The father of one of the young black soldiers who died at the raid's start climbs into the saddle of Skaggs's horse and starts to sing "John Brown's Body" as the colt continues its leisurely walk, dragging not only the Union flag but also its owner's body, tethered to a lug on the horse's saddle. The grief-shocked crowd follows the sable rider, joining in song and pelting the body with rocks. They need this: the battle hymn, the funereal march, the failed attempts to set the body aflame, the ritual stripping of clothes and removal of limbs and fingers, and at last the calloused boredom of rolling what remains of Skaggs into a ravine to tan and rot, to be picked apart by scavenger animals. Tomorrow they will hang a man who arrives in town and seems a little suspicious.

(15) Confession

Shortly before he shipped out, we were walking along Massachusetts Street, stopping at our favorite haunts—listening to records at Love Garden, having an afternoon drink at the Eldridge Hotel, combing stacks at the Dusty Bookshelf—strolling in the early fall with a beautiful ennui. I suggested we drop by the city's historical museum. He'd never been. I told him of the most abject statue of Langston Hughes on display in a hall honoring notable Lawrencians.

A volunteer near the entranceway, an old woman revealing bits of corn chip in her teeth when she smiled, informed us we were the only ones there. We walked through the building, so dark and dusty, lit solely by shafts of sun penetrating the high windows. They had added something new since I'd last been: a multimedia program of significant moments in state history. We skipped around the timeline, stopping on Quantrill's Raid. We were quiet a long time. I wanted to tell him how I felt, to unburden myself, to ask him not to leave. But I knew he didn't feel the same way about me, never had. How impossible it seemed then that any two people ever connected. He controlled the mouse, advancing to the next screen, saying, "Man, that must have been crazy. Can you imagine shit like that ever happened here?" I murmured agreement and asked if he would miss playing guitar while he was over there, but he didn't answer. He simply clicked the S\ᴛᴏᴘ button, rose, and continued down the hall.

(16) The Journey of the Body

By the time Quantrill's raiders leave Lawrence, Union leaders in Kansas City have finally mobilized forces to intercept the guerrillas before they cross into Missouri, where they'll disappear into the brush and thicket, gully and wood, into the very soil, and become ghosts. The Union forces stage two dramatic attempts to stop the rebels but ultimately fail.

Now it is almost twenty-four hours after the ambush began, and with a clutch of Union troops shrinking behind him in the distance, Quantrill feels as though he could sleep for a year, maybe two. He is weary. He knows they'll be safe if they can just make it to Missouri, and he's oppressed by the desire to ride straight to Kate's home and see her face. Amidst all the death has been her memory, the longing to touch her again. Despite this pull, he will take his men to Texas to hide out and let things settle, but as they race for the border there is so much Quantrill doesn't know.

He doesn't know that he'll never receive the recognition he so covets from the Confederate army—no legitimization of him or his men, no General Quantrill; he doesn't know that months from now his men will abandon him, either taking up with George Todd or so racked with guilt over their hand in the burning of Lawrence that they can no longer fight, that only a handful of them will follow him to Kentucky with the intention of continuing on to Washington to assassinate Lincoln; he doesn't know that he'll never get the chance; ambushed by federals, he'll die in Taylorsville, Kentucky, dumped in an idler's grave, farther away from Kate than ever; he doesn't know that his skull will be stolen and that his eye sockets are destined to garage the limp pricks of awkward freshman pledges in a generational fraternity ritual; he doesn't know that it'll be more than a hundred years before his body is exhumed and returned to the loam of Missouri, the people there split on whether to celebrate the occasion or to protest. What he knows now is only a word containing a desire, a wish of coming home, really: *Kate*.

It is morning once again and the last twenty-four hours have taken on the feeling of whole calendars of time. There in the distance, as he crosses into Missouri, the sun appears in the sky, purple shading into blue shading into red, forming slowly up over the far-off hills like a blister, a blemish, a birthmark.

O DEATH

In that year, the South was Redeemed, and with President Hayes having already removed Union troops, something had to be done, for surely nothing good awaited CK Howard and his young family with the return of Democrats to office. Like other black men throughout the Delta, CK had traveled north from his home in Merigold to be part of the meeting in Clarksdale. The hall was packed, bodies pressed against one another, the air heavy with their dank smells and desperation. They listened eagerly for some sign or direction.

"Eighteen hundred an seven-nine spell calamity for colored folk!" boomed the minister.

"What we spose to do?" a voice from the crowd called out.

"I live in Mississip my whole life," said another man, which elicited a rumbling of support. "My family here!"

The minister nodded, and waited for quiet. "But this place is set to return to Hell in no amount of time." He paused. "And if we stay, we die. Whether a return of the lash or the crush on our soul, don't much matter to white folk who feel they been wronged these years last." At that the crowd erupted, neighbors turning to one another while others shouted across the room. "Now, hold on," he pleaded. "God, I'm here to tell you, will show us the way. The Almighty will lead us out of Egypt, this I promise."

"He sure got them words together," CK said to his neighbor.

"Need more than words," the man said quietly, and then, as if boiling up unexpectedly from some hidden place inside him, he shouted at the dais, a voice so strong with intention that it swiveled the heads in the room his way: "What God gon do for us, preach? What, I mean to ask you, *He* gon do?"

In subsequent meetings, throughout the final months of 1878, they would debate the religious and secular implications of the change in political winds—whether it was a sure signal of a coming millenarian End or only the formal institution of an already understood way of life—but when the arguing died down the only consensus remained fear of what lay ahead, and so they turned their attention toward what was to be done. There would be talk of Liberia, of chartered ships that would take them to Africa, of petitioning the president to establish a Negro state somewhere in the territories, of staying and trying to strengthen Republican turnout in the next election. There would be talk of Kansas, the "Eden on the Prairie," of Pap Singleton and the Negro settlements in Hodgeman and Grant counties.

CK didn't know what to do. Merigold was his home, and while most of his kin had passed or already left Bolivar County in the years after the war, it wasn't easy to imagine living anywhere else. But he had his own young family to think about now, his wife, Mil, and their baby, Rachel. He prayed on it nightly, as always, waiting for God to provide some direction, and then one day, coming home from the ginner where he'd taken the last of his unseeded cotton for the season, CK came across the circular, a crumpled handbill lying on the ground. He picked it up and read the advertisement for a newly established town in Kansas whose name was almost familiar, though he'd never once left Mississippi.

"Nicodemus," he said, as he continued walking toward the farmland he rented from a white planter, the tracts where he raised his cotton and where he lived in a small wooden shack with his wife and daughter. He said the name again and felt the incipient rush of near recognition he'd often experienced as vision, a sure sign from God. There was Nicodemus of the Bible, of course, the Pharisee who visited Jesus and later helped Joseph of Arimathea bury His body. But that wasn't the source of the name's mysterious known-ness. Something else, he knew. Slowly, as he read over the leaflet the way his mother had taught him—"Negro colony on the banks of the beautiful Solomon River"—the words started to come back to him. A song he remembered singing as a boy, before the war, bent over sack and bail in the fields alongside his now-dead mother. That was it: a song about a slave who died speaking of the coming freedom and asked to be woken when it came. *Wake Nicodemus*, he hummed to himself. *Wake me up at the first break of day.* He heard those words now as a commandment from his God—it *was* a sign—and he knew now for certain where he'd take his young family. *Wake me up for that great Jubilee.*

Over a year earlier, and five hundred miles away in Kentucky, Talmen Fore had first heard talk of Nicodemus from a man named W. R. Hill, who showed up at Lexington Baptist one Sunday unannounced, whiter than a dogwood in bloom. He claimed to be a minister from Indiana, but land spec seemed the only thing on his mind that day. The audacity—the sheer effrontery—of that white man, talking Kansas, talking all-black towns! Life for the colored man in Kentucky wasn't as bad as it was in the Lower South, Talmen knew, but that wasn't saying much. He had a home for his wife and two children, and drew mostly regular pay as a carpenter. But his house was small and the rent high, and he wasn't allowed to join the new white carpenters' union, which left him taking what he could get from poor folks on his side of town. It was better than it had been before the war—that strange contradiction of being bound to a master in a slave state that had chosen not to secede, that had somehow fought to preserve the Union—but the thought of their own town seemed a danger even to dream. Hill was stubborn in his persistence, however, and preacherly in his delivery. The more he spoke, the more his claims persuaded: rich black sandy loam. Wild horses aplenty. Forests of elm, willow, hackberry, and sycamore for building. Five dollars gets you there by rail and cart. The government was practically giving away land.

And so in the summer of 1877 the initial group of thirty struck out for Kansas, packing all they could—food, pans, clothing, chairs, blankets, tools—first onto the train, where the other passengers inspected them with a skeptical curiosity, and then onto the wagons that took them the last of the way across the arid plains of northwestern Kansas to their new home on the south fork of the Solomon River. It was flat and arid, so different from the wooded hills of central Kentucky, so different from what the white minister had claimed. And yet it was land, theirs for the taking, so they sent back word to Lexington with enough encouragement to spur a second group of three hundred, which included Talmen and his family. They arrived in September of that year, too late in the season to plant and harvest, and had to weather the tough winter in holes they'd burrowed into the hard ground. At night the men huddled in those dugouts with their families, using dried manure to coax a small fire, and stole out in the mornings to surrounding towns to look for work that might see them through to spring. There was nothing. The nearest mercantile center was thirty miles away, at the railhead in Ellis. The soil was parched, nary a horse to be seen, and the only tree for miles was the occasional cottonwood. Disillusioned, over sixty families returned to Kentucky. A posse formed, searching for that liar, W. R. Hill, who'd promised Eden and sold them a desert, and the fearful white man had to sneak out of town under a wagoner's bed of hay.

Things got so bad that winter they nearly starved and were saved only by a group of Osage Indians, returning from their winter hunt in the Rockies, who shared some of their meat with the settlers. At last the third and final group from Kentucky, a lot of almost 150, appeared on the horizon one evening in early March of 1878, looking to Talmen, who was sick and tired, like souls returning to claim their earthly vessels. But their fresh teams of mules and oxen, their new farming implements and provisions, proved to be their salvation.

Even then, however, there were only five harnessed teams to share among their growing numbers, so Talmen broke an entire acre of that heavy soil for wheat-planting with a single spade, wearing it down to a nub. His only help was his eldest, Rawl, a lank boy who at thirteen was already two inches taller than his daddy. It was hard work, with the men in the fields till dark and the women at home with the children and elderly, cooking and gathering dried bones on the prairie to sell to dealers to grind into fertilizer, but there was satisfaction in their self-determined labor, in the emergence of their young town. And for Talmen nothing more spoke to that hard-won hope than after that long winter's thaw when his wife, Eugenia, despite the inauspicious conditions, birthed their second son. One of Nicodemus's firstborn, he was a handsome little boy. They named him after Talmen's father, Isaiah.

After coming across the circular, CK had worked hard to convince Mil they needed to leave, of the surety of his sign from God. He paced around their one-room shack, repeating the preacher's words, talking calamity and exodus, and Mil resisted leaving what was her home too, but finally she relented. So that March of 1879, a year after the final group from Kentucky arrived in Nicodemus, when the ground had thawed and there was the first warmth in the air, when normally CK would have been preparing to seed his fields, they gathered up what little they could carry and made their way south out of Bolivar County. They were still young yet, barely twenty-two, with little weighing them down beyond Rachel. Mil carried the baby and CK shouldered a large pack—some bedding, clothing, a few pots, chipped plates, and of course his Bible—to Greenville. They arrived after two long days of walking and set up camp on the banks of the Mississippi, where they would wait for a steamer that would take them north. They were not alone. Though some of the initial excitement had faded and many had decided to stay and try their luck with the Democrats, plenty of people were still looking to get out if they could, and more and more joined them on the river. Soon, as the days wore on with no boats yet to stop, what had started as a few solitary campsites had turned into a roiling tent town of fleeing colored families.

Steamers coming north from Natchez and Vicksburg passed regularly and every time one neared, folks would run to the banks and shout and wave and watch as it went on its way. "Why you spose they ain't stop for us?" CK said to Mil as he watched another steamer paddle past.

"You know better than to ask after such foolishness," Mil said from inside the tent, where she was feeding Rachel. "They think we got no money."

"Can't fault them their intelligence, then," he said, removing his hat and wiping at his brow. Mil laughed in that way of hers—as if it surprised and then embarrassed her—and CK squatted to peek into the tent. "How's my little queen doing?" he said.

"Rachel hungry, that I know."

"Yessum, sure is," he said. "She need strength for the journey He set us on."

But as more and more boats passed, unwilling to pick them up, the mood on the banks turned grim. Their desperation grew as food dwindled, and soon some of the men were talking of taking a boat by force and others of giving up. At an impromptu meeting CK tried to urge caution, telling them to have faith, that soon enough one would stop.

"Faith sound good from a preacher's mouth, but it ain't taking us out of Mississippi," a man said.

"Ain't a preacher," CK said. "I share my crop, same as you."

Another: "We been out here near three weeks. We'd do better to go back home than starving on these banks."

"No, sir," CK said. "We must believe."

"Believe all you want," the man angered. "You think you ain't a nigger just cause you leave Mississip? Even this place you keep on about—*Nigger* Demus."

"Nicodemus," CK said with a calm certainty that only stoked the man's fury.

"A nigger here, nigger in Kansas. Nigger everywhere," he said. "I'm going home, is all I know. Me and mine. The rest of you know better, you'll do the same."

The man walked off in a huff and CK decided to let him be, turning his attention to the others. "Just a little longer," he said, sweeping across the row of skeptical eyes circling him. "The Lord will give us safe passage, I'm sure it."

Though a few families did turn back, most stayed, crowding along both sides of the river now. However, a few days later, when still no steamer had stopped, a white man showed up on the banks, speaking of jobs at a nearby plantation. "There's work if you want it and you're willing," he said. "I need a few new hands." Several followed and later that day another man, black this time, showed up alone. He called himself Dulcet, and in his hand he carried a small length of sugarcane. CK asked where he was from.

"Up north. Holly Springs."

"Hill country." CK nodded. "What you doing in the Delta?"

"Work," said Dulcet, tapping the sugarcane against the palm of his left hand as he spoke. CK could make out a thin row of holes along the object's smooth rounded curve.

"You play?"

"I blow me some cane here and again." When CK asked for a song, Dulcet said he wasn't in the mood and put the fife in his back pocket. He'd just been fired from a nearby plantation.

"Man from there come by earlier. Took some of ours."

"He got your people on the cheap," Dulcet said, telling of how he'd been talking—just talking—to some of the others about better wages. "Hadn't even said the word *strike*, but word got back to the foreman." He paused, looking around at all the families on the banks. "He knew you all was out here—everyone's talking about it in the towns—so he fired me," Dulcet said, snapping his fingers. He took a quick swig from a clear bottle that seemed to leap out of his pocket. He offered it to CK, but he declined, so Dulcet took another furious swig. The burn of that rotgut whiskey filled up the space between them.

"You alone, then?"

"My wife and kids still there."

"You left your family?" CK said.

Dulcet's plan was to come back for them once he had a place set up in Kansas. "They say there's land plenty there." CK tried to imagine leaving Mil and Rachel behind in Mississippi, but that required a desperation he couldn't summon. Dulcet turned the bottle slowly, watching the crest of the alcohol lower and rise. "Barely let me say goodbye before he run me off." He looked like he might shout at the sky, but then just as quickly seemed to shake the thought away with another drink. "They think we got as much claim to money as their damn mules and gins. We built their wealth and receive nothing for it!"

Dulcet's words were starting to slide into one another, so CK set a steady hand on his shoulder and led him to the tent where Mil was frying pone and bacon rind in the kettle over a fire. Afterward they let him stretch out on their quilt for a tossing, angry kind of sleep.

It wasn't long after Dulcet showed up that a steamer finally stopped and with it came a wild outburst of hoots and hollering, those first sounds of joy on the banks. It was almost April and CK was lying on his back in the tent, Bible facedown on his chest, enjoying the balmy weather. Though his eyes were closed, he wasn't sleeping. He was thinking of Nicodemus. If he thought hard enough, he could see it, that city on the plains. There were sturdy houses of plank and rock, not all of them big, yet none small. And a main street, with several stores, a post office, and a hotel. Not fancy, just enough. And all around those buildings were cattle farms and fields of wheat and corn and soybeans, stretching far enough to test the keen of one's eye. And there was the church, so big as to fit all the people of Nicodemus, who would come each Sunday to sing and pray, and feel love and fear in the presence of the Lord. He could hear them—*Glory be, glory to our Savior!*—and he and Mil and Rachel were there with them, faces turned up toward the sky, singing. But now Mil was calling his name, folding back the flaps of the tent. "Wake up, CK! Ain't you hear? A steamer come. For us." He kept his eyes closed and when she came to shake him, he opened them suddenly and reached for her. She startled and let out a little scream. She wrangled from his grasp—"Got half a mind to get on that boat without you"—

and hurried from the tent, but CK stayed where he was a minute longer, enjoying the wonderful soreness in his stomach and lungs as his body worked to quit that laughter.

In Lexington, Talmen had learned his trade from his father, whom he'd followed around all those years before the war, carrying tools, watching. It was a handy skill, and Eugenia urged Talmen to build a wooden one-room where she and a few of the other women could carry out lessons for the children in town. For years before she and Talmen married she'd taught at a school in Lexington and she championed the importance of education for their children.

"We got a school," Talmen said.

It was true. Eugenia and some of the other women took turns holding class in their dugouts using books borrowed from William Kirltey, one of the few who owned any books.

"Ain't a proper place for a child to learn."

"Ain't a proper place to live either," said Talmen.

Their first dugout had been a flat recession in the ground, covered by a thin layer of wood, that had flooded easily in the spring rains. Next time they burrowed into the south side of a low-rising hill so that the slight slope would provide easy runoff for rain and ice melt. They'd taken strips of the thick prairie sod, gathered after plowing, and cut them into blocks, which they used to build up decently insulated walls to the six-foot-high ceiling. This dugout, a single small cavelike room, was vastly better than their first, but it was nothing like their home in Lexington, which wasn't fancy but at least it had been above ground with several rooms where a person could be alone if he wanted. Over a year into their Kansas experiment, most people were still in the ground. Some had been able to build sod houses, and there were even two made of limestone cut from nearby quarries. But the builders of those homes, S. P.

Roundtree and Thomas Baldwin, were town fathers and men of means. Talmen resented their comfort, when even Z. T. Fletcher had to run his general store, which was generally out of everything, from a dugout.

"You soft-skulled if you spect me to build a school when we living in a hole."

"School first, above ground," Eugenia insisted. "We have a baby now and he and every other will have his schooling."

Trees were harder to come by on the plains, however, and trading for lumber was costly, but when the issue was raised at a town meeting, the vote passed near unanimous. Talmen huffed about it some, but soon he and Rawl were meeting with a dozen or so other men late in the evening to discuss plans for the new schoolhouse. It was the busy sowing season and they could come to it only after a long day working the land, so they'd gather in the failing light of spring and work a few hours more, returning to their dugouts and families in the dark, with eyes so heavy they could barely finish supper. At night Eugenia threw hot ashes from the fire on the dirt floor of the dugout to deter the vermin and once she had seen Rawl and their daughter, Jesse Mae, to bed, she would join Talmen, who was often already asleep. Between them young Isaiah would rest, his swaddle dampened to keep away fleas and bedbugs. With their children almost full-grown, how Isaiah's arrival had surprised them. Their family had been one thing for so long and now so quickly was another.

"Talmen," she whispered one night in bed.

"Mmm," he answered, eyes closed.

"You doing good. You doing right about this schoolhouse."

"I'm doing it for you," he said.

"No, Tal," she said. "You doing it for Isaiah. For all us. You doing it for Nicodemus."

• • •

Imagine: To have left your home in Mississippi, packing all you could carry onto your back and languishing on the banks of a river for nearly a month, watching as others gave up and turned back, only to find safe passage with hardly a fare to offer, having to rely on the kindness of a white steamboat captain who said he couldn't pass up any longer folks in such utter want, and then sailing on a few more days, nearly starving in the dank hull of the ship—to endure all of that guided by what felt in the darkest moments like a singular, quixotic compulsion—only to finally arrive in St. Louis to find thousands of others just like yourself.

What was going on?

CK stepped off the steamer asking that very question aloud. He walked along slowly with Mil and the baby, absorbing the sound and motion of a city far larger than any he'd ever seen. So many colored folks, all crowding around the boats. Some women and children sat somberly at fires while men walked around, either with great purpose or none at all, content to loaf on the levee. The group that CK had come north with, half a hundred or so, moved cautiously in mass, pulled slowly by the current of the city's bustle. A white man in a gray suit approached them.

"Just arrived? Where you folks coming from?" he asked, pencil and paper in hand.

"Mississippi. Every corner, sir," CK said. "I from Bolivar County. Merigold."

The man wrote that down, nodding. It was warm that April afternoon, and sweat matted strands of his brown hair sloppily across his brow, giving his otherwise smart appearance a hint of dishevelment.

"Where you all headed?" He looked up, meeting CK's eyes for the first time.

"Kansas," CK said.

The man laughed.

"What so funny bout that?" said Dulcet.

The man shook his head, amused. "All of you going to Kansas. Amazing." With that, his disposition seemed to change, losing its brusque urgency. He waved his pencil at the teeming streets. "I've been reporting on it for the papers. Never seen anything like it. Kansas Fever, they call it. Negroes from all over the South—Mississippi, Louisiana, Georgia, Tennessee, Texas even. All heading for Kansas."

"All them?"

"Every the last. Each thinking the government is gonna give him land and money just because Kansas was free-soil during the war. No plan whatsoever beyond getting to Kansas. Do that and everything will be okay, they think." He shook his head, apparently pleased to inform them of their misadventure.

"We ain't refugees seeking free houses," CK said. "We emigrants from that young hell behind us."

"They call you exodusters," the newspaperman said.

"We workers," said Dulcet.

"So you two led this group from," he said, pausing as he scanned his notes, "Bolivar County?"

"Ain't no leaders but from above," CK said. "Every black man's a Moses now."

"I like that," the man said, repeating CK's words as he wrote. They left him standing there, writing on his paper, and took in the city. While whites looked on from inside large store windows, blacks mingled in the street in a surprised kind of stupor. After talking with some of the people they passed, CK was able to corroborate what the newspaperman had said: folks had come from all over, and everyone did seem to have their sights set on Kansas. Steamers were arriving, unloading more and more people, but none were boating them on to Kansas yet. Stuck once again, there wasn't much to do but wait and worry and trust that God would deliver them soon enough. They took up residence, like most others, at the Eighth Street Baptist Church, which had opened its doors to these weary travelers. In the crowded basement of that church, people talked, people slept, people grew hungry, people preached the Word, people gamed, people stole, people gossiped, people argued, people cared for the sick, people crowded around when the bread and stew vats came out, people told stories, people played games with the children, people ventured outside into the city to look for work, people returned at night, and others never came back. Everyone waited.

The trouble started when the whites from nearby towns stopped doing business. They'd been quite welcoming at the start, willing sellers and traders when Nicodemus men would hitch up carts and journey to one of these towns—Stockton, Ellis, Bull City, Hill City—for necessities. So in that April of 1879, when Talmen traveled to Ellis, he was surprised to find no one willing to trade for flour, meal, or the extra lumber they needed for the schoolhouse. He went from store to store, to the folks with whom he usually did business, who politely told him they were out of stock, and then to the others, more hostile, who called him names and told him to go on and leave already. It was there in Ellis that Talmen got first wind of the exodus.

"Word out of Kansas City is that St. Louis is overrun with coloreds," Mr. Ryer said when Talmen asked what gave. Ryer had always been friendly to him, and he and Talmen often spent a few idle minutes talking on the back steps of his store.

"What that got to do with us?"

"They say they're coming for Kansas."

"That so?" Talmen said, scratching the grayed stubble on his cheek. "And that has folks here worried, huh?"

Ryer said nothing.

"Don't know nothing bout black folk coming from the Lower. We from Kentucky."

"I know of it."

"We not trying to take nothing from y'all," Talmen said. "Just a spot for ourselves. No harm to no one."

"Look, we never had any problems with you and yourn, but that don't make some here less scared they're gonna be run off by coloreds who want their land. Bad enough with Indians to worry of." Behind the store, away from the main drag, was Ryer's small house, nice-looking, and beyond that was a standing of white oak and sycamore. From where Talmen stood, perspective shrunk even the tallest of these trees to a size he could imagine felling and carrying home across his shoulders, but he knew the reality was that the great oak would crush him if he ever tried something so foolish. "I understand, believe me," Ryer continued. "But you're speaking to the clear of mind, Talmen. Those newspapers speak to the scared."

Talmen turned his attention away from the trees to Ryer.

"Can't you spare us nothing?"

That evening Talmen returned to Nicodemus with what little Mr. Ryer could afford to part with, some cottonwood lumber prone to warp and a sack of poorly milled grain they'd have to parch or boil. It was nearing dark and he figured Rawl to be at work on the schoolhouse, but when Talmen passed by the site on his way into town none of the other men had seen him. It was only when Talmen returned home that he found his son standing outside the dugout, throwing dirt clods at the hillside.

"What's wrong?" Talmen said.

"It's the leastest."

"Isaiah?"

"Yes, sir," said Rawl. "Dr. Newth, he here."

Talmen looked at the door of the dugout, a well-fitting

cover of thick oak that he'd traded for in a scrap shop in Stockton, painted a faded orange by its previous owner.

"Ain't well, Mama say. In his breathing."

The door fit snugly into the sod-walled entranceway but could be removed with a little effort, as Talmen did now, entering the dugout, where he found his Jesse Mae cooking supper over the sod fireplace. Eugenia was rocking the child, a crinkle of concern in her brow. She was standing near the cottonwood center pole that supported the ceiling. She could stand up straight, but Talmen and Dr. Newth had to stoop. The doctor was white and had recently moved to town, as had two other white men who were trying to build stores. It had caused a little concern, but at five hundred to three, it was safe to say it was still an all-black town. And truth be told, they were fortunate for Newth's arrival. Lucky was the frontier town that could claim a doctor. He was a morose man, however, an unfortunate disposition for a man in his trade. He'd just said something to Eugenia and was closing the top of his small cowhide bag, grimacing.

"What's wrong, Genia?"

She shook her head, the sick child at her chest, shushing Talmen for quiet.

When stuck and waiting in a place not your own, CK found, it was hard not to succumb to the feeling that you were living the same day over and again with little prospects for change. So he and Dulcet tried to keep busy, venturing into different parts of the city to look for work, while Mil tended to Rachel and commiserated with others at the church. They split up to cover more territory. CK worried over Dulcet, who sometimes showed up with a few coins and other times with just an awful burn on his breath. But CK did what he could. He knocked on doors, looking for jobs, and when turned away went to another. Every now and then one came through. A few Indian pennies to wash store windows or split wood, make a delivery of some sort to the other side of town. He tried to save for passage to Kansas—they'd left Mississippi with little more than twenty dollars, which had mostly evaporated—but now it seemed they might be stuck in St. Louis forever. People he spoke to in the streets were scared. There was talk that the city was so swamped by refugees they'd all be forced onto boats that would take them back south. As was his way in dark times, CK would smile, maybe place a steady hand on the dithering soul's shoulder, and tell him to keep his faith strong. Everything would be okay. If they questioned how he could be so certain, he'd say, "Because I'm washed in the blood of our Savior." Some grew angry, not wanting to hear any talk of a god that had allowed shackles all those years. Even Dulcet grew tired of his increased speechifying. One day when CK tried to talk to him about Noah's slothful inebriation after the Flood, Dulcet called him foolish for believing in a white man's god after what they'd been through. Stunned to hear such words from his friend, CK could only rejoin, "I'll pray for God to turn your heart."

"How long you pray for the white man to turn his heart?" Dulcet said. "Long enough your knees broke?" They weren't leaving because of God, he said; they were leaving because a black man couldn't get a fair shake in the South, and to illustrate his point he told a story of how before the election he'd worked to get blacks to turn out for the Republicans. "Guess word got around," Dulcet said, "and one night we get some visitors at our home. Bulldozers, threatening to make a good nigger out of me if I don't quit talking about the election. And course I don't, so they come back and set my house on fire." He looked hard at CK. "Burned it to the ground. My home. That's what this about. That's why we leaving."

CK reached to place a hand on Dulcet's shoulder—"I'm sorry, friend"—but Dulcet stormed off in a huff, shaking his head at the bitter memory, and his return later that evening to supper with CK and Mil seemed to seal an unspoken agreement not to discuss the matter any further. Theirs was an argument that could not be resolved, CK knew. It could only be reconciled in light of their common end: getting to Kansas was what mattered. Still, it gave CK pause, not doubt but confusion: How could anyone ignore God's hand in this miracle of common struggle and purpose? They were alive, together, out of Mississippi, on their way to a better life.

Which was not to say CK didn't welcome information that steadied his belief. All that waiting in the church had turned him into quite the gossip, always asking after the latest news. One evening on his way back to the church after having spent the day sweeping out stables, he bumped into that newspaperman again. CK recognized him immediately in that same gray suit. It had been two weeks since the day they arrived and the man didn't seem to remember him. CK introduced himself, asking if he'd heard anything new.

"John Barns," the man said, shaking CK's hand. "Mayor's put a stop on boats carrying coloreds to the city."

"Any talk about steamers leaving for Kansas?"

"Talk of steamers all right," he said. "But not to Kansas. Steamers back south, is the rumor. Townsfolk here are fed up, and planters in the South are sending labor agents to bring coloreds back to the plantations."

"Heard talk of that," CK said, kicking idly at a small rock near his boot.

"Free passage back, they're saying."

"Don't think many will take up that offer."

"You know something I don't?"

CK smiled. "Why we wanna go back to Egypt when we done made it out alive?"

John shook his head, a look of bemused confusion. "Sometimes I don't know whether to laugh or to cry for you people."

"Don't need either from you," CK said, his voice sharpening in a sudden flash of anger, which John seemed not to register.

"What can you tell me about the church where you're staying? What's it like in there?"

"I could tell you everything."

"Go on, then."

CK looked at the ground, coughed into one hand, and held out the other, until John removed a few coins from the small pocket of his vest and dropped them onto his palm.

CK said, "Obliged," and proceeded to describe what he and his family had experienced the last few weeks in the basement of the old church. Or selectively describe, rather. CK painted a pretty picture for John, people cooperating and helping one another, which had been true when they arrived, but lately with tensions rising there had been a lot of arguments, a few that had turned into fights even. He mentioned none of that now. He told him of his friend Dulcet, who played a mean fife that he carried in his coat pocket, entertaining the children with melody and song. As CK spoke, John wrote quickly on his small book of papers. When CK finished, he looked over at John's hurried hand. It looked like a bunch of chicken scratch, mysterious in its illegibility.

"What was it you did back in Mississippi, anyway? You preach?" asked John.

"Nah, ain't much for speaking the Word," CK said, "but I hear it in my head all right." He told him that, like most in Bolivar County, he'd farmed.

"Good profession," said John.

"Difficult where I come from," CK said. "Sharecrop, tenant-farm." He told of how the landowners charged high rents and drew up contracts that made sure they kept the profits when cotton prices were high and the renters took on the debt when they were low, making it impossible to get out of the contract, unless you wanted to go to jail. John wrote none of this down, just listened as he looked out at the water, and when CK finished he said nothing. The two stood silently as the boats rocked calmly in the water, going nowhere. CK enjoyed talking in the warm evening.

Not ready to return to the church yet, he pointed at the newspaper under John's arm and asked, "How you learn that?"

"My daddy wrote for the papers," John said. "Guess I got it in the blood." He smiled, and as if wanting to show off his latest work he unfolded the paper and held it out between the two of them. The headline across the top read "DARKIES DUPED BY FALSE PROMISES!" and John folded it up again.

"What that say?" CK asked, smiling.

John hemmed.

"Just fooling," CK said. "I know what it say."

Again John said nothing.

"You come find me when you ready to write about why we really on this river," CK said and left.

When the boats finally began to leave for Kansas, first they carried the exodusters who could pay, and only then did the relief board raise enough money from private donors to transport those without fare. It was early one morning that CK woke to Dulcet tugging on his arm.

"CK, they here," he said.

CK struggled into wakefulness, shaking his head, rubbing at his eyes.

"The steamers," Dulcet said. "They leaving for Kansas soon."

"What? How you know?"

"Saw a man outside running through the street. Asked where he was going. Said he, 'The boats.' Said I, 'What boats?' Said he, 'Kansas.' Thought he was lying, so I said, 'How you know?' Pushed me, said, 'Get out the way. They filling up and not about to wait a minute longer.' So you know what I do? I goes and gets us three vouchers for passage. Now what you say to that, CK?"

Dulcet slapped him on the shoulder with the vouchers, smiling, proud of himself.

"Time is it?" CK said.

"Before dawn yet. What you wondering after time for? I'm telling you we need to go. We leave for Kansas today."

"What you doing in the street before dawn?" CK said.

People were rousing from sleep around them.

"You want to stay, fine," Dulcet said. "Me, I gon catch that boat."

Talmen and Rawl gathered up all the dried manure they could find, trying to keep as much of that prairie coal on hand so the fire stayed stoked. Eugenia and Jesse Mae took turns holding little Isaiah close, hoping the warmth of the dugout would sweat the cold from his lungs. Folks came bringing what food they could manage, to ask what could be done, but there was little to do beyond praying for the child.

Back in Kentucky they'd lost three children before their second birthdays, so Talmen was no stranger to death. Sometimes he felt as if it followed him, a constant specter. *Death, stay away*, he told the shadowy haunt. *Get behind me, Death*. Talmen needed the boy to survive. Born together, his son and the town seemed connected, their fates intertwined, and in the same way the town needed to survive through difficulty so too did the boy. Talmen tried to stay with Eugenia, but she said the best thing he could do was to make sure the wheat crop delivered on time. So during the days, Talmen and Rawl tended to plowing and sowing the wheat, trying to do the impossible: to drive away thoughts of the sick child, to keep their hands *and* minds on the plow as it burst through the earth and scattered the loose layers of topsoil.

The only time they took Isaiah out of the dugout all week was to go to a meeting so the sick child could receive his blessings. There were three churches in town, one African Methodist Episcopal and two Baptist, all of which met in dugouts except their own Mount Olive, which had recently built a sod house that sat fifty. As they took their seats in church, a neighbor in their pew, Mrs. Baldwin, leaned over and whispered to be sure to come to her place afterward. The Baldwins' large stone house hosted the after-church potluck that had become a weekly tradition. These were crowded affairs with people filling the house so far to excess that oftentimes the gathering extended out the front door to the porch and into the yard. For Talmen the kindness of the gesture was always tarnished by its reminder that most everyone else was still living in the ground. He didn't much care for Thomas Baldwin anyway, a loudmouthed man full of brag, who thought his money turned conjecture into fact. Talmen usually preferred to go straight home after church, but then again, Eugenia and Jesse Mae had been cooped up inside the dugout all week with Isaiah, and his and Rawl's only reprieve was long days in the field.

"Can't we just stay a bit?" said Jesse Mae, who was friends with the Baldwins' youngest daughter, Mercy.

"Might be good for the boy, some fresh air," added Rawl.

Eugenia looked at Talmen, awaiting his verdict. They were all itching to escape that dugout, Talmen included.

And so they went to the stone house and said grace before victuals and sang a few hymns on a well-tuned piano Mercy had just about mastered. Afterward, people sipped coffee and milled around, catching up on farming and family. Talmen had to admit, it felt good to have a nice meal and spend a few hours outside the oppressive dugout. He wasn't much for talking, so he relieved Isaiah from Eugenia's arms and carried him to the kitchen, keeping his boy close to the stove, an unpopular spot in the April warmth that left him eavesdropping on conversations in the other room and trading an occasional word or two with someone sneaking back for seconds or thirds.

Beyond the usual pleasantries of planting and the weather, most of the talk that night was about the exodusters. A few months back, a group of fifty had arrived in Nicodemus from Mississippi, and they'd been welcomed. However, no one knew then that their arrival presaged the current deluge of emigrants coming north, this spectacle that the papers covered in such detail, and now folks in Nicodemus were none too pleased to be associated with that desperate rabble, especially given how difficult it had made business with their white neighbors. It was true. Talmen had seen them grow even stingier since his last visit with Mr. Ryer. Construction on the schoolhouse had all but halted until they could find a mill willing to trade for more lumber. But listening to Baldwin rail against the refugees—with a strength of voice aroused by being in the comfort of his own home—Talmen doubted how different their own situations had been. They hadn't been driven from their homes, of course, but hadn't the settlers of Nicodemus relied on charity—from the Osage Indians, from kindly whites and sympathetic blacks in near and distant towns—to get them on their feet, to give the town even the possibility to succeed? But men like Baldwin could afford to have short memories. The following week, in response to the stories of exodusters burdening towns and services throughout the state, Baldwin would forward a vote at the town meeting, calling for the end of all appeals for outside help, which would pass overwhelmingly. From then on, Nicodemus would survive or perish by her own hand.

Talmen grew tired of the debate, and he and Eugenia and their children left soon after to get Isaiah home for an early bed. But that night Isaiah's breathing worsened and Talmen cursed himself for having taken the child from the dugout. He felt so helpless, watching his son shiver in Eugenia's arms as they waited on Dr. Newth, knowing as he did a father's sad truths of love and death.

They arrived in Wyandotte County aboard the *E. H. Durfee* on April 14, a date CK would never forget, for that was the day they finally set foot in Kansas. The excitement built as they neared the wharf and the steamer's great paddles slowed, its tall stacks puffing their final plumes of smoke into the overcast sky. A light rain had begun. People gathered their families and pushed to the railings to see what free soil looked like. There was crying and then singing as they made their way down the gangplank: "Oh, Kansas! Oh, sweet Kansas!"

Across the water, bustling on the Missouri side of the river, lay Kansas City, and Dulcet stuck his thumbs under his armpits and shook his fingers wildly, saying so long to Missouri and the South, drawing a big round of laughter. There on the waterfront others gathered round, embracing in the rain. Soon everyone, religious or otherwise, was holding hands and kneeling. "It's raining on us now," a loud, ministerial voice called out, "but today that's water from the good Lord given to a free people."

"We made it," Mil said, holding the swaddled Rachel in her arms.

"Not yet," CK said. "Nicodemus is my beacon. Nicodemus is where I'll lay my head."

In anticipation of the exodusters' arrival a relief board had been formed and word was Governor St. John himself was pledging help for the refugees. Till then it was more waiting, and so it was again that they huddled into the crowded confines of a church, this time African Methodist, and bided their time. Strange that you could arrive in Kansas—the very idea of which meant change, a new life—and still be doing the same thing. CK chuckled to himself, musing that first evening as he sat with others around a stove, watching the coffeepots start to boil. Members from the relief board came to visit in the following days with plans to ship refugees to various towns throughout the state so that no single location bore the burden of taking on thousands of so destitute a people. Some took trains to Lawrence and Topeka, others to Hodgeman County. CK, Mil, and Dulcet waited for word on passage to Nicodemus.

The warm weather filled up the church with the stench of sweating bodies and soiled clothing, so they took to sleeping outside, underneath the raised Wyandotte train depot. Word finally came in early May that there would be no direct passage to Nicodemus—the relief board wouldn't send migrants to a place so newly established and distant that they hadn't had a chance to inspect the conditions. That night CK, Mil, and Dulcet conferred about their options under the train depot.

"Figure we can work some and come up with the fare for passage ourselves. Might take a little while," CK said. "You don't have to come, Dulcet. You didn't sign on for no Nicodemus. You can settle yourself anywhere. Bring your family up once you got a place." Dulcet considered this as Mil nursed Rachel, her back to them, nodding at her husband's words.

"You all kin to me now," he said. "Course I coming with."

"All right, then," CK said with a force that betrayed the relief he felt that his friend would join them.

During the days, Mil would rest in the depot's shade with Rachel, listening to the footsteps of expectant travelers scuttling above them every time a train rumbled into town, and CK and Dulcet would set out early in the morning to look for work. CK had some luck at a nearby farm, and Dulcet would try his hand across the water in Kansas City, and they would come back at night tired, crawling under the train depot for supper. Sometimes Dulcet would regale them with stories of the things he'd seen that day in the city, and other times he'd tell them about his family, missing them so. Often he'd blow on his cane late into the night, a dirge or a dance, as his mood dictated. While Mil brought food from the fire, CK and Dulcet would pool their earnings, placing the coins inside the leaves of CK's Bible.

"Tell me about Nicodemus," Dulcet said one night after dinner. He lay back and stretched out, folding his arms behind his head. The smoke from the dying fire snaked lazily in the darkening night. CK turned to Dulcet, tucking his legs under himself.

"I'll tell you bout Nicodemus," CK said, raising his hands. "It's a colored town, course you know. Started a short while ago by folk from Kentuck."

"That's fine and good, but is there work?"

"Plenty that."

"Worked for a colored man for a spell," said Dulcet. "Had a plantation outside Holly Springs. Weren't much different than working for the white man."

"Not this," CK said, sitting up so that he was kneeling now. Mil had set Rachel to bed and was clearing the plates, running river water over them before drying and placing them in the pack. "Every man has a home and a farm to hisself," said CK. "No landlords, no bosses."

"Run by us?"

"It's the truth," he said. "You work your fields for yourself."

"That don't sound half bad."

"Half bad?" CK said, tossing a piece of tinder at his friend. "You hear what I say, Dulcet? You gon have a home. Your own farm. To bring your family back to."

"Now you're talking," Dulcet said, bracing himself on his elbows. "And we gon be neighbors?"

"Right next door," CK said. "We supper together each—"

"What you know about Nicodemus?" Mil said as she took a seat by the fire. "You never been."

It was true; beyond his vision he knew little else but what he'd seen on the handbill he still carried in his pocket.

"I seen it," CK said. "Through my God's eye. He show me."

Mil looked away.

Dulcet lay back down, laughing a single, satisfied laugh. "I gotta give it you, CK," he said. "You ain't know nothing about this town and you act like you fit to be mayor." He laughed again, but quieted quickly. After a moment's pause, he asked, "Tell me what else about Nicodemus."

CK moved his hand slowly before him as if making a careful brushstroke: "It's a beauty like never you saw." Dulcet was starting to believe, he could tell.

"What else?"

"Well, now, you listen," CK began and told Dulcet of the song about Nicodemus, the slave who prophesied freedom and spoke that truth to others. They talked a long time that night, and their excitement carried them out of bed early in the predawn and for several days after, anxious as they were to raise enough money for train fare. They continued to do so until the morning CK woke to find Dulcet gone. He put on his shoes and hustled through town, checking saloons he was too timid to enter and other debauched places where one could lose money so quickly. Nothing. Later CK returned to the depot, ducking under the platform, and met Mil's eyes. Neither said a word. She was holding the Bible and opened the cover. The money was gone. Inside lay the fife. It was light out now, and in the spot of dirt where Dulcet had lain, CK noticed something: a one-word apology, written in the shaky script of a finger dragged through dirt.

The axe had been his father's, but Talmen borrowed the wagon from a neighbor. With Rawl driving, they set out, and when he asked where they were headed, Talmen told him to keep on, saying only, "Outside town a ways."

When they arrived at the oak grove, Talmen dismounted and stood silently a moment, taking in the sight of those tall hardwoods. "How many you figure we need?" said Rawl.

Talmen walked toward a tree, measured it up, and swung quickly, lodging the axe deep in the wood. "Just one." Talmen spoke softly.

"Why ain't we taking more? Sure could use it."

"Now move the wagon over yonder some. No telling which way this gon fall," said Talmen, taking another swing. "When it do, you head that horse, hear? Don't let him spook."

"But why ain't we take more?"

"Son, I need you to hush now."

"Yes, sir," he said.

Rawl was full of questions tonight. Nervous, Talmen figured. Maybe he sensed what his father was up to, that this was no unclaimed spot of land, and that the owner of the claim was white, and, further, that the owner was Ryer, a man who'd been nothing but pretty good to Talmen. And here he was stealing from him so brazenly. Talmen looked over at the house, certain any moment light from a kerosene lamp would illuminate a window. *I'll take what I need*, he imagined telling Ryer as he labored to bring down the tree, *whether you trade or not. You see what you done to me.* Perhaps he would tell Rawl later, try and explain the things a desperate man will do, but for now he didn't care to account for himself. Right now he just needed silence, a demand Rawl met, so that the only sound that passed between them was the hollow crack of the axe. When the oak fell, Talmen chopped half of it into smaller lengths that could be loaded into the wagon and left the other half where it lay.

"But what about—" said Rawl, looking at the abandoned portion.

"Leave it be." Talmen placed his axe in the bed of the wagon and climbed into the cab. "Let's go."

That night, while everyone was asleep in the dugout, Talmen sat outside in the warm early-summer night, stripping bark. He worked late, using the axe and saw to secure enough wood to fashion the top, bottom, and sides that would be needed. It was green, unseasoned wood, but it would have to do. No time for a visit to the mill that might have no time for him. All those years of watching and helping his father build houses, fences, and floors, but never once something so small. He had to trust his eyeballed measurements to be correct. He sat alone on a stool in the starlight and hum of cicadae, his hands resting on the rough denim of his overalls. He wasn't finished, but it was quiet now, and the hammer-and-nails work he had left would wake his family. He would finish in the morning, but for now he just sat there a long time thinking, listening, being still.

Word later came that the mayor of Leavenworth himself had climbed aboard the *Joe Kinney* to stuff a wad of bills in the captain's hand, begging him not to leave any more of these wretched people in his town. "Take them on to Atchison, please," the mayor was rumored to have entreated. Of course CK and Mil knew nothing of it at the time, lodged as they were with the others in the hull of the towing barge. They'd pieced it together only later, when they exited the steamer and walked the banks of the Missouri, met by the cold stares of Atchison townsfolk who were not pleased to see Leavenworth's refuse on their shores.

"Morning, folks," CK said, tipping his hat to the crowd as he and the others carried what was left of their belongings from the steamer.

"Go on back where you come from, why don't you," a voice called out.

CK smiled pleasantly, a calculated gesture of obliviousness that he'd often used to deflect hostility. "Fine day here in Leavenworth," he said, as he helped an old woman struggling to carry an armful of blankets from the ship.

"Ain't Leavenworth ground you standing on, nigger," the voice in the crowd called again. "You's in Atchison here. They don't want you, and us neither."

"Atchison?" CK said, and slowly the pieces started coming together.

Earlier that morning, after Dulcet disappeared with their money, Mil had fumed, cursing his name.

"I don't understand," CK said in a monotone daze. How could a friend who called himself family just up and disappear from your life? Leave you in such a bad spot?

"That darn fool is drinking away our money and you know it."

"No, ma'am," CK said. "He went back for his kin, I'm sure it."

"Believe what you will," she said. "Fact is, that money's gone."

"He'll meet us in Nicodemus," he said, but his words failed to convince even himself.

"How *we* gon get to Nicodemus now?"

She was right, and as he thought about that money—nearly

enough to secure rail tickets—CK's befuddlement dissipated, stoking a slow-burning resentment he struggled neither to voice nor to dwell upon, if only for Mil's sake. Instead he'd made like such a thing could just be shrugged off, saying with new resolution: "We move on." Having little desire to stay in a place that now seemed haunted by Dulcet's betrayal, CK went to the relief board and looked into their options. One of the last free-passage boats, the *Joe Kinney*, was set to leave for Leavenworth later that very morning, and a man on the board said it was a town where one could find steady work. And so he boarded the boat with his family and a new optimism that was almost convincing until now, when they'd arrived in a town that hadn't been their destination.

Those first few days in Atchison were long and without prospect. Just summer heat and hunger. Here there were no relief boards or wealthy donors, and local blacks seemed consumed by a growing indifference to the boatloads of needy refugees who so regularly appeared. CK and Mil had arrived with nearly three hundred others, and many were in a bad way. The hard travel had taken its toll in pneumonia and measles, and their clothes had become little more than rags. There was worry they might even carry yellow fever, so the local authorities concerned themselves with quarantine followed by expulsion, arranging for ships and trains to take the indigents elsewhere. They'd been so overrun with exodusters the last month, they were losing all patience and goodwill. This was not a matter of skin color, the mayor said repeatedly. This was a matter of economics, and Atchison simply couldn't afford to keep giving away food and the like. So it was back to the basement of another crowded church, hoping the hostility would fade, and eventually, as more and more people were transferred, it did, dissolving into mean disregard. CK and Mil took turns ministering to the sick and elderly, praying, listening as they spoke.

"Ain't no Kansas I heard about," said a bone-thin older man, too sick to travel, one night as he lay on his pallet by the fire. CK sat beside him, Bible open on his lap. "Jayhawkers and John the Brown ain't even a memory. 'Eden on the Prairie' ain't even a dream no more." CK raised a tin cup to the man's lips but he shook it off. He was in pain, knew he would soon die, and said he wasn't scared. O Death, be kind to him, thought CK. He'd seen men unafraid of the end and he hoped he could muster the same resolve when Death came for him. But while that would not be the end, lying in the arms of his Savior was something he wasn't yet ready to court.

While most accepted transportation back to Wyandotte or Topeka, CK looked into passage to Nicodemus. The steamer to Atchison had brought them north of Wyandotte but no farther west, leaving them three hundred miles from their destination. A railway would suffice but was costly. He thought of Dulcet, imagined him in a bar, smiling over a bottle of brown liquor, as he captivated others with stories of his journey out of the South. CK carried on an imagined conversation with him as, again, he looked for work. Maybe now Dulcet would stop his scoffing and understand how hard it was to live in a godly way. The lost company of his friend, however, paled now beside the loss of that money. In these times the only salve for CK was Nicodemus. When he felt that wrath come upon him, he'd start to sing "Wake Nicodemus," but now the song was less affirmation of his vision than a guard against succumbing to disillusioned anger.

Defying CK, Mil sought work as well, determined as she was to get out of Atchison. She took up washing and laundering linens for a few families, carrying out the tasks with Rachel on her hip or at her feet. After a few days, CK found steady work in a grain elevator from a man named Roberts, who lived outside of town. Roberts worked right alongside his hired men, putting in a full day, too. He seemed to like CK, and one day as they descended the steps of that towering elevator, along with another man Roberts referred to as "Germany," he offered to let CK stay on as long as he wanted. "You're the hard kind of worker I could use around here," he said. "Ain't that right, Germany? We could use us another two, three like CK."

"They take our jobs," Germany said, his voice heavy with the accent of his home. They were the first words CK had heard him speak beyond the *uh-huh* grunting that shoveling grain necessitated. He was older than CK, bespectacled, and did everything with an air of agitation, whether hauling heavy grain sacks into storage or wiping a smudge from the lens of his glasses with a handkerchief from his back pocket. He repeated himself, Germany did, and set out in the opposite direction, before turning back to say he would see Roberts tomorrow morning, nodding curtly.

This made Roberts laugh. "Don't pay him no mind. He thinks he's white, is all." He took a rag from his denim trousers and dabbed at his forehead, repeating his offer to CK. "Black, white, don't much matter to me, so long as you carry your weight." CK thanked him, but remained resolute on leaving for Nicodemus after he'd raised enough money for train fare. "Whatever suits you," Roberts said, and they continued on in the direction of his farmhouse. "That was the problem with the others, you know," he said a few seconds later. "No workers. Most of your bunch seemed content to wait on charity."

"Plenty willing to work," said CK, feeling comfortable enough with Roberts to speak openly. "But some are sick, need care."

"Whatever they are, they ain't working."

Later CK wanted to explain what he knew Roberts could

never understand: what it felt like to make this journey together, up from where they came from. To suffer sickness and hunger, waiting on boats, penniless, packed into different churches, always being separated or sent to another town. Whether you'd ever spoke a word to them or not, the ones who'd made it this far were as much family as your true-blood kin. But those words wouldn't come to him in the moment. All he could say was: "Well, we here now."

"Yeah"—Roberts smiled, his face mottled from the long day—"can't argue that."

"And now they sending us to every town under a Kansas sky."

"Except the one you want."

"Yes, sir," CK said. "Nicodemus."

"Ah, Nicodemus."

It was Roberts who set CK on the idea of hitching a ride on a supply wagon headed west. "Take a little longer, but cheaper than waiting on that rail line," he said. "Get you closer, too." Roberts went so far as to make inquiries, and toward the end of May, CK and Mil had raised enough to buy passage with a husband-and-wife freighter team whose name CK never troubled himself to learn.

"Can take you as far as Bull City," the husband said. "Got a delivery there, but then we head south, on to Hays. That'll put you close, though. You can catch another freighter from there. Probably walk it even. Ain't but some miles."

"Might could, yes sir," CK said, taking the money from his pocket and handing it to the man. "Much obliged."

They set out from the livery stables in the early morning, CK and Mil cramped in the back of the covered wagon with Rachel, while the husband and wife sat side by side in the cab, driving the team of horses. During the long bumpy days CK played with Rachel, dandling the wide-eyed child—so bewildered by the newness of everything—on his knee as he told tales about what lay ahead in Nicodemus. Sometimes Rachel would coo in response, and he'd say, "I'm telling the truth, my little queen—I swear on it," which sometimes elicited a laugh from Mil in that way CK loved to hear. Tired though they were, deliverance was near.

In the evenings the husband would lead the horses to the trough of whatever town they were passing through and CK would start the fire, while Mil and the wife fixed supper. They ate quietly, though sometimes the white couple indulged CK's joviality, grinning at a joke or story, as if despite themselves. At night CK and Mil removed their belongings to make room for the couple to sleep and would spread their dusty blanket on the ground beneath the wagon, lying down in the warm night with Rachel soughing restlessly between them.

There was a small one-foot rent in the tarpaulin covering that had been rigged to shelter the back of the wagon from which CK liked to look out at the passing land, baffled by the way the landscape of Kansas seemed to change right before his eyes. The way the open prairie went from rolling and tall-grassed in the east to flat and short-grassed the farther west they went along those desolate high plains. Strange that a *place* was actually made up of so many different kinds of places. Wasn't so different from Mississippi when he thought of it, though. He'd rarely left Bolivar County but heard tell of the hill country up north, the sandy gulf to the south, the riverboating east, and the tall piney woods between. And of course there was the burnt-black soil of his own Delta, that gorgeous floodplain between the Yazoo and Mighty Miss. He imagined the underwater humidity of syrupy summer days, the clouds of cotton dotting the horizon in all directions interrupted only by the occasional stand of pecan trees or bald cypress. When he felt the pangs of homesickness, CK would sit and stare for long stretches, humming to himself.

'Twas a long weary night,
we were almost in fear,
that the future was more than Nicodemus knew.
'Twas a long weary night,
but the morning is near,
and the words of our prophet are true.

On the day before they arrived in Bull City, their wagon came upon a long train of Indians, maybe a hundred or so, making their way across the plains. There were a handful of white men in blue tunics on horses directing the scattered group, as if herding cattle.

"Something's wrong with Rachel," Mil said to CK, whose back was turned as he looked out the small window at the strange scene.

"Look at this, would you," he said as he chewed on wild garlic leaves to quench his thirst. He'd seen some Choctaws in and around Bolivar County, but these folks were different, and there was something of the spectacle about them now. They were barely clothed—next to naked, by God—with expressionless faces like beaten leather. A wretched lot, if ever CK had seen one. They walked slowly, in no hurry, it seemed, to arrive at their destination.

"You hear what I say, CK?"

Still he didn't turn, just reached a hand back to shake Mil's leg. The noisome smell of garlic filled the hot wagon and she wafted a piqued hand as she joined him to see what he was fussing about.

She looked on, punctuating her silence with a little *tthit* click in her mouth.

"Look at them, would you," he said. "Ain't they terrible-looking as anything you ever saw? Where you spose them redmen going?"

"Wherever they being put," Mil said, returning to her spot wedged up against a few large sacks of cornmeal. CK tried to imagine where that might be. Where would you go when forced from your home, not knowing your destination? Would you wander forever? "Baby's hot," Mil said, hand to Rachel's head. "I been trying to tell you." CK said nothing, still watching as their wagon left the dismal procession behind, thankful his family knew where their journey would end.

He moved close to his wife, raising two fingers to his daughter's head. "Fever? You sure?" he said skeptically. He took Rachel in his arms.

"You think a mama don't know?"

He rocked the child gently, inspecting her. He didn't realize he was smiling until it had eased from his face. He could feel the warmth inside his daughter. Couldn't be, he thought. Not after what they'd been through. No. He passed Rachel back to Mil. "She feel fine to me," he said.

One of the first ordinances they'd come to decide as a community was to outlaw liquor in Nicodemus. Talmen had never been one for more than the occasional drink, but he craved the tang of that Kentucky corn liquor and was glad he'd snuck a bottle in his clothes truck. He didn't care who knew, either. Damned if anyone was going to say he weren't allowed a drink after losing Isaiah. The night of the funeral, so besot, he walked through town with the bottle in hand. He made his way to the unfinished schoolhouse and went inside. There was no door and the floorboards were warping, a combination of rain-soak and the inferior lumber they'd had to use. There were still some tools lying around, as if any day they might be able to go back to work when the neighboring towns eased up their embargo. He set a hand on the sawhorse, running a finger along the smooth wood. He took a big slug of whiskey, and stared up at the sky through the unfinished roof. Those stars. Slowly he moved to the doorway and leaned against the frame, looking out into the distance. The stone house. Baldwin. It was the only home you could see from there if you didn't know that all around it, barely noticeable below ground, were cramped dugouts full of families. He imagined taking his hammer to every corner of that stone house. He indulged the vision for some time, taking occasional pulls from the bottle as he watched himself chipping away at it until the home was no more than a pile of chalky limestone. His sadness had become anger, and soon that anger tired him. He lowered himself to the floor and fell asleep right there in the door frame, the same spot where Rawl would find him the next morning after Eugenia sent him out to search for his father. She wasn't one bit happy when they returned home, Talmen propped up by Rawl, sweating his drink. She took the bottle and poured out the last of the whiskey right then, giving him the meanest eye she could muster.

In the days that followed, Talmen didn't do much of anything. When Rawl rose early to head out to the fields to prepare for the coming harvest, Talmen slept late and spent the long afternoon hours beneath a cottonwood not far from the banks of the Solomon, where they'd buried Isaiah. It hectored him, Death. It was cruel and it was unrelenting.

After a few days Eugenia came upon Talmen sitting in the shade of the tree, staring a few yards away at the wooden cross he'd fashioned bearing his son's name. She spoke, and when he didn't answer, she lowered herself to take a seat beside him.

"Tal," she said, placing a hand on his leg. They'd hardly spoken twenty words since the funeral—not because of any anger or reproach, but because not speaking of it had been their way of carrying on in the past. But here he was, underneath the cottonwood tree. "What's wrong that you have to sit up here all day?"

"You know why, Genia."

"Your heart is heavy," she said, rubbing her hand over the leg of his overalls.

"I can't leave it behind."

There was a long silence, and they both looked out at the water, a slight breeze passing over them. Last born, first to die, he thought. The awful imbalance of it all.

"Isaiah, he gone, but you still here. Your family still here. We need you." Talmen didn't say anything. "And the wheat will be coming in soon and you know Rawl can't do it all hisself."

"Eugenia," he said.

"Yes," she said, and when he added nothing else, she spoke: "Your heart can sore and you can father. Don't have to favor one to the other."

Talmen looked at the river, silent for a long moment, and then said, "Go on and leave me be a little longer."

"Okay, a little longer then," Eugenia said, but she stayed where she was until Talmen finally moved to stand, giving one hard exhalation, and together they made their way back to the dugout.

The freighter team let them off at the limits of Bull City, the mister—reins still in hand—tipping his cap to CK, and pointing in the direction of the Solomon River. "Bless you, folks," CK said, and watched as the couple made their way into town to deliver their meal and molasses.

Mil said, "We should take her to a doctor now. Here."

"Our girl's fine. We all are—we almost there."

They were so close. He could feel it.

"How you know there's even a doctor in Nicodemus?"

"Of course there is. I seen it in my vision."

"You seen it." Mil looked away, making that clicking sound again in her mouth. "I'm taking her to town now, CK."

"No you ain't," said CK. "You're my wife, you'll do as I say. God start us on this journey together and we gon finish it so. Ain't nothing wrong with any of us that can't be made right in Nicodemus."

CK turned in the direction of the Solomon and began to walk. After a brief pause he heard Mil's footsteps and they continued on until they found the river, and CK stooped by the banks to ladle a hatful of cool water. Slowly he rose and brought some water to Mil and Rachel, and they said nothing to each other for a long time afterward. That night they made their way a little farther on before camping on the bank. Eventually the river would lead them to Nicodemus. The contents of the pack had dwindled on this long journey, having shed some weight at each stop along the way. CK built a fire and set on the coffee, thinned and watery. After trying in vain to catch a jackrabbit that was too elusive in its jagged quickness, they settled for nibbling on the last of their stale bread.

"How she doing?" he said, nodding at Rachel. Their first words in hours.

"What you care?" she said, and pulled Rachel's blanket up so that it covered her neck. It was a cool night and colder still near the water. They slept underneath a quilt with the heat from Rachel's body providing additional warmth. They set out early in the dawn, unable to sleep after the baby began her crying shake. They walked all that morning and stopped in the early afternoon in the shade of some trees. CK eased into the shallow part of the river, dunking his hat under and spilling a refreshing pool over his head.

"We almost there, I can feel it," he said. "Everything's gonna be okay."

Mil was sitting on the ground, leaning against the trunk of a tree, catching her breath. She looked tired and hungry and said nothing. CK filled the tin cups from the pack and brought

water to her. As he waded out again, he looked down into the
river, seeing the occasional fish swim past his legs, and there he
stood while Mil and Rachel took a short nap, splashing around,
trying to catch dinner until his fingers brushed against the tail
of a medium-sized trout and brought him headfirst and all the
way under, soaked. He resurfaced, shooting a thin stream of
water out of his mouth, and smiled at Mil, who'd woken in the
commotion. "Shoot," he said. "Nearly had him." Mil regarded
him, then looked away into the distance.

So they walked and walked, all afternoon, nibbling on the
last handful of coarse grain and seed CK had relieved from the
freighter's shipment.

"How far we?" said Mil.

"We close."

"How close?"

"Closer. I can feel it."

"Quit your feelings already!" she said. "I'll tell you bout
feelings. How bout feeling scared for our daughter? For us
starving on this river?"

"We close, love. Soon, we gon arrive and see what Nicodemus saw—"

"And what happened to Nicodemus? Huh? Where he end
up? He still dead, ain't he!"

Dust caked to Mil's dress, the damp red handkerchief tied
round her head. She moved Rachel to the other side, easing
the weight on her right hip. Rachel began to cry. Mil bounced
her gently and when that failed to calm the child she turned
around and undid the knot holding up the top of her dress.

"The Lord will take care of us," CK said. How old and
weary he felt shouldering the pack.

"That so," Mil said over her shoulder. "*He* spoke to you, did
He?"

"When'd you take on the doubting of Thomas?"

She turned back to face him again.

"And *He* gon take care of Rachel?"

"She washed in the blood, same as us. God been with us the entire time," said CK, exasperated. "Wouldn't have made it this far if He weren't."

She pulled the baby away from her breast and turned her so CK could see his daughter's face. "*He* with her now, is He?" Rachel was shaking, opening her mouth as she searched for the nipple. "*He* the one made my milk dry up?" Mil held Rachel with both hands before her bare chest, unashamed of her top-nakedness.

CK moved close to her. He said, "God wouldn't have us come all this distance only to take her away."

"He done more mysterious things than that."

In one fluid motion—CK's hand darting to the back pocket of his trousers—he grabbed Dulcet's fife, drew back his hand, and brought it down within a few inches of Mil's face. She grimaced but held Rachel firmly, suspended in the air between them. He'd never struck his wife. "That what you want?" he said, drawing the cane away. "You gon drive me to lay hands on you, you know that."

"Go on, then."

He spun left and threw the fife into the water, where it made a light splash, momentarily bobbed, and was gone, taken by the slow pull of the current. He shouted, long and loud, and kicked futilely at the dirt. Mil said nothing. Her breasts, once plump and full, hung low and limp, their roundness gone, leaving depressed folds of extra skin. He took hold of Rachel so Mil could collect herself, but she didn't let go. She held her gaze as hard on him as was her grip on Rachel.

"I want you to remember this," she said.

His eyes fixed on her chest and now he saw the bite marks, the missing part of her left nipple that was nothing more than a bloodless, pink sore. "Cover yourself, love," he said softly, and finally she let go.

It was during that long afternoon and evening that CK finally succumbed to the fear and doubt. His daughter was sick; he couldn't believe otherwise any longer. What would become of them if they didn't soon find food and shelter, a doctor? *We are washed in the blood*, he told himself. He had led his wife and child across the country in search of a place whose existence the grim reality of the journey seemed to test. Had the sign been false? Maybe he'd misremembered the song. Maybe there was never any prophecy. Had the Lord really shown him Nicodemus—those visions that had led him all this way—or had he affirmed his faith only to achieve the end he desired? *Washed in the blood.* He was so tired. Maybe people were never meant to leave their homes. Home, he thought. It had been over three months since they left, but it felt so much longer for what they'd been through. Bolivar County. How lonesome he was to see Mississippi again. *I am washed in the blood.*

Those summer nights allowed them to work past ten, and Talmen and Rawl spent the first few weeks of June bringing in the early wheat harvest. They walked that sea of gold with scythes in hand, reaping the stemmed wheat that they would later separate from the chaff, tie into bundles, and cart off to millers and granaries. It was the busy season, and Talmen was thankful for it because the intense labor kept most thoughts, baleful and otherwise, at bay. Mostly he felt tired or hungry, and those, when he considered such matters, weren't bad things to feel if you knew they could be relieved.

One Sunday night, about eight o'clock, Jesse Mae came running out to the fields. She usually brought them a late supper about this time, and he and Rawl would eat standing up, rushing the food into their mouths before returning to the last few hours of work. But from the sight of his daughter now, breathing so hard, he could see something was the matter. By the time she arrived, she was bent over, trying to catch her breath, and could only muster: "Something happening at that stone house."

Talmen dropped his scythe and began to walk the half mile at a brisk pace. His children followed. He knew Jesse Mae had been at the Baldwins'. On Sundays during the harvest, while he and Rawl worked, Eugenia would take Jesse Mae to church and to the after-gathering. Often Jesse Mae stayed late into the evening, learning piano from Mercy.

"We was practicing our scales when a man come to the door and they started arguing and . . ."

"Go on," Talmen urged, but she struggled to keep up with his long strides and had trouble getting anything else out.

They arrived to take their place in the growing crowd half-circling the stone house. There was an awful commotion of some sort, but Talmen couldn't see anything from the back. He stood on his tiptoes and when that didn't help he pushed to the front, and that's when he saw the two men wrangling in the dirt. Thomas Baldwin and someone he didn't recognize. They were rolling on the ground, drumming fists into each other's middle, positioning for leverage. For all the struggle the town had endured, there'd been little quarreling since settling—a couple of fistfights, one of them a contest between ministers arguing over Bible interpretation—and it was as if no one knew what to do, transfixed as they were by the sudden explosion of violence in the calm summer night. These watchers, Talmen realized as he looked around, were from neighboring dugouts. Mrs. Baldwin shielded Mercy from the scene, screaming for someone to do something, but no one said a word or made a move to break up the fight.

"You no-count criminal—you rotten vagrant!" Baldwin

yelled, pinioned by the silent stranger. There was a woman with a child in her arms, pulling on the man's shoulder, pleading for him to stop. He shook her off, drew back his fist, and quickly struck him over his right eye. Baldwin groaned and rolled onto his side. Then a strange thing happened. The man looked back at the crowd and just sat there as Baldwin regained his wits and started to hit back, repaying the blow a dozen times over. It looked as if he were letting Baldwin hit him, until he finally tipped over and sprawled in the dirt. Baldwin stood over him and kicked his side. He looked at the crowd and screamed, "He tried to break into my house!" He kicked the man again and the stranger's wife cried, trying to bat away his boot. "They exodusters! You see how they are!"

Absent a word, Talmen pushed past the bystanders into the moonlit stretch of dirt where the beaten man and his family lay. Baldwin was possessed of an untethered rage that seemed like it might swing Talmen's way when he stepped between him and the fallen man. Talmen waited for him to make a move, raising his clenched fists. They looked at one another a long second, silent, before Baldwin's face turned from craze to confusion.

"What you doing?" he said.

Talmen looked around at all the eyes trained on him, dropped his hands, and then knelt by the stranger. His eye was swollen shut, blood on his gums and lip. The woman's crying had petered out into a hard kind of breathing. She looked at Talmen, her eyes open wide with uncertain expectation. Talmen helped raise the man to his feet.

"You saw him hit me, Talmen," Baldwin said, and then he turned to the crowd as if to plead his case: "I said they're exodusters! You hear me? They the ones soiling our name."

"Hush your meanness," Talmen said.

"Don't let them get away! They'd be strung up where they come from for what they done."

"No one's doing nothing yet," said Talmen.

He led the strangers into the crowd, parting the mass of onlookers, who made no moves other than to step out of the way, and in that moment it was all human silence outside the stone house, just the sounds of the earth at night around them. Talmen took them to the dugout, propelled only by an instinct that this was the right and only course. Eugenia, too, seemed to be guided by that same unseen hand, going right to the sod fireplace to prepare food at the strangers' appearance. She sent Jesse Mae to the well to draw water and Rawl to call on Dr. Newth.

CK and Mil sat by the fire, she dabbing at his face with a wet rag as he stared into the blue of the flames, wincing when she touched directly on a sore.

"My daughter," Mil said. "She sick."

Eugenia was at the stove boiling beans and salt pork, mixing biscuits in the excess grease and gristle of their earlier supper. "Doctor's on the way," she said. Soon she fixed them a plate and when she set the food before them, she said, "May I?" and motioned at Rachel. Mil handed the baby to Eugenia and took up her plate.

"You gon be right better soon. Just you hang on," Eugenia said as she looked at the child.

Mil watched the older woman handle her baby as she forked food rapidly into her mouth.

"Is it yellow fever?" Mil said.

Eugenia said she felt the fever in the baby and looked hard at her coloring for jaundice, but it was tough to tell there in the night.

"We'll see what Dr. Newth say."

Talmen looked on from a stool in the corner, thinking about what had happened. He'd wanted Baldwin to make a move, so he'd have an excuse to crush him the way he'd once imagined crushing that stone house. It was that desire more than anything else, he knew, that had propelled him forward, not some sense of righteousness that wouldn't stand for seeing a stranger beaten to death in such lawlessness. He didn't even know whether this man deserved defense; he still hadn't said so much as a word.

"Gonna tell us about it already?" Talmen said.

The man sopped his plate clean, then stood, half bent over so as not to hit his head on the ceiling. Talmen motioned at him to follow and removed the orange door to let the dugout cool down.

Outside, CK saw a man heading their way.

"That the doctor?" he said. "He white?"

"Let the man do his job," Talmen said. "Follow me." When CK didn't budge, Talmen assured him they'd come back soon, and CK relented. Talmen led him to the river, where they took a seat under the cottonwood. "My feet," Talmen said, removing his shabby boots. "Darn near rubbed raw from walking that wheat stubble all day." He rose and went to put his feet in the river, sighing heavily as he looked up above him. It was full dark and the stars shined bright in the vast sky. A grave silence had taken hold of CK, but he seemed to listen as Talmen—not knowing what to say to this mute man—spoke. "You exodusters, huh?"

CK nodded.

"Know about long journeys myself," Talmen said, and told of his family's move to Nicodemus, recounting in great detail that first long winter and how they'd been saved only by the Osage and the arrival of that final group from Kentucky last year.

Hearing this unlodged the words that finally allowed CK to speak: "Where everybody at? Where the town? All the buildings—the houses, the church and school?"

"Got a church, not too far," Talmen said. "We working on a school, but ain't finished." He lifted his feet out of the water, one at a time, and let the air send a cool shock through them before dunking them under again. "And people, they all around."

"Where at?"

"In the ground, most of them. Like us." Talmen pointed out the faint wisps of smoke from fires in the distance mingling up into the night.

"In the ground, like a prairie dog?"

"Ain't for long. We gon build us a soddie after next harvest."

"Ain't like I thought." CK shook his head. "Ain't like I thought at all."

"We a young town."

CK considered this a moment: "I spose living free in the ground's a might better than where we come from."

"The Lower?"

CK nodded. "Mississip."

"Had a bunch arrive from there after last winter. Couple months back. February. Group of fifty thereabouts."

"From Mississippi?"

"Sure enough. They settling in right fine."

CK thought of the handbill. So he hadn't been alone in this pursuit. "Wish we'd caught on with them. Didn't leave till March." He recounted the story for Talmen, of the arduous trek, of the waiting and the hunger, of the relief he'd felt earlier at having finally reached Nicodemus, and of how quickly it turned to disappointment and rage. When they had arrived, he and Mil approached the first house—the only house—they saw, whose bright fireplace seemed to bode well. "They was even hymning beautiful songs at the piano," CK said, "and I thought, being Sunday, how rightly to hear our Lord's name praised first thing." He'd knocked, asking that they might come in for some food and medicine for Rachel. Baldwin seemed pleasant enough, he said, but the kindness in his eyes disappeared when he found out CK and Mil were part of the exodus.

"Turned away by one of our own," CK said. "After what we been through?" He shook his head. "That broke me open with wrath I never felt before."

"You hit him first?"

"I did. I lost myself for a time, and when I seen what I done—"

"That's why you stopped when you had him licked?"

CK nodded. They were quiet for a minute before he finally said, "I'm a wicked man. This journey weren't meant for no child. If she don't make it . . ."

"You hard on yourself," Talmen said, still standing in the water. He looked over at Isaiah's grave, near invisible in the dark, thinking he might confide some of the hard things he still felt but thought better of it. There would be time for talking. Now he reckoned they better get back to the dugout to hear what Dr. Newth had to say. Talmen put his boots back on and the two men walked quietly. People weren't likely to take to this young man's family for a while, least of all Baldwin, Talmen knew, and he decided he'd let him work the harvest until he got set up on a claim of his own. He thought this was a kindness he could muster, but the idea soured as he looked out at the smoke from a distant dugout. He remembered the numbers the newspapers had quoted, thinking originally they were an exaggeration to scare white folks, but now he wasn't so sure. What if they were right? What if there were thousands of exodusters?

"How many you reckon come north with you?" he said.

"Us?" said CK. "Ain't figures for that kind of number."

"Where they at?"

"All over Kansas. Some went back south."

All over Kansas, Talmen thought. Maybe they could care for a family or two, but what would they do if that many people came their way? The town would never survive. He looked around him, again focusing on that smoke, and imagined its haze as the dust kicked up from the feet of a thousand weary souls, all coming for Nicodemus.

As they neared, CK could see into the dugout through its uncovered entrance. In the firelight Mil stood next to the dour doctor, who was inspecting Rachel. Talmen entered, but CK stopped at the doorway. He turned around. In the distance, he watched the smoke rise slowly from those holes in the ground, like signs from the great fire below. "Nicodemus," he said, testing whether something would happen, but there was no voice, no vision, no song. "Nicodemus," he whispered again, and nothing came. The name meant nothing anymore but this. He felt alone out there in the coming of full dark, so he turned around and stooped to enter the dugout, surrendering himself to the will of what would come.

When John Romulus Brinkley, a.k.a. the Goat Gland Doctor, decided to publish his memoir, he hired someone else to write the book for him, and fed the man such a load of lies and half-truths that Brinkley succeeded in turning the seasoned biographer into a promising writer of fiction. But Brinkley needn't have done so. His story required no embellishment. The book, *The Life of a Man*, was released long after he was already world famous, and it was a fame, as with his nickname, born of the millions of dollars he made injecting the testicles of Toggenberg goats into men to improve their virility. This was 1920s rural Kansas, a little nowhere town called Milford, but Dr. Brinkley put it on the American and world map, a destination for impotent and infertile men seeking to touch the hem of the Milford Messiah, the Ponce de León of Kansas who'd discovered the rejuvenation of man.

Brinkley was that deadly combination: lucky, smart, and ambitious. Up from nothing to millionaire in a few short years, a kind of garish, backwoods Gatsby. He got in on radio early, purchasing one of the first private stations in the country in 1923, and Brinkley was shrewd in its use. He knew he couldn't simply advertise his procedure on the airwaves. He had to win people over, seduce them, so he filled his programming with musicians and entertainers, going on the air himself only twice a day to give "medical talks" about the wonders of his goat gland operation. The procedure took ten minutes and cost seven hundred dollars. People came by the trainload. He was a charlatan, of course, but, most sexual hangups being psychological, the procedure worked for many. Believing you carried the fecund potency of a bearded, randy billy goat because you had its genitals slipped into your scrotum did wonders for a man's confidence. Seeking to regulate the field, the newly organized American Medical Association made Brinkley its top target, going after him for a decade. Finally, by 1930, the AMA had pressured the Kansas Medical Board to revoke his license to practice and the federal government to revoke his license to broadcast, shutting down what had become in a few short years the most popular radio station in the country. It was a double victory for the AMA. They'd finally got him out of the operating room and off the air. Brinkley was finished, or so they thought.

There's more to the story, but I stop because Will asks if I'm making this up. Actually, it's not a question—he just says that I am, but he does so in an amused way that tells me he believes every word and is only playing his part as interested listener, the receiver of a fantastic tale. Our relationship is six months old, and while the Brinkley story is true, I have already begun to tell the little lies that will become big lies. As in all my previous relationships, I'm pulling away from Will, or pushing him away from me, if there's any difference. He recently moved into the house and will have moved out before I have the chance to finish telling him the story of the Goat Gland Doctor.

Will stands at the stove, his back to me, stirring the vodka sauce for dinner with a long wooden spoon that was once straight but has begun to warp. He repeats his question. The Italian sausage sizzles on a neighboring burner, filling the air of the kitchen with a deliciously brackish fog. A large pot of water boils, awaiting pasta, sending steam over his head, which makes him look like a character in a cartoon who's suddenly become furious, someone who's literally blown his lid. I sit in a chair at the small breakfast table in the corner and turn my attention to the muted television, one of those small lunch-pail-sized ones people keep in their kitchens to watch the morning shows over breakfast, the news at dinner. NBC shows W's face, a story about his upcoming bid for reelection in the fall. He has that look of his, a pained smile that suggests he's still slightly surprised and annoyed to find himself running the country instead of a baseball team.

"Michael," says Will, turning. Dressed in the blue scrubs he wears each day at the clinic, he dries just the tips of the fingers of his left hand on a dish towel slung over his right shoulder. "You're joking, right? Goat glands?"

I shake my head and he asks where I heard the story. "I knew Brinkley's son," I say. "Many years ago—almost thirty—but only a short while. Johnny was his name. He told me about his dad. I didn't believe it either." Will's eyebrows rise, and he nods slowly. I seem to have said this in a way that insinuates Johnny and I were lovers. I do nothing to correct the misapprehension, then offer an olive branch: "Maybe that's what's wrong with me. Maybe I need a pair of goat nuts shot into my sack"—a reference to my suddenly vanished libido, a sore point between us.

Will exhales and moves to the table, squatting so that he's at eye level with me. I can tell he wants to kiss me, but he's been rebuffed enough of late that he's timid and it's like he's bringing his lips to his decrepit grandmother's cheek at the end of a visit. "We've got to get you out of this funk," he says. "What you need is a job. Something to keep you busy." After twenty years at the Wichita Historical Society I was let go when the new state budget slashed our funding. The Society was told to become creative, entrepreneurial, to rely more on private donors. In response it cut its hours of operation in half and fired a third of the staff. Will moved in shortly before this happened and thinks it's responsible for everything wrong in our relationship.

"Maybe I wasn't meant to have a job," I say. "Maybe I was meant to be a home economist. Remember how they used to call it that when we were kids in high school? What a strange phrase. I'll get business cards printed up with that as my title. Michael Kupchick, Home Economist. Sounds more important than Stay-at-Home Faggot."

Will bristles, hates when I use the word, so I find myself saying it more often than I normally would.

"Do I need to remind you what a home economist does, and which one of us is cooking dinner right now?"

"I could learn," I say. "Or maybe I'll start to write again. Sometimes I still feel the itch."

"You planning on penning a bestseller?"

"Are you kidding? I've been producing historical copy for the museum for twenty years. I'd probably end up writing about radical farmers or exodusters."

"Exo-*what*?"

"Never mind."

"Baby," he says, "you *do* need to find a job. We need the money."

We. A ripple of revulsion moves through me. I look over Will's shoulder at the boiling pot. "Don't overcook the penne."

He returns to the stove and I open a bottle of wine, pouring two tall glasses of Shiraz. "They were out there again," he says as he plates the food.

"The lunatics? Still?"

Last month a group called Kansas Families for Life began keeping a daily vigil outside the clinic where Will works, holding photographs of aborted fetuses, shouting at the sunglassed women and couples speed-walking to the entranceway of the health center. As a nurse, Will bears their wrath every time he leaves the building or helps usher a patient to her car. Despite this, he is possessed of a tolerance I find as infuriating as I do ennobling.

"They're only half crazy," he says. "They have their beliefs. We have ours."

"Yeah, but theirs are wrong." I point at the television, where the president speaks at a podium. "And they elect monsters like that."

"Oh, the rhetoric of Good and Evil has begun!" he says dramatically. "You sound just like them."

"Are you one of those self-hating gay Republicans? You should have told me before I let you move in."

"You asked me to move in."

"Did I? Sometimes I forget."

"All right, all right. Enough." We go silent for a spell as we eat and drink. Will doesn't pierce the pasta with his fork. He slides the tines through the body, hooking two at a time, and swipes them through the orange sauce before bringing the fork to his mouth. He does this every time, the unvaried precision of one who makes his life in the medical field. He takes a bite and then laughs softly—a single snort through his nose—muttering something about goat glands. "So you knew this guy's kid. What happened to him?"

"The father or the son?"

"The son," he says, adding flirtatiously, "Johnny."

"He blew his brains out."

"I'm sorry. Were you all—"

"You think George has ever heard of the Goat Gland Doctor?"

"I don't know," says Will, taking another one of his bites. "I'll ask him tomorrow. Probably'd get a kick out of it. Dr. Tiller loves a good story."

• • •

I met Johnny in the summer of 1976, the summer of Bicenten-
nial celebrations. I was twenty-eight, newly out, high on the
promise of the life ahead of me, and he was forty-nine, a drunk
crumbling under the weight of previous disappointments. Naturally we met in a bar. It was a place where I'd had some luck
meeting men, but from Johnny I didn't get sex—I got stories.
Back then I fancied myself a writer. After graduate school in
Lawrence, I'd returned to Wichita and published a collection
of short fiction. Nobody read it, and my publisher told me that
if I was going to make it in this business I needed to write a
novel. I was trying to figure out how to do that when I met
Johnny. He'd come to Wichita for a job he'd recently lost and
was trying to save enough money to send for his daughter, who
many years before had gone to live with his mother in Texas.
We'd spend hours in the evening sipping fifty-cent drafts and
well bourbon, talking. Mostly Johnny talked and I listened. He
told me all about his father, the Goat Gland Doctor. I thought
he was lying—such a character *had* to be invented—but the
story checked out.

I began to think that maybe I'd write my novel about his
father, and soon I was jotting down ideas on cocktail napkins
and taking notes. Johnny didn't seem to mind. In fact, he was
happy for all the attention I gave him. Once I brought him a
copy of my book to show I was serious. He held up the sparse,
white cover with the title running red-lettered across the middle. Johnny flipped through the pages. "*The Thirty-Fourth Star.*
What's it about?" I told him they were stories about Kansas.
"Fiction," he said with a look of distaste. He set the book down
and slid it to me over the damp and sticky wood grain of the bar.
"I don't read make-believe and hocus-pocus. Nonfiction only.
History, biography, memoir—real people doing real things!" It
didn't hurt my feelings. The stories felt distant and had already
begun to bore me. Besides, I'd come to find Johnny charming,

a wonderful, inebriated raconteur. The gin blossom at the tip of his small nose, the patches of thinning auburn hair where I could see his scalp, the way that stench of middle-aged despair disappeared when he was telling a story and his eyes shot wide with conviction. It was okay that our relationship was one-sided. He didn't need me to reciprocate; he needed an audience, a witness, and so I was, if only for a short while.

One morning in late June I walk into the bedroom, toweling off after a hot shower. Will's stretched out on top of the made bed, already dressed, leafing through a copy of *Cigar Aficionado* before work. For reasons I can't fathom he's taken an interest in cigars. At first I thought he was trying to send me some subconscious phallic message, but it seems to be his attempt to transition to middle age with class. It's a small thing to endure, I suppose, but it strikes me as an absurd affectation, these cigars that come in colorful, vibrator-like plastic cases. He eyes me over the top of his magazine and I feel self-conscious of my nakedness. I was handsome as a young man, even into my forties, but the long-haired, lean muscularity of my youth has withered into a bald, skeletal thinness at fifty-six. Sometimes I feel like Nosferatu.

"Did you masturbate in the shower?" he says.

"No," I say, turning around to face my dresser.

"Yes you did. I can tell by the smile on your penis."

I look down at it as I open my socks-and-underwear drawer. He's right. It hangs there between my legs, bobbling a little, like the head of a dog that's successfully returned a Frisbee to its master. I did in fact masturbate in the shower. It was unplanned. I was soaping up and my hands lingered too long downstairs, and I was hard. I knew I could have gotten out of the shower and had the real thing, but I began to go limp as I debated the matter. I wanted so badly to stay in the moment—I hadn't felt the urge in a long time—so I tried to focus on something that would keep me there, and, finally, when I had it, I came all over my hand in a matter of seconds and let the shower's weak pressure wash it off slowly into the drain. The image that had done the trick: that staged photo-op of W in dungarees and a cowboy hat clearing brush at the ranch in Crawford.

"So what if I did?"

"So what? We haven't had sex in five weeks!" He tosses the magazine to the side and sits up on his elbows. Then a devilish smile crosses his face. "Of course, you could come here and get me off too."

"We're both going to be late."

Improvising, I step into briefs and move to the closet, where I pull a crisp, white dress shirt off its hanger and slip it on.

"Where are you going?"

"I have an interview," I lie. "This morning. At the Kansas Aviation Museum."

He comes toward me, his mood softened from anger into an annoyance that won't let him get too angry with me.

"Why didn't you tell me?"

"I didn't want to get your hopes up. What the hell do I know about airplanes?"

He smiles halfway and removes the safety pin bearing the blue ticket from the dry cleaner that's pinned below the last button of my shirt. He tells me I'll do great and snaps the elastic waist of my underwear before heading out.

I spend the morning at the Kansas Aviation Museum, not as an interviewee but as a patron. I walk past displays detailing Wichita's large and largely unknown part in the history and development of American aviation, though in my previous work at the city's Historical Society I've long understood our claim to being the "Air Capital of America": that Cessna and Beechcraft started here and later came Boeing and Learjet, the bomber contracts of World War II that brought the B-52 and doubled the city's population practically overnight. There are replicas of some of the original planes, models of men in early flight suits. I stop before a picture of Clark Gable at the Wichita airport in 1932. He was on a stopover from New York to California. The photographer caught him with a cigarette in one hand and a bemused look on his face, a look that seems to say, *Isn't it weird to see me in Kansas?*

On my way home I pass by Women's Health Care Services and park across the street. The protesters still gather near a tall chain-link fence that was installed to allow patients and workers safe passage to the building after Dr. Tiller was shot in the parking lot almost ten years ago by a woman the media called "an activist." Will had been inside the clinic at the time, had heard the shots and called the police before rushing outside, uncertain whether the gun would be turned on him. Will was unharmed, and Dr. Tiller survived the attack, vowing to continue his work on behalf of women. Will told me the story on an early date, shortly after we were introduced by mutual friends at a party last New Year's Eve, and I wondered aloud how he summoned the courage to continue working at the clinic, knowing there were people out there who could do such a thing. Good and honest and brave Will told me he had to—"Like George says, it's too important not to"—and I thought I could love a man like that. I keep thinking maybe I'll catch a glimpse of him now, walking a patient to her car or sneaking out for—what?—a cigar break, but I never do. When a man from the group spots me and starts walking toward my car, I leave.

I remember one day in the bar that summer when Johnny suddenly pointed to the television, where one of the networks was broadcasting the Democratic National Convention. It was the year in which a simple peanut farmer from Georgia was poised to win the presidency of the United States largely because of his ability to motivate untapped pockets of the electorate, knowingly or not, by professing his faith in evangelical Christianity. "He learned that from my father," Johnny said. I asked what he meant. "Dad was doing this," he said, waving his bourbon-and-water at Carter, "forty-five years ago."

The Goat Gland Doctor's story, I learned, did not end in 1930 when his medical and radio licenses were stripped, not even close. Knowing that the governor appointed the state medical board, Brinkley announced within days of his defeat in court that he was entering the gubernatorial race. Revenge on his mind, he would win the election and appoint choice members to the board so that he could continue to practice in the state. Oh, and he'd be governor of Kansas. It was September, the primaries were over, but in the five weeks leading up to the election, he mounted an independent write-in campaign unlike any before.

He had advantages no other candidate had, namely a fortune in discretionary money to blow and a private radio station to get out the vote twenty-four hours a day. He appealed the revocation of his radio license, an appeal he would lose, but which nevertheless allowed him to stay on the air through the election. He spoke to his fans and followers over the airwaves, presenting himself as the underdog, the messianic outsider who was being persecuted by the establishment, just as Jesus had been. He used his private airplane to keep a campaign pledge to visit every county in the state when most politicians were still putting around in trains. He hired a New York PR firm—a new field then—to advise his campaign, to manage his image and stage photo-ops for the press. He was a pioneer of the sound truck and sent his from town to town, playing recorded speeches from speakers bolted to the roof. But Brinkley's real genius was the campaign rally. He turned his into spectacles such as never before seen, where little politics was spoken. Instead they were like old-time tent revivals, full of sermons, testimonials from audience plants, and performances by musicians from Brinkley's roster of popular radio personalities. Fifty thousand people attended a rally here in Wichita, unprecedented turnout for such an event.

The Republicans and Democrats knew they were in trouble, so they colluded to keep Brinkley from the capital. After all the standard election-day malfeasance to misdirect Brinkley voters and dump ballots, it was still too close to call, the closest election in Kansas history. So in the days afterward, as the danger of a full recount loomed, potentially exposing their fraud, the Republican and Democratic candidates made a deal. The GOP had control of the legislature, so the Dems would fill the governor's mansion this time, and the two would duke it out again in two years when Brinkley, hopefully, had lost interest and moved on. Handshakes and champagne, smoking cigars in the smoke-filled room.

"Dad won it in 1930," Johnny said, chewing loudly on the ice from his empty drink. "They stole it clear out from under him." And he was right. If democracy had properly functioned, the people of Kansas would have elected the Goat Gland Doctor governor, which might not seem like a big deal, but when you consider that the man who won the gubernatorial election in '32, Alf Landon, went on to face FDR in the national election of '36, then you start to see the implications and possibilities of what a rich, proselytizing, antiestablishment candidate with the most powerful radio station in the country might have been able to accomplish nationally.

I couldn't believe it, my hand barely able to keep up with Johnny's dictation as I imagined the novel I'd write about Brinkley. Again Johnny pointed at the television, where Carter was smiling and waving at the large crowd before him shouting his name. "Took them a while, but they saw it worked," he said. "Now they all follow his script."

Will and I spend the night of July 4 over at my friend Ron's place, grilling out and catching up as we watch fireworks from lawn chairs in his backyard. We drink light beer and white wine that chills in a red Igloo cooler of half-melted ice. It's become a tradition of mine to spend the holiday at Ron's. I've brought many boyfriends over the years. Ron recently split with his longtime partner, so it's the first time I meet his young, new flame, Alex. Twenty-five years Ron's junior, Alex is a knockout. Tall, blond, and fair-skinned, he seems to have fallen into a wormhole on some New York City runway and resurfaced in Wichita. When he excuses himself to go to the bathroom, we watch him leave the yard, and then turn our attention to Ron. He laughs, already buzzed, imagining what we're thinking. "I know," he says. "It's crazy. I'm old and depressed—I don't know what he sees in me!"

"He's magnificent," I say.

"Is the sex as good as I'm imagining?" asks Will, elegantly sliding a cigar out of its silver case and raising it to his nose. I look at him like he's just pulled a turd from his breast pocket. Ron shakes his head, leaning back in his chair, trying to summon the words.

"I haven't been fucked like this in a decade."

"I despise you," says Will.

When Alex comes back, we continue to laugh and drink and drink, so that when the fireworks start we're good and drunk. Ron and I rise from our lawn chairs and begin to waltz around the backyard, trying to avoid the croquet mallets and balls no one has used the entire evening, singing, as we always do, "You're a Grand Old Fag" while the bombs burst in air above us. Grown men acting like children. Alex is amused, Will confused. He asks what the hell I'm doing. "I'm celebrating my country! Stop hating my freedom, you terrorist," I say, and Ron cracks up as Alex joins us on the lawn. Will looks at me like, *Do I even know you?* then at Alex's perfect ass, hermetically sealed in tight, dark denim. This is what Ron and I did in previous years with other men we loved longer than the ones watching us now.

It's after midnight when Will and I arrive back home. I head to the kitchen to ward off the coming hangover and he upstairs to change. I pour us two tall glasses of water and spill six ibuprofen capsules onto the counter from the bottle I keep in the spice cabinet. I down mine and pour another glass from the tap when Will appears in his pajamas. He comes up behind me and wraps his arms around me, kisses my neck. I don't pull away. I feel the long-absent attraction move through me, floating up from my toes slowly like champagne bubbles. I turn around and we begin to kiss, pawing at one another, when I catch sight of the answering machine. "Look at all the messages," I say. Fifteen, blinking red.

"Oh no you don't," he says, pulling my mouth back to his.

"What if something's wrong?" I break away from him, then turn back, adding seductively, "Or maybe it's Alex asking to come join us."

As I push the button on the machine, again he comes up behind me and begins rubbing my cock, breathing heavy on my neck. The messages are not from Alex. They are not from family members. One is a prerecorded message from the Democratic nominee for president, Old Stone Face, wishing us a happy Fourth of July and asking us to donate to his campaign. The other fourteen are from a man who identifies himself only as a disciple of Jesus Christ, who says Will works for a murderer and will go to hell for committing genocide against the unborn.

We're silent a moment, and Will lets go of my hard-on.

"Can you imagine if he also knew I was gay?" he says. "Then where would he put me? Hell would be too kind."

"Does this really not worry you?"

"Not much."

He starts to delete the messages.

"What are you doing? Shouldn't we share them with the police, or keep them as evidence?" Then I say, "How the fuck did they get your number?" By which I mean: *How the fuck did they get my number?*

"Look, don't get worked up," he says, sipping his water. "This happens now and again. I used to get stuff like this occasionally, particularly around the elections. It'll go away. George gets this all the time."

"Yeah, and they tried to kill him, remember?"

"That was a crazy person. No one's going to kill me, sweetheart." He rises and embraces me. "This is what they do. They try to intimidate you, scare you so you'll leave town. But this is the worst of it. After the election they'll get bored and stop."

"That's four months away."

"Things will be fine," he says, taking me by the hand and leading me upstairs to the bedroom. "You need to relax." He ushers me to the bed and begins taking off my clothes. At first it's utilitarian, but then I realize he's trying to start with me again. I've lost the mood, though. My head is foggy with drink and the aftertaste of the messages, but Will's upon me. "Relax," he says again. I try to roll away, but he holds me down, lowering himself to my middle. I tell him to stop, but he keeps going. "I want to make you feel good," he says, kissing my waist and tugging at my underwear with his teeth. I squirm, and just as he's taken me in his mouth I'm able to roll to the other side of the bed.

"If you want to make me feel good, rub my fucking feet," I

say and pull the comforter over my shoulder. It's quiet, just our breathing, and then I hear him put on his clothes, followed by the sound of his footsteps padding down the stairs, the slamming of the front door.

And still Brinkley's story wasn't finished. The guy loses the election, can't practice medicine in Kansas, and is barred from broadcasting on American soil, so what's he do? It's 1931, the Depression, and states are looking for anything that might provide an economic boost. He had his pick of several, but decided on Texas. And here's the genius part: knowing radio waves pay no attention to lines on a map, he relocates his hospital to a little town on the Texas side of the Rio Grande and puts his radio station on the other side of the border. Angry with the United States over a recent policy disagreement, the Mexican government was more than willing to give all their wattage to this man who'd become such a pain in the Yankees' ass. As a result, the five thousand watts Brinkley'd had in Milford grew to one million in Villa Acuna, giving the Goat Gland Doctor the most powerful radio station in the world. Sheiks in Saudi Arabia, workers in Russia—on clear nights, just about anyone anywhere could pick up Doc Brinkley's signal. Despite the hard times, his fame and fortune only increased throughout the thirties.

So what became of him? I wondered.

Perhaps understandably, Johnny was vague about his father's demise. He'd only say he was a victim of a witch hunt by the federal government and the American Medical Association. I had to do my own research to truly find out. I learned that in the years leading up to the Second World War, Brinkley became increasingly enamored of fascism. He took his family abroad to Berlin to see the Third Reich firsthand, and at home he tiled his pool with swastikas and the Iron Cross.

Increasingly, his stable of popular musicians like the Carter Family were bumped from the program lineup to make room for appearances by the vanguard of American fascism: William Pelley, Father Coughlin, Fritz Kuhn, Gerald Winrod. This did nothing to deter the attention of the U.S. government and the AMA, the head of which, Morris Fishbein, was Jewish. But, like all great tragic figures, Brinkley was really undone by hubris.

In 1938 Fishbein published an article titled "Modern Medical Charlatans," exposing Brinkley as a quack. Granted, Fishbein had been writing such articles about Brinkley for almost two decades and little had come of it, but Brinkley wanted to be done with the "dirty little Jew" who'd been pestering him all these years, so he sued for libel. Determining whether libel had occurred, however, meant examining whether the goat gland transplantation was a real and viable surgical procedure. Brinkley walked right into his own trap. Soon after he lost the case, charges of fraud came pouring in, as did the wrongful-death suits and court orders for unpaid taxes. Finally caving to U.S. pressure, the Mexican government seized the radio station, closing it for broadcasting Nazi propaganda. Brinkley's health worsened in the long process to adjudicate matters. Johnny was fifteen when his father died of cancer in 1942, bankrupt.

I was so excited by the prospects of my novel that I had trouble sleeping at night, turning it all over in my head, caught up in the epic sweep of a story that struck me as quintessentially American, insofar as it seemed to capture all that was great and terrible about this country. Despite his quarrels with the government, Brinkley loved the United States passionately, grateful for what it had allowed a poor kid from the mountains of North Carolina like himself to become. In fact, according to Johnny, his father often called himself an "Americanist." Not an "American"—that wasn't the right descriptive, didn't quite capture the love and boosterism he felt for the United States. *The Americanist.* I knew this would be the title of my novel. But a problem was emerging: I couldn't find a way into the story. Brinkley's story was already written, and it was real. How could I improve upon, in a novel, what had actually happened, a true narrative that needed no fictionalization? Soon a writerly paralysis took hold of me, one from which I'd never recover.

On the day Will comes home early from work, I'm in the middle of what I've told him is my second full week at the Aviation Museum. Each previous morning I've showered, put on a suit, and left the house, sometimes going to museums, sometimes just driving around, and each evening I tell him about the strange lives of my invented coworkers, the comical encounters I have with patrons. It started off just as a way to get Will off my back about finding a job, then it became fun and I wanted to see how long I could pull it off before coming clean. But on this day, when Will enters the house, he finds me sitting at the kitchen table watching the little TV.

"Busted," I say, smiling.

"I knew it," he says in a voice that is both surprised and not. "How?"

"Because you're a bad liar," he says. He turns off the TV and takes a seat across from me. "I had a feeling you'd be here. I just thought I'd find you in bed with someone else."

"I've become asexual, remember?"

"Don't joke now, Michael."

"You came home because you thought I was cheating on you?"

"No, I came home because a bomb threat was called into the clinic. Dr. Tiller sent everyone home." He pauses. My mouth opens, but words do not come out. "I was shaken up—we all were. I went to find you at the museum. But it was strange.

Even before I went inside, it was, like, I knew. I sat there, staring at the entrance of the building, and I knew: Michael's been lying to me."

"I'm sorry," I say.

"Why have you been doing this?"

"I don't always know when I'm lying."

"Yes you do."

"Sometimes I do."

"Tell me something true," he says. "Right now."

"I don't like hurting people."

"You are a grown fucking man," he says, leaning across the table. "Tell me *something*."

"I worry about you at the clinic, about these people who leave us messages and what they might do."

"That's sweet and unremarkable."

"I don't know why I don't want to sleep with you anymore."

"You're doing it to push me away."

"I don't know why I crave closeness and then pull away when it comes, or why I'm so withholding, or why it's so hard for me to be honest even when I know these are the reasons none of my relationships last."

"Why did you ask me to move in if you knew this would happen?"

"I thought I loved you, and I thought that would make me change, but I don't, and it's only made me worse."

"I see," he says, rising from the table. Only now as I watch him leave the room, realizing it's over, do I feel the desire to chase after him, but I don't, because that will only twist the knife further. At the bottom of the staircase he stops, like he might say something, but then I hear his lumbering footsteps upstairs to the bedroom, the creak of the floorboards as he begins to pack.

• • •

After he told me his father's life story, I saw less of Johnny. This was about the time all the packinghouses left Wichita for western Kansas, where there were no unions to deal with, and Johnny said he'd gotten a job as a foreman at one of the last remaining slaughterhouses. Then one afternoon in August he showed up at the bar. I didn't ask whether he'd been fired or simply stopped going in, or if the job had ever actually existed. He seemed down. He tried to talk about his father again, but they were stories I'd already heard, stories he'd forgotten he told me. "Did I ever tell you how Dad was elected governor of Kansas but they stole it from him?"

I asked Johnny to tell me a story about himself, about what his life had been like. He perked up, and I realized then that throughout his life he'd been someone often asked or expected to speak about his father but never about himself. That's when Johnny told me he'd been a Cold War intelligence officer, working for the CIA. I was dumbfounded. My favorite story was how he'd been embedded with the M-26-7 in Cuba. Desperately in need of press for the revolution, Fidel's group of insurgents welcomed him. Most of the men had never seen an instant camera before and they asked Johnny to take their pictures to send home to family. I tried to imagine Johnny humping through the Sierra Maestra with a group of revolutionaries, memorizing fuel routes and jotting down snippets of overheard conversation to turn over to the Agency when he returned stateside. "Make sure you tell them we are not Communists," implored Fidel. Johnny became particularly close with Raúl Castro, and after a day of difficult hiking they'd drink rum under the starlight of the hot jungle night. One such evening he confided in Raúl that his father had, for a time, been the most famous doctor in America. When Raúl asked what kind of doctor, Johnny demurred, but finally told him after another drink. Raúl began to laugh, spitting out the dark liquor. He said Johnny had to tell this story to their medic, calling out for him in the middle of the night, *"Ernesto, ven aquí!"* I couldn't get the picture out of my head: Johnny telling the story of his charlatan-*cum*-fascist father to Che Guevara on the eve of the Cuban revolution. It seemed impossible, but so had everything Johnny told me. I didn't know what was true anymore, or whether it mattered.

On what would turn out to be one of our last days together, Johnny asked how my novel was coming. He was calling me Mikey by then, like he was my uncle, like he'd known me a long time, though we'd been acquaintances for only five or six weeks. That's exactly what he said: "Mikey, how's the novel coming?" I was surprised. I could count on one hand the number of times he'd asked me a question more substantive than what I cared to drink. I was honest. I told him it wasn't going very well. Maybe he was right, I said. Maybe I was wasting my time with fiction. How could it trump a story as wonderfully true as his father's? "Ha! I told you," he said, slapping me on the back. "Real people doing real things—that's what folks want to read!"

Shortly thereafter he was gone. There was no goodbye, no final bender. He just stopped showing up at the bar. About a month afterward he put a Luger to his head and pulled the trigger, though I didn't find out about it until much later, when I tried to track down a number or address for him to see what he was up to.

Assuming my pension from the state will still exist in a few years, I'd like to retire when I'm of age and see if I might begin to write again. I'd like to tell Johnny's story. I filter through my memories of him on occasion, trying to remember the things he said and to imagine what his life had been like before he decided to end it.

As it is now, I've taken part-time work in special collections at the Wichita State University library. Each day I pass by Women's Health Care Services on my way home. I remember Will saying that the protesters would go away after the election, but it's well into the New Year and they are still holding their vigil outside the clinic. Sometimes I park and watch them, wondering if I might catch a glimpse of Will, but I never do. I look at them, these people I've long despised as intolerant and ignorant, and I try to imagine my way into their lives. In my mind I follow them home to their spouses and children. I sit down at their dinner tables and listen to their conversations and observe the ways in which they love one another, trying to understand how they believe in what they do, and it seems that if I could successfully do that, then I could also imagine a way in which they would act differently, would think differently, would stop their threats, pack up their vigil, and think of another way they might serve and honor God. But each day when I drive by the clinic they are still there.

HARD FEELINGS

[Stillness, 1952]

Thirty minutes' break was what he was allowed for lunch. Twelve forty-five to one fifteen usually, but if there was a lunchtime rush, Mr. Stoughton sometimes asked him to stay on longer. He didn't mind that, though. Didn't take but one hundred seconds to eat his sandwich—the army had taught him how to eat without chewing, how to feel sated without tasting—which left a whole heap of time to relax. Sometimes he sat in the back room of the store, among the boxed-up appliances and stacks of white-walled tires, thinking, picking over a weeks-old newspaper. Other times, like today, he went for a walk along Massachusetts Street, looking in storefronts, maybe picking up a cup of coffee to warm his hands. He wasn't hungry yet and decided he'd eat when he got back from his stroll.

"Thomas," Mr. Stoughton called after him as he stepped out onto the sidewalk. He stopped where he was, paused momentarily, and turned. His boss stood in the doorway of the store he'd owned since the interlude between the wars, just a tad over twenty years. Mr. Stoughton had a thin, clean-shaven face, and the last of his graying hair blew wildly from his head now in the breeze. "Your jacket," he said. "It's winter."

Thomas nodded, said, "Yes, sir," but only stood there as his black tie suddenly billowed from where it had hung still against the ironed crisp of his white shirt. "It don't bother me none, sir. I prefer it."

"I can't afford you getting sick on me, son," Mr. Stoughton said in a harsh tone, but then added, kindly: "Wouldn't do either of us any good, you laid up at home."

Thomas smiled. That was Mr. Stoughton's way; his hardness could soften so quickly. Thomas considered him a good, fair boss.

"No, sir. I reckon I just might drive Verna mad, were I that." So he went inside to the back room and took his blue jacket of thin canvas that suited him well enough even in the harshest of Lawrence's winters. Mr. Stoughton let one cheek rise as Thomas held it up to show him, then said curtly, "Twenty minutes today, Thomas. Mr. Merton is coming at one to pick up that oven. You'll need to load it for him."

"Yes, sir," he said, pulling on his coat as he exited the store again. He walked north, in the direction of the river and railroad, the direction he took each evening home. Sometimes at night he stopped on the bridge to regard the languid flow of the Kaw, or paused near the tracks to feel the hot breath of the Santa Fe rushing past. Now he walked a block to the corner of Eighth and Massachusetts, where he took his coat off and slung it over his arm. He liked the cold. It softened the starch of his shirt the same way it softened the starchy way his insides sometimes felt. Out here, on these brief ambles downtown, he remembered himself. He felt stillness. There were places he couldn't go, but that was okay, since he knew the ones he could. Usually on these walks he'd stop in at Green's newsstand and look at the bright covers of magazines, scan the black headlines of gray papers for news about Korea.

Then he'd stroll up to Sixth and cross to the other side of Massachusetts and continue east to New Hampshire, near the *Lawrence Journal World* offices. He remembered the night, more than ten years ago now, when he had been coming home late on a Sunday in early December. He was eighteen, only just done with schooling, and he'd told his parents he was helping clean up the church after the weekend services. But what he had done instead was walk right past the AME and toward the cul-de-sac where Angela Geeshie lived in a small house with peeling yellow paint and a sunken front porch, a house, he thought, that were it a face would be wrinkled and yawning. It was dark. He went around the side and stood below her bedroom window, following her movements through the thin gauze of her window curtain as she prepared for sleep. She was a beautiful dark form walking around the room under the soft light from a dying bulb until she finally settled in bed with a book. He'd almost done something brave that night in declaring his love, and perhaps he might have summoned the nerve were it not for the sigh of the porch's warped boards, exhaling under new weight. Mr. Geeshie's evening pipe. The night was still, and the only sound was the conversation Mr. Geeshie and that yellow house seemed to be having, one of groans and echoes and breath. Thomas waited for him to finish, then hustled in the direction of home, burning in cowardice, when he noticed the crowd gathered around the *Journal World*'s offices. Negroes and whites, near equally. All standing there in the cold, reading dispatches the staff collected right off the AP wires and posted in the windows about the attack in Hawaii, a place that had barely existed until the moment Thomas heard a white man nearby pronounce it and make it real.

Now Thomas passed right on by the press and turned left, heading into East Lawrence, a neighborhood of colored folks mostly, some Indians. He stopped into Willy's for a swallow of hot coffee. He asked after the time, and Willy, in his clean white shirt and dirty white apron, pointed at the cola-clock on the wall. He had thirteen minutes, no need to rush. He sipped

his coffee and thought about how that sight stayed with him—
Negro and white commiserating on the fate of the country they
found themselves living in—all through his years in the war.
It had been strange coming home to Lawrence afterward. The
Sunflower Ordnance Works, a rocket powder factory outside
of town, had flooded Lawrence with men looking for work,
and soon followed the taverns and establishments in which they
could lose their wages. Was it enough to say the town had
grown? Every able-bodied couple, he and Verna included, had
a baby. No, simple growth wasn't enough; it was *change*, which
was more than numbers. It was evident, whether people were
talking about it or trying to *not* talk about it, which is what he
was asked to do by the man at Menninger's the previous week.

Verna had been on him since last spring about making an
appointment.

"They are the best in the country," she said, "and only thirty
minutes away."

"The best at what?" he said.

"Psychology, dear. Psychiatry." He looked at her sharp, gave
her that lemon-sucking face he did when she put on airs and
conversed over his head. "At talking to people who've been
through what you have. Who've seen what you saw." She told
him how Dr. Menninger himself had been made a brigadier
general by the army for his work with soldiers during the war.
"Someone you can talk to."

"We talking fine right now, Vern. I know my letters."

He was reluctant, but Verna was a good woman, and her
love was true, so when she persisted, as was her way, he finally
relented, if only to ease her nag. He didn't care for driving—it
unsettled him—so she took him the twenty-five miles to Topeka, and as they made their way to the clinic they saw the
group of colored folks standing on a downtown street corner
holding signs. *Negroes Acting As Crazy People*, he thought, which

tickled him. He knew he wasn't a humorous man, so when it came he had to savor it. When Verna asked what he was so pleased about, he kept it for himself, and neither remarked a word as they drove past the group. The issue came up a short while later, however, when the doctor asked Thomas about his military training in a segregated unit. It took a while for him to feel comfortable speaking to a white man, despite the doctor's sincere entreaties. Finally he did so, figuring worst case they'd send him home and he'd be done with the whole nuisance.

The colored units were mostly made up of men from the Deep South or the Northeast, whom the military trained in the Midwest before shipping off to Europe. There was tension in that rural-urban division, and Thomas had felt stuck in between the two, unable to stake a claim in either camp. He was from nowhere, and the others didn't know what to make of a Negro who wasn't country and wasn't city. "We different enough as it is without adding color to it," Thomas told the doctor. Sure, the black man walked a harder road, but there wasn't much good done in crowing about it. "That's why this trouble here in Topeka ain't about to serve Negroes nothing. I been in a schoolroom with white folk and don't mean to repeat it." He'd attended KU for a semester after coming home from the war and suffered the threats and cold silence. Enrollment had exploded, the campus overrun with students, but most often, except for the class in which he'd met Verna, he was the only Negro in the room. More than anything it was the staring that made it impossible to concentrate. He couldn't focus on the words his professors were saying. He tried to stay inside himself, as he'd always done, but that's when doing so began to feel like watching a slab of stone slide over the top of your tomb. And so he'd dropped out and went to work at Stoughton's. The lone consolation of his short time in college had been meeting Verna, who was so serious about her schooling she was able to endure what he could not. "Now we trying to put our kids in that situation?" he said to the doc. "No one's as good and evil as a child. Black or white."

Now Thomas walked through a basement flea market bearing the name of that Missouri guerrilla who'd once burned Lawrence to the ground. He sometimes came here and browsed the strange debris and wares pedaled by vendors. He came upon a man with long silver hair and sunken eyes. He was Indian, but there were no tribal pieces. His booth was made up of varied military supplies and paraphernalia. There were uniforms from the Great War, ceremonial sabers with gold handles, mud-caked Civil War bullets, mint Confederate money, and ornate helmets that had once belonged to soldiers from other countries fighting other wars. On a shelf next to some tarnished medals sat a grenade, the pin still holding the spoon in place. It looked like the Mark II bombs Thomas had hurled in the war. He picked it up.

"Easy now," the man said. "Liable to blow us sky high." He was sitting on a stool, balancing a shoebox on his knees that served as his register. "You fight in it?" Thomas neither shook his head nor nodded. "Me too. Can you believe it?"

"What?" Thomas said.

"Us, fighting for them."

Thomas continued to examine the grenade, turning it under the light.

"Flip it over," the man said. On the bottom of the bomb was a white cap. "Hollowed out." He was laughing now. "*Had* you, didn't I? You could pull that pin and all you'd hear was the heartbeat of the world."

The clock on the wall showed it was time to go. He hustled to Stoughton's and into the backroom. He had two minutes to eat. From his makeshift locker—really just an old metal nail tin—he took out the sandwich Verna had made him that morning: bologna on white, mustard on the bottom slice only. He sat on a stack of three used tires Mr. Stoughton bought on the cheap and sometimes resold to poorer customers. He braced the sandwich on his leg and removed the grenade from his pocket. He set it on the ground between his feet and stared at it as he unwrapped his lunch from the waxed paper and ate quickly.

When Mr. Stoughton appeared, popping his head through the black curtain, Thomas had both hands on the crust and there was no time to pick up the grenade. Mr. Stoughton asked if he was ready. Mr. Merton had arrived to pick up his oven. "Yes, sir," Thomas said, chewing furiously. Mr. Stoughton started to turn back, but stopped, having caught sight of the object at his feet.

"What is that, Thomas? Is that—?"

"Ain't nothing," he said, swallowing the last bite and picking up the weapon.

"My God, what are you—"

"Ain't nothing to worry about." He turned the grenade upside down to show Stoughton there was no danger.

"Is this some kind of joke? Do you think this stunt is funny? What would customers think if they saw it?" Thomas said nothing. "This is a fireable offense," Mr. Stoughton whispered so no one out front would hear. Thomas dropped his head. They were silent a few moments, then Mr. Stoughton said, "What are you going to do with it?"

"Don't know." Thomas shook his head. There were all these things, hard to feel and hard to name, swirling inside him, and he didn't know why, let alone what one was ever expected to do with them.

Mr. Stoughton had little sense of what to make of it all, his Negro employee and his grenade. He stepped fully into the back room, letting the curtain fall behind him.

"Are you okay, Thomas?"

He looked up and smiled. "Yes, sir. Thank you."

"Take a minute to get yourself together, then meet me out front. We've got work to do." He took Thomas in for a long second before turning to leave.

Mr. Stoughton walked to the register where Merton waited. He began filling out the bill of sale but was still thinking of Thomas. What was it about the Negro that unsettled him so? He'd had few workers better and more dependable. Did as told. Never complained, never said boo. But the young man vexed him. His quiet, his stillness. So unsettlingly self-contained. He considered firing him, but decided against it; he was a good worker with a new family—a young girl, plus a baby on the way—and he'd fought in the war. Served his country. Whatever went on inside his head, however, Stoughton didn't want a glimpse, for it was either everything or nothing, and neither seemed innocuous. This was what he was thinking about later that evening as he shut his eyes and lowered his head over knotted fingers. He was trying to pray to God but could think only of the confounding blackness inside his young employee's head. Don't worry it any longer, he told himself, and then looked up at his wife and smiled. "Dinner looks lovely, dear. Thank you."

[The Men, 1968]

That May, we met in the Lawrence High School cafeteria to voice our demands—black teachers, black counselors, black history, black cheerleaders, black homecoming queen, more representation—to the school administration. We presented it to them calmly and plainly, no flash, no high talk. My brother Brian couldn't be bothered, but Mother came with me and we sat next to Rodney and his father. Principal Medley listened and nodded, and when he spoke he said that as a red-headed man he too knew what it was like to feel oppressed. "Few realize the burdens of being different," he said. We left the meeting with assurances that steps would be taken. But when we came back to school the following September we found nothing but a couple books on Negro history in the library.

I forget whether it was Mike or Rodney who came up with the idea for the walkout, but by then all of us were a little under the spell of Honeyboy, who'd appeared in Lawrence the previous year in braids and black leather, and it very well might have been at his urging. Honeyboy was not colored, not Negro, not even black. Honeyboy was Black. Regardless, if it wasn't his idea, he'd at least given us the okay. We didn't tell anyone, not even our parents. That following morning we met in the library—thirty-seven of us—and marched through the hallways, gathering numbers along the way. The sea of white faces parted, some scared, some amused. "Looks like they've opened a fried chicken stand in the cafeteria," someone called out. "Hide your women and your watermelon," cried another. We said nothing, just turned down the main corridor, and that's when I saw Brian. He was standing by his locker, talking to a couple of white boys. Bearded freaks in bandanas and beads. I ran ahead of the group and pulled his arm to come on.

"Lay off," he said, shaking me away. He wasn't but a sophomore and thought he already knew all there was. He said he was staying right there, and I told him he best get his black ass outside.

"Chill, Petal," one of the freaks said, setting his hand on my shoulder. He was wearing sunglasses with no lenses and his shirt was opened to his belly button. "We're rapping."

I put my palm right into that hairless chest and pushed him back against the locker.

"You best not lay hands on me again."

He formed his hand into a peace sign, said he was a pacifist.

"Better go with your sister, Bug," the other one said, looking just as crazy-minded as the other. Overalls with no shirt underneath, an American flag tied around his waist.

"Bug?" I said. "What he mean by that?" It was the first time I'd heard his nickname, the name his friends called him, the name he'd go by up until the day he disappeared a decade later after leaving a commune in Colorado, never to be seen again. Every once in a while I'll bump into one of the old heads here in Lawrence—they're all respectable lawyers or bankers now—and they'll ask about him. "Any word from Bug? He ever turn up? I bet he's still out there."

"It's what they call me," my brother said with a shrug.

I pointed at the one in overalls.

"His name is Brian."

He thought on that a long moment, biting his lip as if in deep contemplation, and said, "I can accept that."

We ran to catch up to the walkout, Brian dragging his big feet the whole way. We joined the group just as they made it outside the main entrance of school. I was standing next to Rodney and he took hold of my hand. We turned around and what a sight that was. All those white faces in schoolroom windows, wondering what the hell we were up to. A few teachers had come outside, asking what was going on. We said nothing, turned, and marched to the community center, where Honeyboy waited.

Later that night, when we got home, word had spread.

"You better have an explanation," Mother said. "The school has been calling all afternoon."

Brian gave her a quick kiss to the cheek as he brushed past her and disappeared into his room. A few seconds later the metallic sound of rock and roll behind his closed door. She turned to me: "Well?" I tried to explain to her what we were doing.

She'd been at the meeting the previous spring. She knew the problems at the high school and had come out in support.

"They ain't done nothing for us since May, Mama," I said.

"I am your mother, not your mama."

"They buy a few books and hire a part-time colored counselor and expect us to go back to the fields?"

"Would you listen to yourself?"

"We done asking for things. We taking them!"

"How can you expect to be taken seriously when you sound like—"

"Like what? Sound black?"

"Ineloquent," she said. "You're acting ignorant, Petal."

"Which one of us acting?"

Mother had her education and saw to it that her children did too, but oh how our affectations nettled each other.

"You need to be smarter than them," she said. She paused, sat down on the couch. She had an unsettling way of remaining composed at all times, and her only tell at that moment was the way she ran her hand over the lace stitching in the couch's pink floral pattern. "Progress is made through thoughtful, patient work—not through rash decision-making. Not through coercion. Look what we did with the swimming pool."

For a decade she'd been part of various groups trying to integrate private pools, so we'd have somewhere to swim in the summer. When that failed, they fought to have ballot measures introduced that would create a municipal swimming pool. It was voted down in '56, '61, and '63, but had finally passed the previous year. That was how change happened, she said. That's the thing. It wasn't that Mother accepted the way things were. She'd been involved, had taken me to marches since I was little. She knew things at LHS were rotten for us. What we were really debating that night in the front room was strategy, but I couldn't see that, couldn't see her reticence as anything but betrayal.

"You know they call it 'coon lagoon,' don't you?" I shook my head: "Crumbs."

"Pardon?"

"The white man drops crumbs and you stoop to pick them up and say thank you."

"Don't sharpen your tone with me, Petal."

But I was too worked up. I could hear it in my own voice: Honeyboy's words, his inflection.

"Grateful to be a nigger."

She rose slowly from the couch.

"You see what that done to Daddy. Sitting in a room by hisself in Topeka."

Mother was looking at the floor, as if she weren't listening to a word I was saying.

"To be black the way they want us to be in this country can't help but make you crazy. Something wrong with you if you ain't!"

The force of her slap sent me backward, the shock of it—Mother had never laid a hand on me—made me crouch and, despite myself, cry. She didn't say anything, just turned and calmly walked away. I heard the creak of the staircase and then the slow clack of her heels on the wooden floor upstairs as she made her way to the bedroom and quietly shut the door behind her.

I snuck out that night, made my way to Rodney's house across town. It was unusually warm that September and I began to perspire. When I arrived, I tapped on Rodney's window and a few moments later he opened it as he held a finger to his lips. He listened hard for a few seconds to hear if anyone had stirred and then hoisted me up into his room. I was still worked up hotter than hell and whispered all sorts of familial blasphemies to poor Rodney. I called my very own mother a high-yellow bitch. I called Brian a cracker-lover. I called Daddy a

mad Uncle Tom. Shame on me. I resented my mother's skin,
her intelligence. I resented her comportment, her gradualism.
I resented her privilege, which I'd enjoyed and benefitted from
because her father and grandfather had managed the near impossible: to become successful businessmen in Kansas City at a
time when colored folk were lucky to find work as a bootblack.
I resented that we had a nice house and white neighbors. Why
didn't we live with our people on the east side of town? I was a
wet-faced, angry mess, and Rodney held me until it was out of
my system, my eyes sore and my throat strained.

I took the long way home that night, walking down Massachusetts Street, looking in store windows. I stopped when
I came to Stoughton's appliance store. It was dark, only the
faint glow of a light left on in a back room. Daddy had once
worked there when I was young. I tried to imagine him standing behind the register or carrying something to a customer's
car. I saw him smiling at the customer, a white man in a camel
topcoat and feathered hat. "Yes, sir. You're welcome. Thank
you, sir."

The next morning I made my way to Veteran's Park, where
we had agreed to set up our own black school, right across the
street from LHS. Rodney called it symbolic, Honeyboy called
it revolutionary. We set up tables and chairs, a tent. By this time
word had spread about our alternative school and black people
showed up to hold signs, show support, to teach classes on the
stories and history excised from our regular schoolbooks. The
park was humming. There were reporters covering the story,
asking questions about our demands. "But Principal Medley
says you have a colored teacher at LHS," one of them said.

Rodney responded, "He's a Negro. He's not black. There's
a difference."

We would all return to school in the coming days, satisfied
with having made our point. The administration would meet

some of our demands. We'd have black cheerleaders. Rodney
and I were seniors. We would graduate and go to KU the following year and join the Black Student Union. In two years
Rodney would be shot as he fled from the police. In ten Brian
would disappear. In thirteen Daddy would pass away, still in
the sanitarium. Those beautiful men: dead, vanished, or insane. And then there would be only me and Mother.

She showed up that day in Veteran's Park. I first saw her
standing at the periphery, on the sidewalk, dressed up in a way
that embarrassed me at the time. I was still smarting from the
previous night and we didn't speak, but we stood close enough
to eavesdrop on what the other was saying. This was how we
sometimes communicated. Honeyboy approached her. "Verna,
thank you for coming."

"My name is Mrs. Johnson," she said.

Honeyboy seemed to know Mother didn't care for him, and
he let go a little nervous laugh. "Of course, Mrs. Johnson," he
said, adding, "ma'am."

"I heard you need teachers," she said, and he led her to a
group of people, some sitting in chairs, some sitting on the
grass, all waiting to hear her speak.

Mother.

[It Just So Happens You Have Many Concerns, 1961]

The pleasant sound of two fresh inches of snow crunching under the slow spin of your tires on a January morning. It's too
cold to make them walk, so you've dropped Petal and Brian at
school and now you make your way to the doctor. You don't
take the most direct route. You have a few minutes, so you
take the Oldsmobile to the north end of Massachusetts Street,
near the Kaw River, and turn south. The lampposts wear the
newly fallen snow like stoles. There are red-and-white bows on

street-corner signs, holly wreaths in storefront windows, and unlit Christmas lights still snake through the trees, though it is the middle of January.

Tonight you will watch the Kansas President's Farewell Address with a group you've come to be acquainted with. This group, the Lawrence League for the Practice of Democracy, gets together to discuss, debate, and propose plans for furthering equality in Lawrence. It is intended to be an interracial gathering of like-minded folks from the university and the town, but it is mostly white faculty members and their wives, a few forward-thinking folks from local church groups. You are one of two Negroes—sometimes three, when Sherelle can get off from work—and there is one Oriental from the Chemistry Department. Recently your work has been focused on integrating swimming pools. The previous summer you picketed the Plunge, a private swim club that doesn't admit Negroes. Unsuccessful, the demonstration was denounced as a Communist plot by the Lawrence Committee for a Free America and the Save America from Communism Council. Everyone belongs to a group, a society, a committee, a council, and yours will now turn its attention toward generating funds for an integrated city pool.

But you're not thinking of that now. For now you are concerned with keeping the appointment you've scheduled, so you continue south on Massachusetts, past the candy-cane swirl of barbershops, past Raney's Drugstore, past Weaver's department store. You still can't pass Stoughton's without looking in, half expecting to see Tommy.

At the doctor's office, you take off your long, winter fur and sling it over your arm. You draw stares from the white girls in reception, the white patients in the waiting room. "Verna Johnson," you say and fill out paperwork, as instructed. You take a seat and rest your small purse on your lap, resisting the urge to itch the spot where the nylon under your mint-colored dress has snagged a rogue hair. You will not scratch under their collective gaze. When he calls you back—a silver-haired man, whose indulgence of bay rum overpowers even the anesthetized nothing-smell of the medical office—he takes you to a small room near the back. It doesn't say COLORED on the door, but you know this is where he takes the few Negro patients he has. Not many can afford private treatment. Daughter of a well-to-do real estate executive in Kansas City who has made his father's business profitable by managing to sell homes in redlined white-fled neighborhoods, you can.

He looks at your chart, and though it says why you've come, he asks anyway. When you tell him, he asks if you're married.

"Yes," you say, which is true, though sometimes you tell people you will never see again that your husband has passed away.

"May I ask why you would like oral contraception?"

He seems to know he's being inappropriate. He closes the chart but quickly opens it back up, feigning a second glance at something he might have misread. It would be easy enough to say that you and your husband have two children and two children is all you desire to have, but you don't. You cannot tell him the truth, which is that you've not made love to your husband in eight years; which is that you're seeing one of the men from the group you'll be attending tonight. You cannot tell him that this man is white, nor that he is married to a woman who also attends the group and with whom you are friendly. You cannot tell him that this man was a professor of yours years ago at KU and that the affair started before Tommy went to Topeka. You cannot tell him any of this, and your privilege allows you to know you don't have to, and you tell him so.

Though he has been allowed to for over a year, your doctor is hesitant to prescribe the Pill, believing that it encourages promiscuity. But he has a bigger concern: population growth. The figures are staggering and sometimes he finds himself awakened in the middle of the night by the image of a planet shrinking until it is the size of a marble residing in the bellybutton of a pregnant woman. He does not subscribe to the eugenicist theories of his medical forebears, but the numbers don't lie. Higher birthrates in racial minorities meant more children born into poverty, which meant the need for more social services, which meant more government involvement and higher taxes, all of which were minor nuisances that distracted from the real overarching problem: the finite supply of necessary resources to keep the species alive.

You don't know that he's considering all of this in the long silence that has come between the two of you before he relents, writes the prescription, and retreats to an empty adjacent room to wash his hands before seeing his next patient. Right now you are struck by the certain fear that he knows you're sleeping with a married white man.

Neither of you knows the complexities of the other.

You have poor kin in Mississippi who were sterilized without their consent or knowledge, who have wondered aloud why God won't bless them with a child as He has you, and many years from now, when the duplicity is revealed and thousands of folks begin the long process of seeking legal recourse, you will recall the silence in this office, on this day in January, when there was new snow on the ground and President Eisenhower, Ike from Abilene, Kansas, was to give his farewell address.

[The Leastest, 1970]

We. We live on the Farm. We snort and smoke and drink and fuck. We inject things meant for barnyard animals. Cow speed!

Tranquilizers! We make a living selling shitty ragweed to dealers in Florida who use it to cut the good stuff that comes up
from South America. K-pot, ditch weed! Which grows wild in
the fields outside of Lawrence, brought here in the hooves of
Texas steer in the days of the old cattle drives. We're on the Silk
Road for drugs, the meeting place of every east-west/north-
south drug runner. Baghdad on the Kaw. Highway 40 SDS.
We are the Kaw Valley Hemp Pickers! We are from towns
most have never heard of—Coats, Seneca, Sublette, Holcomb—
and we've dropped out of school and landed in communes and
stash houses in and around Lawrence, which is burning, burning, burning. This is the summer the cops have killed Rodney Burnside, and three nights later they shot that white kid
outside the Gaslight. Now there are fires every night, bombs,
arson, snipers in windows shooting cop cars. People are arming
themselves: the Panthers in east Lawrence, the Lawrence Liber-
ation Front in Oread, the Klan and the Minutemen at the police station, scared citizens in their homes, clutching shotguns.
Everyone is on edge, and we want only to roll the fattest jay
and exhale a mushroom cloud on the city, but right now there
is little interest in drugs. Right now the market has spoken and
people want guns, and so we will deliver weapons we have no
clue how to use.

The cache arrives in the trunk of a green '62 Skylark, driven
by bleary-eyed Weathermen who've been driving for twenty
hours straight, headed for a meeting in California. Two dykes.
They've been put in touch with us by a guy who knows a guy
who once scribbled the address of the Farm on a piece of paper
and then swallowed that piece of paper. We direct them to pull
around back so their car stays out of sight from the road. We
watch them unload the package and switch license plates. We
are to run the guns to the Panthers, who will hand us an enve-

lope of money. They want us to go now, but Lawrence is under curfew. It's too hot, we tell them. We'll go in the morning. "Don't double-cross us, or we'll blow this place to fuck," they say, and we nod.

"Wouldn't dream of it," we say. "We're on your side." They look us up and down and tell us that we are not on their side. They are not a chatty pair. When they speak, it's mostly to tell us about the big meeting in California they can't tell us anything about. They do not partake of the spliff we pass. They ask us if we've read Lenin and we say we are the walrus. They are not amused. We are lost causes, at best human shields for a future bank expropriation. They will allow themselves a bowl of hippie gruel, three hours of sleep, and nothing more before they resume driving. They tell us when we wake they will be gone and we will forget their faces and the make of their car. "If I hear from the Panthers that you didn't deliver the package," says the one who looks uncannily like John Brown, "I'll personally come back and blow this place sky high. You won't even know it's coming."

If it must be so, we tell them, we'd prefer not to know it's coming.

The other one is also thin but with blond hair that looks to have been dyed even blonder. She is, in fact, blonde on blonde. Is that what Dylan meant? We'll debate this later when the dykes have gone to bed, tripping outside under the lonesome stars. She looks at me and asks, "Why aren't you a Panther?"

I rise from my chair quickly, muster a straight-faced anger.

"That's some racist shit," I say in a voice not my own.

Blondie is caught off guard, scoots her chair back. She is about to apologize when John Brown's gaunt, woodeny face says, "We're antiracist."

"Show me," I say.

"Show you?" says Brown.

"Show me how antiracist you are," I say. "Kiss my black feet."

To my amazement they actually do so. They lower their weary white bodies to the floor, their heads hovering over my sandals like I'm Jesus Himself, and we can't hold it in any longer. We crack up, our eyes fill with tears. We shoot ropes of snot from our noses. We fall out of chairs. We haven't laughed like this in at least half an hour.

"Fucking cunts," says Blondie.

"Fucking dicks," adds Brown. As they leave the kitchen, she stops and says, "Deliver the guns tomorrow, or sky high, I'll do it. I'll send this place to the fucking moon."

In the morning—perhaps we've woken, or maybe the sun has only come up—they're gone. We snoop through the cache: two rifles, a bunch of handguns, a few grenades. In case the cops pull the truck over, we decide it's best if not everyone goes. Can't risk the whole Farm getting busted. Rutabaga twirls in circles—a light-blue flash of clacking beads and chains—chanting his gibberish, and then stops on a dime and says he's in. His mantra this morning is: "I'll go." Scare Baby says we need someone else. He looks at Mr. B, and Mr. B looks at Wishy, who is pregnant and splayed out on the couch.

"Maybe you should go, Bug," says Mr. B.

Scare Baby agrees: "The Panthers'll deal easier with you."

"Just don't tell them to kiss your feet," says Wishy, trying to joke, but no one laughs. She is wearing only a dish towel that she's fashioned into a loincloth. Her long blond hair falls past her nipples. I tell her to shut up and put on something besides a diaper. I'm edgy and short-tempered because I haven't yet taken anything this morning.

"Hey," says Mr. B, resting a hand on my chest. "She has a pretty face. Her diaper is lovely."

So then it's me and Rutabaga in the red truck, driving into town. The package is in the flat bed, tied up in a blanket and covered by a heavy tarp weighted down by rocks. I watch my speed, check the rearview, and Rutabaga speaks words I do not understand. We don't know much about him. He showed up at the Farm a few months ago, saying he'd just come from India. He'd studied with the maharishi and now his name was Rudra Veda. He asked if he could be our guru. Sure, Rutabaga, we said. We could use a guru.

We turn onto Mass Street, driving slowly past South Park, where there's some sort of demonstration going on. A hundred years ago, this was the street Quantrill's guerrillas rode up and down, looting stores and killing townsfolk in the name of the Confederacy. The shit you remember from school, even when you've dropped out.

I pull the truck over in front of Strawberry Fields. Ruta-baga doesn't ask why, just gets out like it's a planned stop. It's already hot and I think that maybe after we make the drop we can swing by the pool to cool off. A church bell tolls, its sound hanging long and lonesome in the summer air. We go inside and I buy some papers and a one-hitter to give to Wishy when we return, a peace offering. Rutabaga stares at a case of crystals for a while, mumbling to himself, before picking up a necklace that has a many-armed figure hanging from the end. He holds the idol close to his face, and then he puts the necklace around his neck and leaves the store. "We'll take that too," I say to the girl at the counter.

Outside, the bells still ring. They unsettle me and I wish I'd gotten high before leaving. I'm itchy, aching, already feeling hollow in my bones. I roll a cigarette and a police car creeps by. Rutabaga waves and I tell him to knock it off. "The fuck is going on with these bells?" I say. "It's not even Sunday, is it?"

"It's okay," Rutabaga says. "I hear them too."

I tell him let's get this over with.

When we get to Afro House, there are several guys in full Panther dress standing watch on the porch. It's all black denim and berets over there. One approaches the truck and I tell him we have the package. He looks at Rutabaga, then at me, takes the toothpick from his mouth, and tells us to pull around the side of the house. Before we've even gotten out of the car, two others have thrown back the tarps and taken the package through a back door. We follow them, but there's a big cat standing guard at the door. "We haven't been paid yet," I say. He says I can come in but Rutabaga can't. "He's cool," I say. "He's not white anymore. He's Indian." He pauses a moment to remove his beret and wipe away sweat before leading us inside and down a flight of stairs to the basement. It's a cellar they've fashioned into a war room. There is a map of Lawrence with certain areas highlighted and marked beneath the black stencil: *Fight Pig Amerika*. Pictures of Che, Ho, and Malcolm— the gang's all here—on the wall, and maybe two dozen Most Wanted posters bearing the face of the cop who shot Rodney. *Wanted for Murder*, they say. *Ten Pigs for Our Brother*. Another shows Rodney's face above the words: *He Was Ready—Are You?* Seven or eight Panthers follow us in and take seats on the ratty couches to our left and right. Before us stands Honeyboy. The package lies on the floor before him and he squats to inspect it, then looks at us a long moment.

"The fuck you doing here, peckerwood faggot?" he says.

"It's okay," I say. "He's with me."

"I wasn't talking about him." He stands and moves close to me, leans in an inch away from my face. "Look at you in your sandals and beads." He slowly circles around me. "You worse than Uncle Tom. Ain't never seen anything as backwards as a hippie nigga."

"I'm not the one wearing sunglasses in a dark basement."

He pushes me. "Motherfucker, I will end you."

"Stop!" a voice from behind calls. Though I haven't seen her in over a year, of course I recognize it.

"He my brother."

Petal enters the cellar and won't make eye contact with me. She's looking at Honeyboy, who seems to think she's joking, but then it clicks and he stares at me hard. "Shit, I remember you." He waves over his shoulder to a fat man with a cigar box by his foot. "Pay these goofy-looking motherfuckers."

"Let there be commerce between us," smiles Rutabaga, the tips of his fingers touching, forming a tent on his chest.

"Show these hippie capitalists the door."

Petal follows us outside. She looks just as absurd as the others. I ask if she's got a minute. She glances back at her comrades in the doorway and nods at them. "A minute," she says. I tell Rutabaga to scoot over so the three of us can fit in the cab of the truck and Petal tells him that's not going to work and points to the truck bed. He complies without comment, hopping in and scooting to the side. We are silent as I drive, and I watch Rutabaga studying the god on his necklace out back. The last time I saw Petal was right before I dropped out of LHS and moved to the Farm. It was the last time I saw Mother as well. The three of us had gone to see Daddy in Topeka. Petal and Mother argued the entire time about the war, about politics, about school, and by the time we got to the sanitarium they were no longer speaking to each other. They brought Daddy out to the foyer and we took seats around him on a couch. Mom visited him every week, Petal and I less frequently, but this was how it always was. The three of us sitting around him, wondering if he'll ever say anything again. He just sat there, rubbing his hand over his leg as Mom gave him the week's news. She told him how after two years the city had finally built the swimming pool just in time for the summer heat.

"Petal and Brian are going to the opening, aren't you all?" she said. I looked at Petal and she was slumping in her chair, shaking her head. It was hard trying to talk to someone who never answered. I said, yeah, we sure were.

I park the car on Eighth and tell Rutabaga to wait there. Petal and I walk quietly a minute and there's just the sound of the bells ringing. I tell her I'm gonna go crazy if they don't stop.

"They ringing it forty-four thousand times for the war dead."

"Good thing I live in the country now."

"Of course they only counting they own dead. Ain't enough bells in town to ring for all the Vietnamese."

When we get to Mass Street, I tell her I'm sorry about Rodney.

"After his funeral," she says, "we marched from the church to the cemetery, right up Mass. Had his casket on a hearse pulled by a couple ponies. Crackers on the sidewalks and in store windows just staring. You could feel how scared they was. That's when I knew we were gonna win."

We have stopped in front of Stoughton's. She asks if I remember this place. One time when I was little, before he fully cracked, Daddy brought me here to meet his old boss. I don't remember Stoughton's face, but I can hear his voice. "This is your youngest?" he'd said. "Yes, sir," Daddy answered. "This Brian, my leastest." My *leastest*. Where had he gotten that? The kind of expression Mother probably tried to coach out of him. It's one of the few things I remember him ever saying. He and Stoughton spoke a minute more—about what I don't remember—and then we left and continued down Mass Street.

The store is empty now. CLOSED INDEFINITELY, a sign says. Petal cranes her neck to see the roof, where the brick is scorched, the upper-floor windows blown out.

"That night, after we put Rodney in the ground, I threw the Molotov right through that window. I hoped he was in there."

"Who?"

She says nothing. We were never particularly close, but we've never felt as far apart as we do now. There is a moment where we meet eyes and she puts a hand to my face and it seems like she might say something important, but when she finally does speak, she says only, "Good work on that package," and pauses a moment. "Now forget you ever saw it or me and whoever gave it to you. Get the fuck out of here and keep your head down." She turns and leaves and I'm standing in front of Stoughton's appliance store, where my father once worked, and still the bells toll.

A DEFENSE OF HISTORY

As instructed, the Assistant arrives at the campus library early on Friday. This despite not being what one would call a morning person. He needs coffee ASAP, which makes his location convenient. Among undergrads, the library is more commonly and aptly referred to as "the place where Starbucks is." He shivers in November's autumnal chill as he waits for the Historian, a professor in the department where he is pursuing his Ph.D., the one who has beckoned him here at this early hour, the attractive older woman upon whom he has the most innocuous of crushes and whom he hopes will guide his own studies when he's ready to dissertate in a couple of years. Still finishing his coursework, the Assistant was appointed to help her with research this semester, a post that until now has mostly entailed tracking down a few articles for her book project on the People's Party.

"Populists," she said when they met in her office back in early September to discuss her research. "Radical agrarians. You're familiar?"

The Assistant learned quickly that in this environment there is nothing worse than showing intellectual uncertainty, and nodded with a confidence that wouldn't, on pain of death, betray the fact that he had no idea what she was talking about. Afterward, waiting in the interminable line at the bookstore to purchase texts for his classes, he took out his smartphone.

Populist Party (United States)

People's Party	
Founded	1884
Dissolved	1908
Preceded by	United States Greenback Party
Succeeded by	Progressives
Ideology	Populism, bimetallism
Political position	Left-wing
International affiliation	None
Politics of the United States Political parties	

The **People's Party**, later erroneously also known as the **Populist Party** (derived from "Populist" which is the adjective which describes the members of this party) was a short-lived political party in the United States in the late 19th century. It flourished particularly among western farmers, based largely on its opposition to the gold standard. The party did not remain a lasting feature most probably because it had been so closely identified with the free silver movement which did not resonate with urban voters and ceased to become a major issue as the U.S. came out of the recession of the 1890s. The very term "populist" has since become a generic term in the U.S. for politics which appeals to the common in opposition to established interests.

—WIKIPEDIA ENTRY, 2010

The research has been interesting and his duties minimal, but yesterday he received an e-mail from the Historian asking if he was going to be around this weekend and whether he might be able to help with her research at the library. There was urgency in her tone, a faint allusion to an imminent deadline of sorts. He'd planned to drive the two hours home to spend a long weekend with his parents. His mother is sick and has been undergoing treatment throughout the summer and fall, something he's avoided facing since school started up, and the Historian's request gave his continued avoidance an air of legitimacy. "Of course we understand your school obligations," his dad said, clearly bummed, when the Assistant called to cancel. "I'll give Mom your love."

When the Historian arrives, they enter the building through the slow-sliding automatic doors, purchase coffees, and take the elevator to the fifth floor, where they find an empty conference room. The Historian is slim and fit, an obsessive user of a personal home Elliptical, the Assistant would wager. Her hair is red, cut short, textured, and styled messy, and her face has an angularity that gives her a hint of masculinity that makes her seem both sexy and fierce. If she made a pop album, it would be called *Sexy/Fierce*. Instead of a backpack or briefcase, she tows behind her a roller bag too large for overhead stowage in an airplane. It makes her seem older than she is—mid-forties, he'd guess, but clearly passes for late thirties. He helps her lift her luggage onto the large, rectangular table. "This is my war room for the weekend," she says, unzipping the bag to reveal stacks of yellow legal pads tattooed with blue ink, as well as books from her home and office.

Properly caffeinated, the Historian lays out the game plane. Her book proposal on the Populists is due on Monday. She has three days to figure out her angle on these radical farmers and work up a pitch. She wants him to focus on primary sources today, to see if he can't find something interesting, something she's overlooked. "Take notes on anything that seems relevant," she says, tossing him a clean legal pad. *Relevant to what?* he wonders. He takes it and puts it in his messenger bag. "Transcribe, make photocopies if necessary." He stares at her, faintly nodding, waiting for more direction. He's unsure where to begin, but too embarrassed to say he's unsure where to begin. "This is good training for your own research," she tells him, ushering him out of the room with a powerful little nod toward the door. "I'll be in here if you need me." As he makes his way down the hall, he hears the Historian call out, "Thank you!"

The time has come when it is necessary in our own defense that the working people of this country, the farmers, mechanics, day laborers and all men and women who earn their living by hands or brains, organize against usurpation. . . . This is not a movement against the merchant, the lawyer, the beggar or anyone else, but a great uprising of the people. They say we want to destroy capital. But we want to restore the supremacy of the people, and we propose to do it.

—WILLIAM PEFFER, POPULIST SENATOR, KANSAS, 1891

Equal rights for all and special privileges to none.

—SLOGAN OF THE PEOPLE'S PARTY, 1891

It's been a little while since he's considered the matter, so the Assistant recounts what he knows. In the decades after the Civil War, farmers were crippled by agricultural debt, and by the 1880s the country was deep in recession. They organized alliances in the South and Midwest to press for economic relief and governmental reform, but the Democrats and Republicans did little to alleviate the situation of the farmers. The grassroots push for an independent third party that would do something grew rapidly, spurring the formation of state parties that won major electoral victories in 1891, as in Kansas, and within a year the national People's Party was founded. The Assistant wonders how he'd never heard of the Populists before. His entire life spent in the state and it took coming here to Manhattan, Kansas, to the state's agricultural college, to find out about them. How does that happen?

I am the innocent victim of a bloodless revolution—a sort of turnip crusade, as it were.

—JOHN JAMES INGALLS, REPUBLICAN SENATOR, KANSAS, UPON HIS DEFEAT BY POPULIST WILLIAM PEFFER, 1891

And I say now to you as my final admonition, not knowing that I shall meet you again, raise less corn and wheat, and more hell.

—MARY LEASE, KANSAS POPULIST, ADDRESSING A GATHERING OF FARMERS, 1891

For nearly five decades the Assistant's grandfather, who considered himself an Eisenhower Republican, was a farmer in western Kansas. He died when the Assistant was young, but from what he remembers he could never imagine his grandfather raising less wheat and more hell. The Assistant feels drowsy, could use a little break, so he picks up another coffee, exits the library, and calls home to see how his mother is doing. She's in partial remission and there's constant fear and likelihood of recurrence. Throughout the awful summer, he'd driven her to appointments and sat in waiting rooms and worried, while at home he'd read to her from her favorite chapters in the Bible. All the while she grew frailer and frailer but her optimism and fortitude didn't diminish the way the Assistant's had. That was what was tough to face: her equanimity in the face of it all. It was either denial or acceptance, and both were unsettling because they led to the same end.

The Assistant's father answers the phone and tells him that Mom is resting, so the Assistant asks about Grandpa, the farmer. "Dad was a man full of contradictions," says the Assistant's father. "He hated farming but did it anyway. He lobbied for and relied upon government subsidies that kept his farm afloat, and then voted a straight Republican ticket each election." The Assistant asks if he's ever heard of the People's Party. "The what?" his father answers. "Is that some new commie outfit on campus?" The Assistant tells him he needs to get back to work.

It's only right that the Conference come at the call of Kansans, for on her plains was shed the first blood in the struggle that freed six million slaves, and on her soil was fought the first battle which is to free sixty-three million industrial slaves.

—WILLIAM F. RIGHTMIRE'S OPENING REMARKS AT THE
CINCINNATI CONFERENCE THAT WAS TO CREATE
THE NATIONAL PEOPLE'S PARTY, 1891

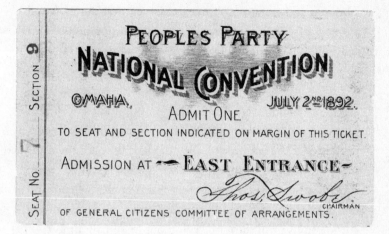

The Assistant feels a slight preference for the yellow highlighter over the green. He studies a Xerox he's made of the Omaha Platform, the Populists' first unified statement of their policies and beliefs. *Wealth belongs to him who creates it*, he highlights. *The interests of rural and civic labor are the same; their enemies identical.* Their platform called for government control of transportation and communication: *The time has come when the railroad corporations will either own the people or the people must own the railroads.* They also demanded the direct election of senators, an eight-hour workday, a progressive income tax, and the free coinage of silver to create a more flexible currency that would protect farmers from inflation and debt. *The land, including all natural sources of wealth, is the heritage of the people and should not be monopolized.*

Just then the Assistant realizes the Historian is looking over his shoulder. "The Omaha Platform," she says. "My God, isn't it beautiful?" The Assistant opens his mouth and the Historian raises a hand to stop him. He wants to ask what exactly it is he's supposed to be looking for. "Just going to pee," she whispers, walking away from his table. "Carry on."

The new movement proposes to take care of the men and women of this country and not the corporations. This movement is a protest against corporate aggression.

—POPULIST PRESIDENTIAL CANDIDATE
JAMES BAIRD WEAVER, 1892

I have no qualms of conscience about commanding the corporations of the country to obey the law, they are the creatures of the law; all that they have the law gives to them; and the people of this country, especially the farmers and the workmen, have been trampled upon by these railway corporations until they are crying out in despair almost.

—WILLIAM PEFFER, POPULIST SENATOR, KANSAS, 1893

A movement against unchecked corporate power in the 1890s? Fittingly, the Assistant ponders that as he waits in line for another coffee at Starbucks. As a twenty-seven-year-old man in 2010, he sometimes feels like they, corporations, are some modern phenomenon unique to his personal life chronology, like MTV or the Internet.

While the Populists lost the national election of 1892, they did garner eight percent of the national vote and won four states outright, the Assistant learns, making their showing kinda phenomenal considering the party was less than a year old. And here in the Kansas state elections the Populists made even bigger gains, electing their entire state ticket.

> It is the mission of Kansas to protect and advance the moral and material interests of all its citizens. . . . The grandeur of civilization shall be emphasized by the dawn of a new era, in which the people shall reign; and, if found necessary, they will "expand the powers of government to solve the enigma of the times."
>
> —KANSAS GOVERNOR LORENZO D. LEWELLING,
> INAUGURAL ADDRESS, 1893

> We have come today to remove the seat of government of Kansas from the Santa Fe [Railroad] offices, back to the Statehouse where it belongs.
>
> —"SOCKLESS JERRY" SIMPSON, POPULIST CONGRESSMAN
> FROM KANSAS'S SEVENTH DISTRICT, 1892

Late in the afternoon, the Assistant comes across the story of an incident he'd never heard of before called "The Legislative War," one so unbelievable he literally writes *WTF?* in the margins of the book where he found it. According to this account, it was perhaps the only attempt ever made in this country at "social revolution in the classic sense: violent seizure of the apparatus of government accompanied by class warfare in the streets." The conflict was between the Republicans and Populists over contested election returns that would decide the balance of power in the Kansas statehouse in 1893. Neither side gave ground, and for more than a month the legislature was a divided body, with Republicans using the chamber in the morning and the Populists in the afternoon. Little was accomplished and frustration grew as threats issued from both sides, until finally the schism led to armed conflict. The Populists locked the Republicans out, and the Republican speaker of the House used a sledgehammer to break down the doors and gain entrance to the chamber. Fistfights broke out on the House floor, while outside members of both parties armed themselves. Populist governor Lorenzo Lewelling sent in the militia to restore order, declaring: "We are here by the will of the people and will disperse only at the point of the bayonet." The hostilities went on for days.

What is an almost-revolution like? the Assistant wonders now, looking away from the machine where he examines old newspapers on microfiche. A fleeting vision: he is marching with the disquieted masses, storming the capital in expropriated SWAT gear. There is urgency and anger. Fists are raised. A grappling hook might be involved.

"ANARCHY!"

"ANARCHISTIC!"

"THE JACOBINS!"

"Is the Kansas Trouble the Incipiency
of a National Anarchist Uprising?"

—February headlines from *The Kansas City Mail,*
The Wichita Daily Eagle, The Marion Times,
and *The Kansas City Gazette,* 1893

It appears to be the determination of the opposing factions
in the Kansas House to superadd to the stupidity of a sense-
less deadlock the crime of an open revolution.

—*KANSAS CITY STAR,* 1893

When things calmed down, however, the upstart Populists
were blamed for the affair. This was the beginning of the end
for the party, the Assistant learns. Though they would win state
elections in Kansas in 1896, it was the national election of that
same year that would prove fatal.

While the party's numbers had increased sharply in a few short years, Populist strength was largely concentrated in regional pockets of the South, Midwest, and West. Without additional support, which meant merging with one of the major parties, it would be impossible for them to have a chance of winning a national election. And so it was that the issue of silver, a minor plank of the Omaha Platform, became the central issue in the debate over fusion. The People's Party advocated bimetallism, the use of gold and silver as currency, to increase the money supply and alleviate the debt farmers and the poor had taken on throughout a decade of economic depression. The pro-gold financial elite in the Northeast, who were also the creditors for most of the country's debt and benefited from staying on the gold standard, supported the Republicans. The Democrats, backed by silver mine owners in the western states, decided to make the free coinage of silver a central issue in the presidential election in an effort to win Populist support. Their young charismatic presidential candidate, William Jennings Bryan, electrified many with his fiery rhetoric.

Having behind us the producing masses of this nation and the world, supported by the commercial interests, the laboring interests and the toilers everywhere, we will answer their demand for a gold standard by saying to them: you shall not press down upon the brow of labor this crown of thorns, you shall not crucify mankind upon a cross of gold.

—WILLIAM JENNINGS BRYAN, 1896

THE SACRILEGIOUS CANDIDATE.

Is the Populist party ready to be dumped into the lap of [the Democrats]? Are the men who have been fighting the battle of humanity in this country for twenty years willing to acknowledge all they wanted was a change in basic money? Are we ready to sacrifice all the demands of the Omaha Platform on the cross of silver?

—ABE STEINBERGER, KANSAS POPULIST, 1896

If Populism means nothing more than free coinage of silver, there is no excuse for the existence of such a party.

—WILLIAM PEFFER, POPULIST SENATOR, KANSAS, 1896

The party that was going to pay off all the debts of the people by legislation, that was going to even up the inequalities of life that come from inequalities of the brain, the party that was going to stop the smart man from getting the best of the stupid chump, the party that was going to do what God himself couldn't do—make men equal. . . . And

all that is left of this great nightmare is a roomful of sad
visages, seedy citizens and a terrible past.

—WILLIAM ALLEN WHITE, REPUBLICAN NEWSPAPERMAN

FROM EMPORIA, KANSAS, 1895

After Bryan lost to William McKinley in 1896, the People's
Party ceased to be relevant at the national level. The Kansas
Populists were voted out of office in 1898, and by 1900 most
had either given up on politics or become Socialists. In the
ensuing decade much of the Populist platform was either en-
acted or on the way, championed by the very Republicans,
rebranding themselves as Progressives, who'd opposed them
initially.

We caught the Populists in swimming and stole all their clothing except the frayed underdrawers of free silver.

—WILLIAM ALLEN WHITE,
REPUBLICAN TURNED BULL MOOSER, 1940

I met some of my old Republican opponents today and they said to me: "Oh, Jerry, you ought to be in Kansas now. Kansas is all Populist now." Yes, I said to them, you are the conservative businessmen of the state, and doubtless all wisdom is lodged with you, but you are just learning now what the farmers of the state knew fourteen years ago.

—"SOCKLESS JERRY" SIMPSON,
FORMER POPULIST CONGRESSMAN, KANSAS, 1905

The Assistant keeps at it all afternoon and into the evening, occasionally catching sight of the Historian walking somewhere with extreme purpose or scribbling furiously on a legal pad. He's been so wrapped up that he's forgotten to eat lunch, and with the dinner hours nearing he's tired and ravenous. When a voice comes over the PA to tell them the library will be closing in fifteen minutes, the Historian appears.

"What the hell kind of university library closes at six?" she says. "In my day they were open all night—you could bunk up with a transient if you wished."

"Sounds great."

"It was! I got so much work done."

He follows her to the conference room down the hall where she packs up her absurd luggage, and they walk toward the elevator. On the ride down, his stomach makes increasingly loud thundery sounds, which both agree tacitly not to acknowledge.

"How did it go today?" she says as they exit the library.

"Good, I guess, but I don't really know what I'm looking for."

"You're doing the right thing. I just want a lot of source material to consider once I figure out my argument. It's bound to click soon. Usually it comes out of nowhere. Who knows, maybe it'll hit me on the walk home."

She turns to leave, saying she'll see him tomorrow. She lives close to campus, the Assistant thinks as the Historian and her bag roll away. He wonders what her house is like and for a brief moment considers following her before deciding that's an absolutely terrible idea. He returns to his apartment to supper on Hot Pockets and Sunny D, the dinner of folks everywhere who don't even compete in the race, but it's been a long day and, well, so what if he likes his Hot Pockets. He plops onto his futon, which is employed permanently in its couch function because it's broken, and turns on the TV, which gets a single, fuzzy channel. Through the garish swirl of bad reception he can just make out a detective show of some sort, which he watches semi-awake, followed by another detective show of some sort—a spin-off of the first perhaps—before the late local news comes on. During his time in graduate school he's become a lazy citizen, neglectful of affairs local and otherwise. He has a general sense of things, overhearing bits of conversation at school, ignorantly *uh-huh*ing as one of his parents references some incident or other. But mostly, as they say, he's fallen out of the loop. Sometimes on the phone his mother will ask, "Do you live in a cave or something?" and he'll look around his three-hundred-square-foot apartment at the stacks of books and mounds of dirty clothes and consider answering in the affirmative.

Tonight there's a story about a massive Tea Party rally in Washington against the expansion of health care. He actually has heard about this, thanks to good ole Dad's middle-age flirtation with libertarianism, his father's love-hate relationship with the Republican mainstream. Sitting on the coffee table next to a half-empty Sunny D is the legal pad he took notes on today. He picks it up and begins to doodle absentmindedly as he listens to the TV. It's strange when the newscaster uses the term *populist movement* in reference to the Tea Party, these people whose rage seems both real and subsidized by billionaires. They are the complete opposite of the Populist Movement the Assistant has spent the day researching that wanted to use government to help the rural and urban working poor at the expense of the rich and corporations. These small-*p* populists seem to want to destroy government to protect Big Business at their own expense. Oh, and personal freedom, that's a big deal for them. From their cold dead hands or something. No, that's guns, which is also apparently about personal freedom, so maybe it is the same thing. He's heard all the Tea Party talking points from his dad, and the Assistant listens quietly, not bothering to voice suspicion of his freedom to be uninsured, that opportunity to accrue massive and insurmountable poverty-trapping debt in future visits to the ER if he so chooses— second only perhaps to the poor's sacred freedom to starve.

Actually, once he didn't listen quietly. Once this summer, in fact, when his mother had just come home from the hospital and his father was ranting at clips of the president on TV, the Assistant said, "What about Mom? What if she didn't have insurance? What if you all had to take on the debt of her surgeries and treatment and medication?"

"You leave Mom out of this," his father had said. "Don't you dare make this personal." And then Dad went ahead and made it very personal: "Say we actually had national health care. Do you know what would have happened if Mom didn't have surgery right away? If she had to wait weeks or months in line behind others?"

They'd caught the disease early, but it was an aggressive form, and his dad had taken her to Kansas City immediately, to the best treatment center in the region. While his father did not analogize the situation to those new barroom juke-boxes he'd seen in some of the bars near campus whereby one can pay more money to cut to the front of the song queue, the Assistant's mind went there immediately. No, there was no mention of line-cutting, let alone the fifty million people not even allowed to wait in line at present, and yet the terrible thought of Mom languishing there as the disease consumed her insides did penetrate the Assistant like a lance through the chest. Mom. The Assistant sets the legal pad aside and thinks of calling home, but the clock on top of the TV that he's never properly reset after last month's power outage says it's 3:17 p.m., which means it's 10:32 p.m., much too late to phone.

The next morning the Assistant makes his way back to the library. Still half-asleep, he notices clusters of purple-and-white-clad students staggering around campus. One young man is literally army-crawling across the quad in purple over-alls. What is going on? There's something of a zombie apocalypse about the scene. Maybe this is a dream. But then it hits him: home football game! The Assistant has never been up early enough on a Saturday to actually witness this, but here he is in the midst of ritual. In Manhattan, Kansas, two things are sacrosanct: football and farming.

The library has just opened and the Assistant figures the Historian might already be in the war room, but when he arrives at the fifth-floor conference room he finds someone else there: a young female student sitting at the head of the table before her laptop, wearing headphones and giggling. She has on pink sweatpants tucked into furry winter boots as well as a men's undershirt, as if the bottom half of her were prepared for winter while the top was still summering. Oh *hell* no, he thinks. He stands in the doorway until she looks up from the computer screen to take notice of him. He switches his messenger bag from one shoulder to the other, meaning: Do you know who the fuck I am? She goes back to watching her dumb show or dumb movie or whatever the hell it is she's watching, but the Assistant just stands there glowering until finally, vanquished, she rises, unplugs her power cable from the wall and brushes past him, refusing to close the laptop, which she bumbles awkwardly as she relocates to a common area down the hall. The girl is rail thin, but the seat of her sweatpants says *Juicy* in cursive, which is strange, but also better than having *Fat Ass* written across your butt, whatever its actual size, he concedes.

When the Historian arrives, the Assistant wants to tell her how he defended her honor, or protected their turf, or drew a line in the sand, but can't find the right bromide and lets it go. They've got work to do anyway. She's dropped the sexy-fierce pantsuit of yesterday in favor of snug blue jeans and a well-worn Liz Phair concert tee from the early nineties, which is sexy in its own way. Sexy-casual. He wants to ask how her walk home was yesterday evening, whether the idea came to her, but he can see she's agitated and there's little time to waste with pleasantries.

"You're on secondary sources today," she says.

"Okay."

"You can start here." She motions toward The Bag, which somehow seems to have put on a few lbs. since yesterday.

"Okay."

"But you might also run a search, check the databases, and see if anything interesting turns up."

"Okay."

Her directives still sound a little like "Go walk around for several hours and write down everything you see," but he'll do his best. The Historian unloads books from The Bag and pushes the stack across the table slowly toward him. The books at the top skirt the edge, about to fall, but stop, leaning precariously, as if held there by some unseen wad of chewing gum. A biblio-Pisa. He decides he'll work in a carrel near the computers and takes the books low into his arms and clamps his chin on the top to steady them for the hazardous walk down the hall. "We'll meet up later and see where we stand," the Historian calls after him, a command the Assistant can acknowledge only with the slightest turn of his head.

> Kansas was probably the most radical state in the Union in the 1890s, and leftwing efforts continued there for decades.
> —WILLIAM C. PRATT, "HISTORIANS AND THE LOST WORLD OF KANSAS RADICALISM," 2008

The Populists in Kansas, however, were never successful in uniting the rural with the urban political elements. . . . The agrarians, in their struggles against bankers, railroads, mercantile interests, and sound money men, held little appeal to the average urban workers who confronted quite different problems and adversaries. . . . The Populists, however, left a good legacy of labor legislation despite workers failing to reciprocate with political support for agrarians.

—R. ALTON LEE, *FARMERS VS. WAGE EARNERS: ORGANIZED LABOR IN KANSAS, 1860–1960*, 2005

Parry, parry. Riposte:

Populism was never just a farmers' movement, even in its earliest stages, and agrarian radicalism always encompassed more than just farmers whether they be "subsistence yeomen" or "petty producers." And I do not think farmers would have accomplished nearly as much as they did had the movement been limited to farmers from the beginning.

—O. GENE CLANTON, *A COMMON HUMANITY: KANSAS POPULISM AND THE BATTLE FOR JUSTICE AND EQUALITY, 1854–1903*, 2004

The Assistant's carrel is overrun with small, variously colored sticky tabs that he uses to note passages the Historian might find helpful. He discovers a yellow tab affixed to his coffee cup. Mysteriously, too, one on a neighboring chair. Colored red.

In their struggle, Populists learned a great truth: cultures are hard to change. Their attempt to do so, however, provides a measure of the seriousness of their movement. Populism thus cannot be seen as a moment of triumph, but as a moment of democratic promise. It was a spirit of egalitarian hope, expressed in the actions of two million beings—not in the prose of a platform, however creative, and not, ultimately, even in the third party, but in a self-generated culture of collective dignity and individual longing. As a movement of people, it was expansive, passionate, flawed, creative—above all, enhancing in its assertion of human striving. That was Populism in the nineteenth century.

—LAWRENCE GOODWYN, *THE POPULIST MOMENT: A SHORT HISTORY OF THE AGRARIAN REVOLT IN AMERICA*, 1978

The interpretative volleying of historians. The Assistant recalls his father's fondness for saying that opinions are like assholes: everyone's got one.

The interpretations of Populism have run a considerable gamut. John Hicks's *Populist Revolt* (1931) saw it as interest-group politics using popular control of the government and government action to regulate corporations and political conspiracy. Chester Destler in his 1946 account de-emphasized the regional aspects and saw the People's Party as part and parcel of long-held radical beliefs on natural rights. . . . Robert McMath, in *American Populism: A Social History* (1993), emphasized that Populism was especially strong in Kansas because the mainstream party response to farm problems was ridicule and intransigence. Had there been some bend in the Republican establishment, perhaps there need not have been such a fracture. Worth Robert Miller has found the picture still not orderly after one hundred years of analysis. . . . The movement does not fit neatly into a standard ideological category. Miller concluded, "It was a thoroughly American, nonsocialist, anticapitalist movement that called for enough change in the institutions of land, transportation, and money to be considered moderately radical."

—CRAIG MINER, *KANSAS: THE HISTORY OF THE SUNFLOWER STATE: 1854–2000*, 2002

He wonders what angle the Historian will take.

The Assistant, spitballing: Populists as some kind of anti-agribusiness/sustainable-farming avant-garde? Possible title: *Organic Revolution*.

A study of populist outrage: the People's Party and the Tea Party? Possible title: *Grassroots vs. Corporate Roots*.

Then the Assistant comes across this:

The grievances and solutions articulated by the People's Party have been the source of much historiographical conflict. In the 1950s Richard Hofstadter portrayed the Populists as an assortment of angry, reactionary rustics, dreaming of preindustrial times rather than facing the permanence of recent changes. Others found the Populists a far-sighted group of reformers concerned with America's industrial future.

—THOMAS FRANK, "THE LEVIATHAN WITH TENTACLES OF STEEL: RAILROADS IN THE MINDS OF KANSAS POPULISTS," 1989

Which rings a bell from earlier research. *Hofstadter*, the name keeps coming up. The Assistant scans the H columns of the indexes in the books on his desk.

Hofstadter was no specialist on Populism, but his treatment in this book changed the direction of scholarship on the topic. No other account had such an impact on the study of farm movements. He explored the darker side of populism, focusing on its illiberal tendencies. In his eyes, Populists indulged in conspiratorial thinking, nativism, and anti-Semitism. *The Age of Reform* won the Pulitzer Prize for History in 1956 and, to this day, is acknowledged by many as one of the most influential works by a post–World War II historian.

—WILLIAM C. PRATT, "HISTORIANS AND THE LOST
WORLD OF KANSAS RADICALISM," 2008

The Assistant fancies himself old school, still favoring the book-as-object that one can touch and smell, and in which one can underline and spill coffee. But in 2010 the writing, so to speak, is on the wall, and he wonders how long before he will capitulate and buy a goddamn e-reader. A menacing gloom overtakes the Assistant as he searches the stacks to find a copy of Hofstadter's book, already missing these last precious days before everything is finally digitized.

The Populists looked backward with longing to the lost agrarian Eden, to the republican America of the early years of the nineteenth century in which there were few million-aires and, as they saw it, no beggars, when labor had excellent prospects and the farmer had abundance, when statesmen still responded to the will of the people and there was no such thing as the money power. What they meant—though they did not express themselves in such terms—was that they would like to restore the conditions prevailing before the development of industrialism and the commercialization of agriculture. . . . In Populist thought the farmer is not a speculating businessman, victimized by the risk economy of which he is a part, but rather a wounded yeoman, preyed

upon by those who are alien to the life of folkish virtue.
—RICHARD HOFSTADTER, *THE AGE OF REFORM*, 1955

The Library of Googlexandria.

In the books that have been written about the Populist movement, only passing mention has been made of its significant provincialism; little has been said of its relations with nativism and nationalism; nothing has been said of its tincture of anti-Semitism.
—RICHARD HOFSTADTER, *THE AGE OF REFORM*, 1955

The Age of Reform serves up a pupu platter of vitriol and condescension that spurs the Assistant to write *cheese dick* in the margins of page 156. Hofstadter, the Assistant feels confident in asserting, is not only misguided in his analysis, but also kind of a jerk; however, he's aware of a certain strain of Stockholm syndrome particular to academe in which the researcher comes to overly sympathize with the researched. He's protective of his Populists as a mother hen now that they've kidnapped him from his own work, his responsibilities, his life.

Later in the afternoon, the Historian pops over to see if he wants to "powwow."

"Sure, let's powwow," he answers. Now that she's introduced the word, he can think of nothing but it. "I could use some more coffee. How about we powwow downstairs?"

"My treat."

At Starbucks he orders his third venti dark roast of the day, and she a grande Americano and a cake pop. "Goddamn, I love these things," she says as they take a seat. The quasi-fart smell of burnt coffee hovers over everything. "You'll never believe what I saw two undergrads doing in the stacks."

"I believe you," he says, and she laughs before consuming the rest of her cake pop as though she were a sword-swallower. "So, what did you want to"—*don't say powwow*—"talk about?"

She takes a swig from her drink, shaking her head.

"I don't know," she says. "It's like I've hit a wall. I can't figure out my argument, and the proposal is due the day after tomorrow." She pauses a moment. "I don't suppose you came across anything interesting."

He tells her about coming across Hofstadter, and she says *The Age of Reform* was a seminal book and largely responsible for shaping public perception of the Populists as "ignorant, pitchfork-wielding rubes, screaming about silver. But refuting Hofstadter has driven the field for the last fifty years. I want to do something new." She takes a sip of her drink and adds: "I *need* to do something new."

"What do you mean?"

She grimaces, seeming to weigh whether she wants to answer, and finally says, "I have a two-book deal with the publisher."

"Okay," he says. "That's great, right?"

"Not when the first book bombs." She pauses. "Mine did." This admission of failure feels like intimacy; he's been admitted into her confidence. Suddenly he wants to tell her every dopey thing he's ever done, every sin committed. "And the second book is contingent on a proposal, which I submitted last month, but they weren't impressed. Not provocative. Too safe, they said. They gave me one more chance. That's what's due Monday."

"What happens if they don't like the new proposal?"

"They kill the book," she says. She seems to recognize his silence as confusion and explains: "I've taken money for one book that did poorly and a second I couldn't deliver."

"So you'd have to give the money back?"

"Normally that would be the case." She says this with a smile that is unsettling because she's clearly upset. "Except I've spent it all." The Assistant recalls a high school girlfriend who would double over in fits of laughter in moments of great despair or misfortune. "That's how I bought my house."

Neither of them says anything for a few moments.

"It's not just the money, though," she says. She looks at her Americano, slowly turning it in circles. "I've been here for a while, and I'm used to it, but with a successful book I could . . ." She doesn't finish the sentence, but doesn't need to. The Assistant realizes she is a woman who never once imagined she'd spend the majority of her life in Manhattan, Kansas, the Little Apple.

He wants to help, doesn't like the idea of somebody murdering her book or fucking with her domicile situation, and tells her the ideas that came to him while researching, but she dismisses *Organic Revolution* and *Grassroots vs. Corporate Roots* with a look of squinting, silent disfavor. Later, when the library closes and they leave, she says they're good attempts but just not right for this particular project. Across campus shine the bright lights of the football stadium. The cold night air does something strange to the oracular voice of the announcer so that only every fifth word is understandable.

"Well, what're you up to?" she asks.

"I better check into the game. My teammates need me," he says, nodding in the direction of the stadium. "You?"

"Home. I'm gonna work a while longer." She starts to turn, but stops. "If you want, you could come over and we can work together. I'll order a pizza or something . . . but you're probably—"

"Thanks, but I'm pretty beat. I should—"

"Of course," she says, "of course," shaking her head, clearly regretful she extended the invitation.

"But I can help again tomorrow, if you'd like."

"That would be great. I appreciate it."

She says goodbye and leaves. For twenty seconds or so he simply watches her go, but then his feet begin to move in her direction, and ten minutes later the Assistant is standing on the opposite side of the street, watching as she lugs The Bag up her front porch, unlocks the door, and enters. The pretty yellow bungalow is just the kind of place he would have imagined her in. *What am I doing?* he thinks, as he crosses the street and stands behind a tall oak tree. She flips on lights and moves from room to room. Finally she seems to settle on the kitchen and the Assistant skulks over to some holly bushes on the side of the house. *What am I doing?* She uses a black wine key to open a bottle and pours a glass of what he suspects is Shiraz. *This isn't that weird. She invited me over, after all, so I came over. That's all this is.* The Historian sits at the small kitchen table, staring at her wineglass—thinking what?—and then suddenly begins to cry. Like *really* cry. Head down on the table, shoulders shaking. He's pretty sure this qualifies as weeping. These do not seem like tears over only a failed book proposal; these are tears of existential worry. He's seen something he shouldn't have, which tends to happen when you spy on people, when you are engaged in activity of the pervert/voyeur/stalker variety. *What the hell am I doing?* He leaves quickly, cursing himself. *I'm the worst. What was I thinking? Idiot!*

"I'm so sorry," the Assistant says the next morning when he finds the Historian waiting outside the library.

"For what?" she says, turning his way.

He looks at the tall building.

"For being late."

"Don't sweat it," she says. "Place isn't even open yet. Apparently on Sundays they don't open till noon." They both just stare at the library as though awed by its capricious sense of operating hours. "Buy you breakfast?"

They walk to a diner off campus and sit in a booth near

the back. It's not busy, the calm before the post-church storm. She's wearing a Yo La Tengo shirt today and he wonders how long she'll keep up the concert-tees-from-my-twenties theme. Today is the rare occasion she looks her age, whatever that is. She appears exhausted, proverbial bags under the eyes like she hasn't slept, or like if she has slept she probably spent the time crying. Sleep-crying. Talk about a wet dream. He thinks of her last night, his shameful encroachment on her privacy. And yet, part of him is glad he saw what he did. To behold the suffering of others can be illuminating and strangely bond-forming. Perhaps that's so because most of the time we don't, can't, or won't, he realizes, apropos of his own strange relationship to his mother's illness. He wants to tell the Historian about it, how sometimes at unexpected moments his body, too, will spontaneously combust in wet, lugubrious sorrow.

"I had a great night," the Historian says.

"You did?"

"I think I figured it out. My angle for the proposal."

"You did?"

"I did—thanks to you."

She tells him how she'd all but given up on it when she thought back to their conversation earlier in the day and re-called something he'd said. For a brief moment he's thrilled.

"You want to use *Organic Revolution!*" he interjects.

"Oh," she says, "no. No, I don't."

"*Grassroots vs. Corporate Roots?*" he whimpers, which she re-fuses to dignify with a response.

"You brought up Hofstadter and *The Age of Reform*."

"I did."

"And I said refuting Hofstadter was old hat."

"You did."

"And that's when I had the idea," she says, her eyebrows raised, a slight opening of the mouth. "An apologia." She says this uncertainly at first, as if only testing out how it sounds, but it's just a matter of seconds before she avers, "I will defend Richard Hofstadter." And like that, lured by the provocative potential of so-unfashionable-it's-fashionable contrarianism, her hammer has forged an angle.

The Assistant, with the earnestness of his seven-year-old self: "But he was wrong."

"Maybe," she says. "Doesn't really matter, though."

"Doesn't matter?"

"What matters is carving out space in the scholarly debate. There is no right, no ultimate position. There's only interpretation."

Interpretations are like assholes, the Assistant wants to say. Everyone's got one.

"Besides, this is the kind of thing the publisher likes. Something controversial."

"It *does* matter," he says. "You can't defend him."

He feels both nervous and confident in eschewing his usual deference. In the hierarchy of their shared world, he's supposed to know he is basically toilet paper stuck to her stiletto. Normally he does, but he can't help himself. He's gone into mother-hen mode. For a fleeting moment he imagines "Sockless Jerry," William Peffer, and Mary Lease lying completely still in their graves, smiling. Equal rights for all, special privileges to none.

"Excuse me?"

But he also likes the Historian and wants to help her.

"I can do whatever I want," she says, a slight your-move edge in her voice. Her eyes narrow a tad, as though if she really wanted to she could summon laser beams that would shred him into confetti.

"Of course you can," the Assistant says.

For about half a second he felt like a hero, but then she iced over and readied ocular lasers, and now they fill the rest of their time with silent eating and occasional remarks that carry a we're-still-cool-right? subtext. And they are still cool, it seems. Despite their fatigue, at least they have a goal. His mission is no longer to wander out into the world, writing down everything he sees. In the war room the Historian tells him to focus on compiling information on Hofstadter. She's going to begin drafting the proposal. Before he leaves, she asks for his legal pads, the primary and secondary sources he's taken notes on the past two days. "Oh right," he says, removing them from his messenger bag and sliding them her way across the table.

The most influential book ever published on the history of twentieth-century America.
—ALAN BRINKLEY, HISTORIAN, ON HOFSTADTER'S
THE AGE OF REFORM, 1985

Hofstadter's ground-breaking work came in using social psychology concepts to explain political history. He explored subconscious motives such as social status anxiety, anti-intellectualism, irrational fear, and paranoia—as they propelled political discourse and action in politics.
—WIKIPEDIA ENTRY, 2010

There's no question that Hofstadter's writing was wonderful. But his understanding of the American past now seems narrow and flawed, and marked, inevitably, by the preoccupations of a generation that lived through Hitler and Stalin, by a gnawing anxiety that some kind of American fascism, a vicious right-wing movement coming out of the heartland, was not only possible but likely. . . . Hofstadter's "status politics" thesis held that the Populists were driven to irrationality and paranoia by anxiety over their declining status in an America where rural life and its values were being supplanted by an urban industrial society. Populism, in this view, was a form of reactionary resistance to modernity. Here Hofstadter was the Jewish New York intellectual anxiously looking for traces of proto-fascism somewhere in middle America. He saw Joe McCarthy as a potential American Hitler and believed he had found the roots of American fascism among rural Protestants in the Midwest. It was history by analogy—but the analogy didn't work.

—JON WIENER, "AMERICA, THROUGH
A GLASS DARKLY," 2006

I still think his position is as biased by his urban background and by the new conservatism as the work of older historians was biased by their rural background and traditional agrarian sympathies.

—MERLE CURTI, HOFSTADTER'S DISSERTATION ADVISOR
AT COLUMBIA UNIVERSITY, 1955

The Assistant takes a break to get more coffee. He's fading and there are still several hours to go. He should have just worn a beer helmet that holstered twin venti dark roasts this weekend. His research chapeau.

The Populists saw the principal source of injustice and economic suffering in rural America in what they called "the money power." In Hofstadter's analysis, this was evidence of irrational paranoia, of "psychic disturbances." Moreover, Hofstadter argued that these denunciations of "the money power" were deeply anti-Semitic. . . . The problem with this analysis, aside from the paucity of evidence, was that anti-Semitic rhetoric was hardly a monopoly of rural Midwestern Protestants in post–Civil War America. The Protestant elites in East Coast cities were probably more anti-Semitic, and Irish Catholic immigrants in Eastern cities had no love for Jews either.

—JON WIENER, "AMERICA, THROUGH
A GLASS DARKLY," 2006

While Hofstadter's misreading has a quality of grandeur, the source of his difficulty is not hard to locate: he managed to frame his interpretation of the intellectual content of Populism without recourse to a single reference to the planks of the Omaha Platform of the People's Party or to any economic, political, or cultural experiences that led to the creation of those goals. Indeed, there is no indication in his text that he was aware of these experiences.

—LAWRENCE GOODWYN, *The Populist Moment:*
A Short History of the Agrarian Revolt
in America, 1978

This being Hofstadter's most pointed-out flaw as a historian: an aversion to consulting the historical record.

In a liberal society the historian is free to try to dissociate myths from reality, but that same impulse to myth-making that moves his fellow man is also at work in him.

—RICHARD HOFSTADTER, 1956

The Assistant wakes under the gentle hand of the Historian. "Hey there," she says. "You okay?" He's fallen asleep on top of a picture of Hofstadter he printed out from the Internet. A bead of drool has dampened the paper and now dried, giving Hofstadter the impression of entirely elective plastic surgery gone awry. The Assistant nods, not quite verbal yet. He does not feel rested. It was the kind of nap that only makes you more tired. "Closing time," she says. "Buy you a coffee on the way out?" It does not feel humanly possible to ingest more coffee than he has the last three days. He shakes his head and begins packing things up. He hands her the legal pad with today's findings on Hofstadter. "Your notes have been very helpful. You found some great stuff," she says. "I finished a draft of the proposal. It would be great to have another set of eyes on it, though. I wonder if you might look it over before I submit it to the publisher tomorrow morning. I'll e-mail it to you tonight." He tells her sure and they leave together. "I'm beat," she says, yawning. "But it's a good kind of tired"—*speak for yourself*—"like we earned it." She thanks him for his help. "Obviously I couldn't have done it without you." She moves a centimeter toward him, which for a quick second feels like the beginnings of an embrace, but she stops and just pats him once, awkwardly, in the general vicinity of his shoulder. "Go get some rest, okay?" she says and turns to leave. Watching her go, he feels the slightest nostalgia for the godforsaken Bag.

Back at his apartment, the Assistant climbs into bed, intending only to redeem what he can of his truncated nap but wakes thirteen hours later. His body has performed some weird kind of intervention. *Look, homie. We love you very much, but you're not taking care of yourself so we're unplugging you for a while. We're doing this for your own good.* He staggers over to his desk, which is a repurposed card table he bought at Walmart for twenty dollars when he started grad school two years ago. He checks his e-mail and finds seven from the Historian. The first of which arrived yesterday evening with the proposal attached, and they appeared steadily every few hours throughout the night and morning, sometimes with a new draft attached, sometimes with a thinly veiled entreaty disguised as a joke and full of exclamation points and *ha-ha!*s. It's the e-mail trail of a crazy person; her body has not performed an intervention. The most recent e-mail from less than an hour ago, 6:27 a.m., said something to the effect that she needs to submit the proposal by 8:00 a.m. and could he pretty pretty pretty *pretty* please for the love of God read it ASAP! She would be soooooooooooooooooooooooo grateful!

Quickly he opens the attachment of the latest draft and reads. He's disappointed when he remembers the core of her argument, which is really Hofstadter's specious argument, denigrating the Populists. Maybe the book will become famous and he can perform a respectful takedown of it in a few years with his own work on the subject.

As he reads on to the second page, she makes the case for the importance of her book, its relevance to the field, and gives a synopsis, outlining the structure and timeline for the completion of the book. In the section titled "Research Plan," she provides samples of the sort of evidence she hopes to incorporate into the project, and that's when he sees some of his notes. He's still a little groggy, but it's strange. One note in particular seems off. "They are in fact reactionary betrayers of the term *populist* who want to carry forward a regressive agenda that will overwhelmingly harm the majority of the population." Who the hell said that? It's attributed in the proposal to William Allen White, the famous newspaperman from Emporia, Kansas, ardent Republican and fierce critic of the Populists. But he didn't say that, did he? Then it hits him: White *didn't* say it—the Assistant did. Or, rather, he wrote it. Friday night, when he was watching the news story on the Tea Party rally, he'd been scribbling on the pad and written down the thought, carrying on an imaginary argument with his dad, perhaps the germ that led him to *Grassroots vs. Corporate Roots* the following afternoon. He must have written it on his pad close enough to a William Allen White quote for her to have mistakenly attributed it to White. Surely she wouldn't have knowingly done so. There are other quotes from his notes, correctly transcribed but taken out of context, and they're presented in such a way as to move the Historian's thesis a notch above conjecture. *Your notes have been very helpful.*

The Assistant had been an English major as an undergrad and recalls something he read long ago in a Brit-lit survey, Shelley's *A Defence of Poetry*, in which the great Romantic argued that poets are the "unacknowledged legislators of the world." If this is so, the Assistant realizes, then historians are the autocrats.

Next to the keyboard, the Assistant's phone suddenly buzzes. For a moment he thinks the Historian has given up on e-mail and changed tactics, but it's not her. It's a text from Mom. Each morning she sends him a Bible verse for the day. The Assistant and God have been at an impasse since he was sixteen, and while he used to find these messages annoying, now he sort of looks forward to them. *"Therefore, as God's chosen people, holy and dearly loved, clothe yourselves with compassion, kindness, humility, gentleness and patience." Colossians 3:12.* Then a second text arrives: *Missed u this weekend. May B nxt? Thinking uf u. Luv Mom.*

The Assistant wants to be compassionate, kind, humble, gentle, and patient. He also wants to be honest and responsible. The clock on his phone, the only accurate clock in his apartment, says 7:31 a.m. He thinks of the Historian and her crumbling book deal, desperate to leave a place she doesn't want to be, crying into her wine each night in her little yellow bungalow. Maybe the notes aren't wrong after all. Maybe this is how history works. Maybe interpretations *are* like assholes. The clock: 7:33 a.m.

Sorry for the delay—totally crashed when I got home! he types in response to the Historian's last e-mail. *Just a couple of minor things.* He points out a typo and a comma splice. *I'm glad to have been of help*, he types. *Best of luck—fingers crossed!*

He stares at the screen, the cursor blinking, and then he hits SEND.

GOOD MEN A LONG TIME GONE

Ricky had wiped down the counter and was checking the level on his well liquors when his first customers—Doris, Charlene, and Kathy—walked through the door. Instinctively, he looked at the clock, 5:17, and then at the calendar, which was from the previous year, 1992, but was flipped to the correct month, July, so he moved the corresponding date ahead one slot. Second Thursday, he realized. It would be a late night.

The bar—the Doc Holliday Inn and Lounge, which had never included an inn of any sort, and which most people just called Doc's—was located on the far western edge of Dodge City, just past the less frequented of two discount supermarkets on Wyatt Earp Boulevard but not quite to the closest of several industrial slaughterhouses. In the late seventies, these packinghouses—Cargill, National Beef, IBP, ConAg, D&L—had followed tax incentives west to be closer to feedlots and to escape union contracts in Kansas City and Wichita, making boomtowns of Dodge, Liberal, and Garden City the way oil and railroads had a century prior. They drew a large pool of unskilled laborers to towns that had been losing population for decades, providing them with a constant source of employment. But the work was difficult and dangerous, and turnover was rampant. Some quit immediately, some after a month, but there was always somebody new to fill the spot. Few lasted a year, let alone several, but those who did shared a kind of bond, the hard-won cachet it took to work whatever horror show came along the chain day after day, to live with joint pain so unrelenting you could no longer lay your hand flat. It was this specific niche—the lifers of the nearby D&L plant—who were Ricky's regulars. Most nights a handful of them would swing by for a postshift shot and a beer, and one or two might even stay late to watch a game and work himself through a pack of Winstons and a dozen dollar-and-a-quarter draws, but tonight was payday, and just about everyone showed up when the checks were cut.

They arrived in the manner their labor divided them. First in were the packagers, this trio of women who worked the line, preparing the shrink-wrapped cuts for shipping to wholesalers. They were followed by Bob, a stunner, whose job was to lead the cattle into holding pens, put the captive bolt to their skulls, and pull the trigger, as well as Ray, a line supervisor. The shacklers, stickers, and steamers—a group of six who together hoisted the unconscious cow from the kill floor to the overhead rail, slit the jugular, drained the blood, removed the hide, and hosed down the carcass—followed shortly thereafter. Then there was a break in the flow of arrivals, twenty minutes or so, because though everyone showered and changed clothes after their shift, the splitters' and eviscerators' work, separating the edible from the offal, was especially dirty, and despite the equipment—the chain-mail apron, the armguards and mesh gloves, the hard hats and industrial goggles—filth would inevitably find its way around, so Dolan and Byrd needed extra time to soak and scrub a second lather of Lava soap onto their skin. Last to arrive were Hector, Dan, and Carlos, the butchers, who showed up after everyone else because they were the artists, and so they took their time. They could usually be found in the locker room late, towels around waists, wet hair dripping onto the slippery tile, comparing knives and techniques, bragging of cuts.

What was it about Doc's that they liked? There was nothing special about the place, and that's what made it special. Unlike other bars that tried too hard, Doc's was not seeking to win their affection, which made them want to give it away all the more. It was small, with a capacity of forty that it exceeded only on the weekends. Its walls were paneled wood grain and dotted by the occasional clock or piece of racing memorabilia bearing the sponsorship of a beer company no one was certain still existed: Falstaff, Utica Club, Grain Belt. Pushed back against the wall opposite the bar were four booths, the carmine vinyl of which was stretched and torn, some holes slapped over with duct tape while others exposed their foamy camel-colored insides. There was a pool table in the back, and one could get a clean shot from all but three angles where the *Death Wish* pinball machine prevented full extension of the cue. To be "Bronsoned" was to find your ball in this no-man's-land, and every player avoided it like the plague. There was a jukebox stocked with records that hadn't changed since Ricky took over in 1979. In the way of food, there was a chip rack, fifty cents a pop, and a red Hot Nuts machine that dispensed at a quarter a turn. Ricky made use of a small stove in the back, where he'd cook burgers using ground chuck delivered straight from D&L and serve them to customers on thin paper napkins the width of a sanitary pad. It was the only thing on the menu, and there was nothing like a long night of drinking to convince customers they were the best burgers in town.

The ladies sat in their usual spot, three stools front and center, elbows up on the bar. Doris no longer drank, but she'd stop in for a while because her husband was sick and bedridden, which made the house feel oppressive. She'd have an occasional shot glass's worth of pink champagne if there was cause to celebrate, though she usually just sat sipping a tumbler of tonic neat. Kathy and Charlene waited on a round of SoCo.

Afterward, they'd switch to beer because they'd need their wherewithal to accept or deflect the inevitable advances of the men, especially Dolan. Who for the time being was sipping a can of Pabst as he sent the cambering pinball over Charles Bronson's leathered scowl. Byrd sat in a booth, talking to the only other black man in the bar, a shackler named Asie, a fact he'd become conscious of only two days later, as he stooped to pour gas into his mower, thinking back on the night and what had happened, and how it was strange that it didn't feel strange or isolating that he and Asie happened to be sitting by themselves for a time. The butchers stood at the pool table, debating which of the three would have to team up with Dolan in the first game of the night.

Bob lowered himself onto his favorite corner stool by the television, and Ray and Sal occupied the neighboring two on the short side of the L-shaped bar. The Scotch-taped stools were as familiar as their recliners at home, accepting the curvature of their butts like regal death masks. Bob had given them a ride because Ray got hit with a DWI coming home from Doc's the previous Saturday. Feeling a sense of indebtedness for the lift, Ray called out: "Give us a trinity of the High Life at this end. Drafts. Put them on my tab." As Ricky pulled clean glasses from the dry-rack, Ray rocked side to side on his seat. "My hemorrhoids send their regards, Ricky," he said, then nodded at Doris, Charlene, and Kathy as if to say, "*Ladies . . .*"

Doris was in her late forties, still good at her job, but not one to project sexual fantasies onto. She was the self-appointed lookout for the two younger women, and because everyone had eyes for Charlene, Ray focused his flirtations on Kathy, who at thirty-six was half pretty and had an ass he sometimes fantasized beating with a flyswatter. "Kathy with a *K*," he said to her now, "when you gonna let me make a dishonest woman of you? We won't tell your husband." It was harmless. The fact that nothing would ever happen with Kathy was what made this permissible. She knew it too, which is why she could answer "I don't eat red meat, Tonto," and still make Ray laugh.

Bob wore a white undershirt that stretched over his big belly and tucked into a pair of dark dungarees, which were held up by a pair of crimson-and-blue clip-on suspenders. He removed his ball cap, setting it beside his beer, and turned his attention to the only television in the bar, an old nineteen-inch Magnavox with rabbit ears that picked up a handful of stations, most importantly channel three, which broadcast Royals games. Bob was a loyal fan and this was George Brett's final season with the team. Out of respect, he'd made a pledge to watch every Royals game he could. And while he'd never betray these feelings to the others at Doc's, where he sat stoically sipping his beer, he was grateful for having had the privilege of watching a player like Brett—three thousand hits, flirting with .400 in '80, the World Series in '85—compete, grateful and mystified at the way Brett's excellence on the field had somehow made his own unremarkable life feel a bit better. Foolish but true, he knew, and perhaps that's why he felt a sense of loss as he watched Number 5 assume his familiar lean-back stance in the box and chase a low-and-outside for a third strike.

He finished the last of his beer and pushed the empty glass toward Ricky.

"Another beer, Bob-O?" Ray said.

"Not this time."

"Come on, stay a while," said Byrd, who'd left Asie in the booth to come order another round.

This was all part of the ritual, the routine. Bob only ever stayed for one beer, but the fun was in pressuring him to stay for a second. The wild incentives. *Charlene will show us her titties.* Or: *I'll buy one for the whole fucking bar if you stay for another.* But Bob would never bite. He'd just put on his cap and, already on his way to the door, simply raise a splay-fingered hand over his shoulder as a goodbye.

"One day I'm gonna have that kind of discipline!" said Ray. "I feel like we should be clapping."

"He ought to have a plaque on the wall," said Byrd in his slow manner of speech. "*Here drank Steady Bob, model of moderation.*"

Doris added: "You'll never get rich on him, Ricky."

Ricky shook his head, grinning as he dunked glasses in the bleach water and rinsed them.

Beside Ray sat Sal, silent, content to let the others do the talking. His real name was Adolfo, but one day after a few weeks on the job, as he sat in the break room, Ray told him: "As your friend and supervisor, I feel I must advise you against calling yourself Adolf." At that point Adolfo knew almost no English, and it took a week to understand why Ray was always talking to him about some guy named Sal.

"Sal," because Adolfo was from El Salvador. He'd come north in 1983, fleeing the civil war, and he had the wounds to prove it. His face was scarred badly from the Guardia's attempt to gain intel about the rebels. It was something he would forget about, the scars lining his face, only to be reminded in the reactions of others—the piercing stares when they thought he wasn't looking, the quick dart of eyes when they knew he was—and he'd look at the ground and feel shame and anger. Throughout the previous decade of civil war and insurgence many had emigrated from Central America, and recruiting agents, sent by the packing plants, lined the border, drawing cheap and unskilled workers to towns throughout the Middle West. Hector was from Guatemala. Carlos, Honduras. Still others came from Nicaragua. Different as they and their cultures were, to most whites in Dodge they all looked the same, spoke the same language, and were generally referred to with the catchall "Mexican" or "beaner." But Sal was different. He didn't look *Mexican*. He was indigenous Pipil, his face longer, broader, darker in color, which Ray had recognized immediately, and which caused him to take special interest in Sal. "You and me are Indians, brother," he'd explained to Sal. "We invented this continent before they stole it."

Ray was part of the first group hired when D&L opened in 1980, and he'd outlasted almost everyone in his cohort. He was a good worker, talented, and had proved himself skilled and knowledgeable about the plant's various operations so as to be moved by management to a supervisory role. Ray had been at the plant for three years when Sal arrived, and he'd looked out for him from the start. He set Sal up as a shackler, where he stayed for nearly a decade, until last month, when he'd been moved to Exsanguination, thanks to Ray putting in a few good words to management. It meant more hours, a bump in pay. It was coveted but gruesome work, and Ray wasn't sure how his soft-spoken friend would handle it. But on the first day of the switch, when Sal was shadowing him, Ray tested him to see if he had the stomach for it. Thinking Sal might hesitate, Ray watched him calmly take the knife from his hand and cleanly sever the throat of a cow shackled hindquarters up. He did it three more times in quick succession without pause. Exhilarated, proud even, Ray cried: "I knew it! You're like one of those farts no one can hear but it kills the entire room."

Now in the bar, Ray signaled Ricky for another round. He let out the ponytail, and his long black hair fell to his chest, the ends of a few strands finding their way over the lip of his beer. He nudged Sal and they walked back to the pool table, where Hector and Dan were preparing to take on Dolan and Carlos.

"How about the two of us jump in?" said Ray.

"How about you wait your turn," said Dolan. "You ain't boss in here."

Ray laughed at the kid's practiced bravado. Dolan was six-foot-five, and at twenty-seven young enough to hit the gym for ninety minutes before coming in to work a ten-hour on the line. He bought Wranglers and western shirts a half-size small to accentuate his body's brawn. Ray stage-whispered to Carlos: "You gotta watch out for your partner over there, Captain Tube Sock. He'll go after anything that bends over. Don't risk it—use the bridge." Nestled in the small of his back, attached to his belt, Ray wore a leather sheath, barely noticeable, containing a knife shaped like an arrowhead. An elder had given it to him while Ray was visiting his wife Lorna's family on the rez in Oklahoma. More good luck charm than anything. He took it out and offered it to Carlos: "Here, take this. You might need protection."

"No knives in the bar," Dolan said, but he sounded like a tattling child and regretted speaking up. It was true, though: Ricky had banned knives after a night the previous winter when a couple of the butchers brought their tools into the bar and injured themselves horsing around.

"What, this little thing?" said Ray, turning the knife under the light. "I just use this to scratch my butthole."

"How about you shut your facehole so we can play?" Dolan said.

Ray made a childish face, like his feelings had been hurt as he slid the knife back in the sheath. He fished out a couple quarters from his pocket and set them on the rail to stake his place in the queue, then moved over to the lone high-top where Sal was sitting. He continued to stare at Dolan.

"Fuck you looking at, Ray?"

"I was just thinking."

"You shouldn't do that."

"I was wondering what you must've looked like at birth, crawling out the pussy of that giant ear of corn."

Hector collapsed onto the pool table, ruining the rack he was trying to center and had to start over. Dolan ignored their laughter and moved into position to break. He sized it up, turning the cue slowly over palm and knuckle, and then did a series of three quick practice shots just to the left of the cue ball. Finally he was ready and brought back his shooting arm, a slight tremor betraying the power he was trying to harness for the shot.

"Okay, fine. You win," Ray said to Sal, who stared back silently. "You can buy me a drink."

Despite the varied accents and idioms, Sal had gotten by easy enough with so many Spanish speakers at the plant. Ray pushed him to learn English, though. "I want to know about your home, what the Indians are like down there," he said. "Besides, I need someone I can tell a fucking joke to." So, early on he'd begun inviting Sal over for dinner at his small two-bedroom house, where Lorna would fix supper while they sat at the kitchen table and talked. Or, rather, Ray talked and Sal tried to follow. Ray would bounce his young son Daniel on his knee, periodically sending the giggling boy into the air above his head. He tried to tell Sal about his and Lorna's people, the Kiowa, and of the Plains Indian Wars after the Civil War, but Ray spoke too fast, the words bleeding together. The less Sal followed, the more Ray began to embellish and lie. He claimed Satanata, the great Kiowa war chief, had been his great-great-grandfather, and was outraged when Sal didn't know who that was. He said scalping was a lie created to demonize Indians. Finally, he said that when the white man went to the moon, he found Kiowa and Cheyenne, who instead of relocating to Indian Territory had rowed a special canoe into outer space. Lorna, stirring a pot on the stove, laughed softly through her nose. Sal followed none of it.

"I see the problem," Ray said one day back in those early years of their friendship as he drove Sal home after their shift. "You're like the teacher says about my boy—a visual learner." So that weekend he took Sal to the Boot Hill Museum downtown. It was a tourist trap made up to look like Dodge had in 1876 with reconstructed saloons and period-style shops and crafts. "Most of this is bullshit," he said as they entered the museum, passing exhibits on Wyatt Earp, Bat Masterson, and other famous residents of old Dodge. There were tableaux of cowboys sitting around the campfire, and another of a frontier woman rocking in her cabin. Ray stopped in front of a figure of a smiling Indian in native dress holding a peace pipe in one hand and a bird in the other. "This almost hurts my feelings more than anything," he said. Then, from the corner of his eye, he saw the life-size buffalo diorama. "Ah, there it is," he said. "This is what I wanted to show you."

Ray led Sal over to the exhibit that explained how the Plains Indians of the area had once depended on bison for food and clothing. When the whites came and the Indians resisted relocation, the settlers began to kill the buffalo and so began the decade of slaughter, the 1870s, when the army machine-gunned the great herds and left the meat to rot in the plains. The goal was not profit but the extermination of the native food supply so they would leave their land, which they eventually did, and in twenty years the number of buffalo dropped from seventy-five million to near extinction. Sal had been practicing reading in bed each night and took in the exhibit's informational cards slowly, understanding about sixty percent of the content. But Ray was right: it was the picture that made the most sense. It was black and white and showed a massive pile of bison bones that Sal couldn't fully grasp the scale of until he saw the little man, a dot holding a skull, standing on top of the mound. "The Great Massacre," the caption above the photo read. This Sal understood.

It would take him several more months before he knew the language well enough to tell Ray the story of his own people's Great Massacre, *la Matanza*, when the Pipil Indians rose up against the fascist government. Promising dialogue and pardons, the government invited the peasants and workers into a public square to air their grievances and proceeded to shoot them all. The army killed so many people that no one knew the exact number, perhaps forty thousand, most of them indigenous Pipil who worked on the coffee *fincas* in western Salvador for the country's oligarchs. This was in 1932, more than thirty years before Sal was born, but his grandfathers and grandmothers, the great uncles and aunts he'd never know, all died in the uprising. An entire generation gone, as if never born. And after the violence came the real genocide, when to save themselves from further reprisal the Pipil erased their culture. They took up Spanish, burned their native clothing, and married non-Pipil to dilute the blood that made them look so much like the people pictured in the new history books that celebrated the government's heroic victory over the traitorous Communists and feral Indians. Sal's parents were both Pipil, but most of the other kids in the village where he'd grown up were mestizo, and he'd only ever heard Nahut spoken late at night as his parents whispered to each other in bed before falling asleep. When he'd ask them about it the next morning, they'd pretend not to know what he was talking about. "You must have been dreaming," they'd say.

Time passed in that strange barroom manner, by turns laggard and fleet, Hector literally feeling in sync with the earth's revolution as he sat in the booth, listening to Carlos go on about his girlfriend not giving it up, while Asie went to the bar to check the score of the game he expected to be in the middle of the third inning only to find a postgame interview with José

Lind on the Magnavox. Charlene was in her own dilatory circle of hell, half listening to Doris natter away. She and Kathy
both liked Doris, prefacing every behind-her-back critique or
bashing with just that phrase, but she could set up camp all
night, spouting aphorisms she'd come across in the Cracker
Barrel gift shop. What was especially annoying was that Doris
seemed to know it was annoying—they were right, she did—
and she took a cruel pleasure in playing killjoy. Lacking Charlene's looks and Kathy's wit, she exercised the power she did
have: the ability to mitigate theirs. She played up her role as
matriarch, adopting the style of dress and manner of speech
of a certain kind of woman she might become in another ten
or fifteen years. "Goodnight, girls," she said to them as she finally rose from her stool. "Be each other's shepherd now, okay?
Call if you need me." To drag it out a little longer, she took
her time—thirteen interminably awkward seconds after saying goodbye—to dig through the bowels of her purse for tip
money, laying on the counter a couple half-torn bills destined
for eternal pop-machine rebuff.

Within seconds of her exit, Dolan made his way to the stool
still warm with the heat of Doris's hams. "I threw that last
game just so I could see your pretty face," he whispered in
Charlene's ear. She was twenty-five and in her third year at the
plant, the first two of which she had spent in a long-distance
marriage to her high school sweetheart, who worked on an oil
rig in Alaska. When her marriage fell apart, the news that she
was single spread through the plant like lighter fluid ablaze, and
despite the don't-rush-into-anything prudence Doris had cau-
tioned, it felt good to be so desired. She narrowed her brown
eyes at Dolan, meaning: Go on, tell me more.

Ray sat beside Kathy, doodling on a cocktail napkin. He'd
switched to bourbon, and Ricky was setting another rocks glass
before him when Brewgner entered the bar. He took a seat on

the stool next to Ray and ordered a Miller, which Ricky knew to serve with a glass of ice because Brewgner's doctor had told him that if he couldn't quit drinking, for his liver's sake, he at least needed to water it down. Like Ray, Brewgner was part of the original group of new hires at D&L, so he had seniority, but unlike Ray he had no interest in management. He'd worked himself up to Exsanguination and stayed there until recently, when he developed carpal tunnel in his knife hand. He'd been out on workman's comp for two months. He was wearing a wrist guard he'd used years earlier during a short-lived stint in a bowling league. Answering a question Ray hadn't asked, he said, "My wrist feels perfect."

"Don't look perfect," said Ray, not taking his eyes off the drawing.

"I'm ready to come back next week."

"Good, I'll let management know we've got a new secretary coming in."

"I'm serious, Ray."

Ray examined his drawing, clicking the ballpoint he'd been using bearing the name of a local real estate agent who'd passed away the previous year. He had a talent for drawing, cartoons mostly, and for a time when he was younger thought he might pursue it, but now he just did it to entertain his kids. This one was a picture of an Indian wearing a headband with a single feather, one hand holding a meat cleaver and the other giving an oversized thumbs-up. The wet bottom of his glass had formed an annular frame around the small figure. He slid it down the bar to Kathy on his left.

"I want you to have this," he said.

She picked it up and studied it.

"Wait, I forgot to sign it."

She passed it back to him and quickly he drew a massive erection on the figure and returned it to her. "It's a self-portrait."

"I need to talk to you," Brewgner said, pulling Ray's attention away from Kathy. He needed back on the line, he said. Workman's comp was a pittance and he was behind on the mortgage.

"They're not gonna take you back," said Ray flatly, honestly. Management had made it clear that they wanted someone younger, quicker, more productive.

"Who'd they get?"

"Sal's taken over your hours."

"Of course you take care of your friend," he said. "I been here since the beginning, same as you. He ain't one of us."

"There is no us, paleface," said Ray. "If you're gonna gripe like a bitch, gripe about the fact that he pulls his count before you're halfway through."

Brewgner and Ray had never particularly liked each other, but it pissed him off that Ray wouldn't go to bat for him, given their shared history at D&L. Brewgner steadied his voice and leaned close to Ray. "Look, I didn't want to say anything, but Ruby's sick. Cancer. Treatment's expensive." At the moment this was a lie, but in three years Ruby would indeed discover the stomach cancer that would take her life in four. "I'll do anything—put me in packaging if you have to. I need a job, Ray."

"What do you want me to do about it?"

Knowing Ray's weakness for gambling, he played his only hand: "Gimme a chance to win it."

In the years after that trip to Boot Hill, as he became fluent, Sal would learn how to answer when Ray asked him to tell stories about what it was like back home. What did El Salvador look like, what did he do, what did he eat? Ray wanted to know it all. Sal described the jagged beauty of the southwestern highlands, the quiet stillness of his village versus the bustle of nearby Izalco, where he and his father would take their crops to market. Since he'd arrived in the United States, Sal had been single and kept his hair short, but Ray was tickled to learn it had once been long, down to his waist, and that he'd known the love of a good woman. Ofelia. "You were like the original man out there! Wandering around with your long-ass hair and jungle woman, eating plantains and shit. You probably swung from the trees, didn't you?" When Sal arrived in Dodge, Ray hadn't even known there was a civil war being fought in Salvador, and he'd become aware of it only when he finally asked about the scars on Sal's face.

Throughout the early years of the war Sal's village had remained isolated from the fighting, he told Ray, but one day the FMLN showed up, part of their effort to bring campesinos in the rural regions of the country to the side of the revolution. They demanded to be fed and housed, forcing every male villager to stop farming and start training, learning to fight. In the evenings in the open square there were mandatory classes on political theory and economics. There was some sense in what they were preaching, but his support for the revolution was coerced. Sal mostly wanted them to leave. The occupation didn't last long, less than three months, but at the time, living with the rebels felt interminable. "So you go from Adam in the Garden to Dennis-fucking-Banks—you expect me to believe that? What happened?"

When the government learned of the cell in Sal's village, they sent the Guardia. The rebels got wind of it and urged everyone to leave, but many stayed, to their peril. The Guardia arrived and decapitated the remaining men and left them hanging upside down from trees as a warning. The women they raped, before and sometimes after slitting their throats, and they bashed children's heads against rocks to save bullets. "How'd you get away?" said Ray. That's when Sal told him about the scars, that the Guardia had tortured him, carving up his face, demanding information about the FMLN, before they'd got drunk and passed out, allowing him to sneak away.

This was a lie. Here is the story Sal had never told anyone:

He'd fought with Ofelia about heeding the rebels' warning, but she wouldn't leave her family, and her family, like his, wouldn't leave the village. In anger, he cursed her stubbornness and left, thinking she'd follow if he did, but she never came, her loyalty to her family trumping her love for him. Guilty and ashamed that he'd left his love and his family to slaughter, he tried to kill himself while at the refugee camp in Guatemala, where he'd gone after returning home to discover the inevitable horror. He held the knifepoint to his breast for a long time, imagining the cool blade sliding into the tender muscle of his heart, but couldn't go through with it. He began to cry at his cowardice, and then he cut up his face so he would never forget it.

Everybody, each one of them in the bar, suffered their shame in private, and for that they were as lonely as they were connected.

For the past hour Sal had been sitting at the bar, staring at the mute infomercial that had come on after the late news. For forty dollars you could buy an aerosol can that spray-painted hair onto your bald spot. Bored, he left to take a seat by the pool table just as Brewgner sunk a game winner in the side pocket.

"Best two out of three," said Ray.

"What's in it for me? I already got what I wanted."

Ray asked Sal to get a round, and when he was gone said, "Maybe I can sweeten the pot."

It was just past eleven, and everyone was crowded up to the bar, trying to get a drink, or packed into a booth, devouring burgers. Sal held up two fingers as he approached. Somehow Ricky managed it all with aplomb, hurrying to the stove to turn burgers and then returning to eyeball generous pours from the well. The time Dolan had put in with Charlene was paying off. He was calling her Charlie and she was starting to consider the possibility that she would let him take her home. Hector and Byrd sat in a booth with Dan and Carlos, devouring the first of two burgers apiece, pausing momentarily to make a joke. "I think I remember this one from last week," said Dan, studying his burger.

Having dropped the first game, Ray was now obliged to find a job for Brewgner at the plant. It would take some coaxing of the bosses, but he could find something in Packaging or Rendering easily enough. Now, however, Ray promised that if Brewgner won again he could return to his old position. It wasn't that the thought of demoting Sal from his new post didn't cross his mind. It was that under the heady glow of competitive wager it didn't seem possible. Didn't hurt, of course, that if Ray won he'd collect Brewgner's final two work-comp checks. There was no way he'd lose.

"You put these on *my* tab, right?" said Ray when Sal returned with two more bourbons. Sal nodded yes, though he'd placed them on his own. Brewgner was on the far side of the table, his back to them, chalking his cue. Sal asked what the bet was. "It's nothing. Whoever loses has to drink buffalo sweat. I got this." Buffalo sweat was what they called the cocktail produced when Ricky wrung out the rags he used to wipe down the bar into a single shot glass. Every few weeks some poor bastard lost a friendly bet and had to suck one down. Suddenly Ray cried, "Oh shit, I forgot my theme song," and ran over to the juke. He selected "Wasted Days and Wasted Nights," smiling as Freddy Fender's voice filled Doc's. "No wonder I lost the first game," he said, playing a little air guitar with his cue.

Sal knew this was no bet about drinking a vile shot of liquor.

Despite Ray's jovial calm, Sal could see the gambler's intensity. It was payday; he was betting against his check. He'd seen the highs and lows of Ray's gambling over the years, and had benefitted from it, too. His friend had always been generous. Used to be, if Ray won—be it cards, pool, darts, whatever—they'd end up in a room at the Thunderbird with a couple of whores from the boulevard for an hour or two before Ray had to get back home. Last winter, however, they'd passed out after sharing a chubby blonde who'd infuriated Ray when she said Sal had to fuck her from behind. Those scars, she said, made her want to puke. Ray pulled his knife on her but she showed no fear or regret; she said cutting cost extra. Exasperated, he put the knife away and unzipped his fly.

Later Ray returned home unapologetic, stinking of another woman. Lorna had been out searching all night. "If you're not gonna give it to me," he said, "I'll find it somewhere." She told him not to talk to her about needs. They had three kids, plus they sent money to her sister and mother on the rez. Their house was a dump, the boiler needed to be replaced, and the truck was always breaking down. "I don't want this life anymore," she told him and left the house. A minute later Ray chased her down, falling to his knees and wrapping his arms around her waist, pleading, apologizing. "I'll last for thirty seconds without you and the kids." He was a bastard, he said. He had the heart of a prairie dog. "Come back to me, baby." That was her opportunity to leave. She wanted to, considered it, and then thought of the kids. If it was this bad now, what would it be like with no money coming in? She told Ray he needed to bring his paycheck home. No more gambling, she said. No other women. And he'd cried, swearing allegiance and fidelity—a promise he'd kept thus far—leading her back inside, where, still dirty with the sex of the other woman, he made love to her against the kitchen counter.

Not long after that, Lorna had confided in Sal about her concerns. He was over at their place for dinner and Ray had run out to the store to pick up an ingredient—cayenne, Sal still recalled—Lorna needed for a dish. There was a lull in the cooking, the kids were watching TV in the back room, and they sat at the kitchen table. She'd told him about the gambling, money concerns, how she'd almost left. "Ray's great, the kids love him, but he's . . . Ray." Then she started to cry, but quickly changed the subject, trying to laugh it off. "How about you—got your eye on anyone?" She smiled, a single, persistent tear still lodged in the corner of her eye. But he didn't want her to back off, to close the door she'd already opened. In that moment he wanted to confess his own shame and sadness. He wanted to tell her the truth about his scars and said so. "What happened?" she said, leaning across the table to put her hands on his face. Her soft touch over his old wounds. But as he began to speak, Ray entered through the front door and she took her hands away. "Not too much of this, baby," Ray said, holding the red spice container. "I don't want to be screaming on the toilet tomorrow."

Brewgner was short but lean, bald, with an overbite so extreme that he looked like a character in a horror movie in the early stages of transmogrifying into a werewolf. It was unsettling to look at him and he knew it. He stared at Ray across the pool table, the scattered constellation of a good break between them. The table was open, Brewgner's shot. Ray grabbed the crotch of his jeans, cupping his testicles, and plopped them on the silver ornamental work of the corner pocket Brewgner was eyeing for the three ball. "Don't let them scare you," he said. Ray had won the second game easily and was anxious to vanquish Brewgner in the third. Brewgner wasn't worried. Sure, Ray had gone on a tear in the second game, but he had dumped a couple shots on purpose to speed the process along, to feed Ray's confidence, to set him up for a game-three comeuppance. Brewgner leaned forward, sized up the three, and staked his claim to the lows. He'd struck the ball hard but with control so that the cue didn't fly all over the table, a leave that allowed him soft tap-ins on the seven and five before he missed on the two. Ray took over and quickly combo'd the twelve off the ten. He whistled as he took a long, slow strut around the table. He knocked in the ten and banked the fourteen into the side pocket, and then had a two-ball run that ended with the cue following the fifteen into the pocket. "I meant to do that," he said. "You look like you could use some help."

When Lorna showed up with June, their youngest, at her chest, Brewgner was in the midst of taking a commanding lead, capitalizing on Ray's scratch. It took Ray a moment to notice her standing there beside Sal, and then a few moments more, him just staring at her, to react. In so many ways it was completely normal to see his wife and best friend watching him, whispering. It was Byrd's ridiculing from the front of the bar—"Look out, Ray, your old lady's on the warpath"—that provoked him to say something. To be dragged out of Doc's by your wife was one of the greater indignities in the D&L universe.

"The fuck are you doing here, woman?" said Ray.

"Like it was hard to know where you'd be," she said.

It was bubbling in him now. He had to let it out, and it had to be mean if he was going to preempt further ridicule and hazing at work.

"With my baby! Are you crazy or just stupid? We have rules in here—no knives, no babies!" As he continued to perform his anger for the bar, Lorna slowly approached him and when he finally quieted, she whispered: "Give me your paycheck and you can make your scene. I won't care whether you ever come home again." He reached in his pocket and gave her his check and pay stub. Then she turned and left as everyone stared at her. Asie nodded, said, "Night, Lorna."

"That's right—leave! Go change a diaper. You're stinking up the Doc Holliday Inn and Lounge!" Ray yelled. Sal followed after her as Ray shouted at everyone staring back at him: "Fuck are you looking at?" They returned to their drinks and conversation, and Ray felt a little relief. It seemed to have worked. No one was likely to tease him about the incident tomorrow. Brewgner tapped his stick against the table. It was Ray's shot. "You think I'm rattled?" he said. "I become a goddamn artist at this table when I'm angry."

Outside, Lorna sat in the driver's seat of Ray's pickup. She rolled down the window as Sal approached. The heat of July was still in the air and the soft light of a toenail moon made the red of the truck's hood glow. Inside the cab were all three kids. Daniel, ten now, sat next to Russell, four, who held Baby June. They were in their pajamas. In unison the two older children said, "Hello, Uncle Sal" sleepily.

"That went well," said Lorna. She was wearing one of Ray's shirts, red-check and pearl-snap. Her hair was black and fell longer than Ray's, almost to her breasts. "I hate him," she said. To prevent herself from crying she started the engine. Sal wanted to reach in and turn it off. Tired, upset, beautiful, did she know that he was in love with her, that he'd longed for her for years? Did Ray, for that matter? Sal took hold of her hand that was hanging out the window. She squeezed his hand twice and smiled sadly. "Thank you for calling me. It's not your job to look after him." She attempted to let go, but he held fast to her. "Are you okay?" she said. He was acting strange, quieter than usual, if such a thing were possible, and he leaned forward through the window. She pulled back—"Don't"—and looked at the children crowded against each other on the bench seat, who stared back at them. "I have to get the kids home." She shifted into gear and she was gone.

Sal went back inside the bar and made his way to the high-top, where Ray was pointing his cue at Brewgner: "You bush-league sonofabitch!" He swung the stick toward the image of Bronson on the pinball machine. "You've placed my ball under the spell of this man with a tanned vagina for a face."

"It wasn't intentional, Ray," said Brewgner.

"The hell it wasn't. We have a code here—you don't Bronson another man!"

Brewgner hadn't meant to. He didn't need to, he was on the cusp of victory as it was. A gambler like Ray would almost always beat himself, which was why Brewgner let him move the cue ball a few inches so he could get a clean shot. But Ray was rattled, convinced this, like everything that evening, was only a small part of a vast conspiracy to keep him from winning, a notion seemingly confirmed when the eight followed the eleven into the corner pocket.

"Oops," said Brewgner, smiling.

Ray stared at the pocket in disbelief. He tossed his cue onto the table, sending the remaining balls scattershot. Brewgner returned his stick to the rack on the wall and walked toward Ray.

"Doesn't mean anything," said Ray. "You're done at the plant."

Brewgner grabbed hold of Ray's shirt. "You made a bet."

"I didn't sign anything," he said, pushing Brewgner's hand away.

"The hell you didn't. On your word, Ray. You bet on your word, like we always do."

They were in each other's face now and Sal approached to intercede. Everyone in the bar was good and tight and no one up front knew a fight was about to break out. Sal pushed them apart.

"Tell him," Brewgner said to Ray. "Go ahead."

"Enough," said Ray. "We'll talk. The three of us. Out back." Once again he told Sal to go get them another round. "Three whiskeys. On me."

A few minutes later, after the trip to the bar and a stop at the pisser, Sal made his way to join them outside, a pyramid of tumblers clamped between his hands. There wasn't much back there, just a gravel lot, empty but for an abandoned Buick where people sometimes went to smoke a joint or fool around. He nudged open the screen door with his boot and for a moment saw nothing, just the darkness and fuzzy starlight of a humid summer night. There was the sound, though—like hooves on cobblestone—and in the distance he saw Ray running down the road, those boot heels clacking away on the pavement. Sal called out to him. Ray stopped and turned around. That's when Sal sensed something off to his left, beside the rear tires of the Buick. Brewgner prostrate on the ground. Ray waved his hand a few times—what did that mean?—before taking off again.

Sal dropped the glasses and approached Brewgner, kneeling next to the fallen man. His left hand was covering his stomach, his shirt blood-soaked. Sal moved the hand to inspect the wound and saw Ray's knife lodged in Brewgner's stomach. Ray had got him good, the kind of cut that didn't look like much but would bleed you to death if you let it. Brewgner's eyes were shut and Sal put two fingers to his neck. There was still a pulse. Sal looked back at the bar. Through the screen door the light inside illuminated the familiar spectacle of a late-night wind-down, people leaning against the bar, wearily suppressing yawns, boozily swaying. They would all be heading home soon. Sal thought of taking the knife and running, then of calling for help. Neither avenue was actually a way out.

All roads led back to Ray. One way or another his friend would pay. Sal froze. For a brief moment he was filled with the rush of excitement that Lorna would be alone.

While he was still half turned, looking back at Doc's, the knife entered Sal's neck below the left ear—Brewgner's eyes suddenly opening, his hand thrusting forth from his belly—and severed the left carotid artery, a clean swoop that continued across the neck to the internal jugular vein, stopping just past the far side of the trachea when Brewgner's arm reached full extension. It was over before Sal had a chance to register pain, though as he fell backward he knew what had happened and what would. He looked up at the sky, but what he saw in his mind's eye was the knife making its silent progress along his throat. The cut wasn't complete, but it was enough. He had 83 seconds to live.

It was twenty minutes past closing when Ricky finally started the arduous process of getting everyone to leave. "Closing time," he would shout, and they'd nod and return to their conversations. He'd kill the juke, wipe down the rail, and then begin gathering the glasses from the tables, saying, "Finish your drinks. Time to leave." Again they would nod and return to their conversations. A few minutes would pass and then he could bring the anger: "Come on, you bastards, I want to go home!" Only then would they slowly make their way to the bar to settle their tabs, fumbling for wallets, while Ricky figured their totals, punching a number that sounded right into the ancient register and making change.

There was the mad rush for a final piss that turned the men's bathroom into a virtual clown car: Asie splattering the toilet seat in the stall, Dan and Byrd at the urinals, their streams in audible competition, and Hector, unable to wait, pissing so hard in the sink that it seemed he might bore a hole through the enamel. Kathy had already paid and left, giving a ride that was nothing more than a ride to Carlos, who'd drunk too much and left his car in the parking lot. Slowly, the men exited the bathroom and made their way to the front exit, fishing for the keys in their pockets, figuring out who was giving a ride to whom. They needed to go home and get some sleep or else they'd suffer under the watch of line supervisors who would write them up—three and you were out—for slowing down the chain or not pulling their count.

In a minute they would all be gone and Ricky would count the tips and wash the last of the glasses. He'd find Ray, Sal, and Brewgner's tabs unpaid and set them next to the register to remember to collect on the next time they came in. He had a few more things to do but was already thinking about the joint in his shirt pocket that he'd smoke out back under the stars.

Dodge City, you open sore. Where Ray bursts through the front door, dripping sweat, telling Lorna to get the kids in the truck. Where Dolan, in the cab of his Ranger with Charlene, sensing the onset of whiskey dick, rejects the advances he's worked so hard to engender, something that leaves them both feeling ashamed and embarrassed when he simply drops her off outside her apartment and speeds away before she's made it inside. Where Doris, unable to sleep, watches television well into the early morning while her cancer-sick husband snores in the bedroom. And where Bob, two hours passed out after another Royals loss, momentarily wakes to flip his pillow to the cool underside when he hears the siren of a passing ambulance sound through the neighborhood. But then it's quiet and he's asleep again, his hand extending through the sheet tangle to the empty space on the other side of the bed.

WHAT IS TO BE DONE?

Part I: Dinsmoor

1.

He dreamed of concrete. And so, upon his retirement in 1905, from teaching and farming, from fighting, first on battlefields of the Civil War and later on political campaigns of the 1890s—from sixty-two years in the American maelstrom—Samuel Perry Dinsmoor bought the half-acre lot, moving with his wife and children from the outskirts of town to the center of Lucas, where his neighbors, who'd long termed the man a *freethinker*, looked on with moderate curiosity as he began to construct the fence surrounding his property, a fence he fashioned from cement paste and crushed stone. The July 20, 1906, edition of the *Lucas Independent* deemed him a "genius" and his fence "the noblest in town."

2.

Then, the log cabin. Of stone. What was it about the hardness of things that attracted him so? The "logs" were narrow slabs of post-rock limestone, quarried and cut to lengths of Dinsmoor's specification, some as long as twenty-seven feet. After all the heavy lifting, the horse-drawn carting, the shooting pains and shoving into place, there stood an eleven-room cabin. Dinsmoor would follow his wife, Frances, from empty room to empty room, the limestone sending a cold shock through his uncovered feet, listening as she planned discrete decorative schemes that he'd undermine by placing a stuffed bald eagle in every room.

Twenty years before, they had moved to Kansas from Illinois, where Dinsmoor had been a schoolteacher, in order to farm and raise their family. Now, with their children grown, long since gone off to start their own families in other towns, Dinsmoor and Frances harbored an unspoken desire that they all might return to live under one roof again. But except for occasional visits, most nights it was just the two of them in the large stone cabin, quietly rocking in their chairs, him reading and her sewing. He alternated between the Bible and political newspapers like the *Appeal to Reason*. Periodically he'd shatter the silence with an outburst, rising suddenly from his seat as he wagged the Good Book over his head: "See! See! Jesus was the first socialist!" Frances would look at her husband pacing around the room, lecturing to an imaginary classroom of students, the way he once had to living and breathing pupils, and then still the swing of his rocking chair and return to her sewing.

3.

All those years before, when the war had stolen him from youth, he'd followed the 116th Ohio Infantry from Tuppers Plain to the hospital tents of Martinsburg, Virginia (later West Virginia), where he put down his gun and became a regimental nurse, stretchering in familiar faces of the dead on damp canvas sheets and holding down strangers whose whiskeyed screams before the surgeon's saw burned his eyes. And then one day came word it was over, and he helped to take down the field tent and center pole, which they set fire to right there on the spot because, they were told, there would be no more fighting. But it wasn't enough to convince, so he saddled his horse and made his way to Appomattox to witness the formal closure. The relief on Lee's face, he remarked. He thought of those severed limbs, which he'd had to pick up and place in a bloody stack in the corner of the field tent, as he sat on a stool outside in the early summer mornings, so many years later, muddling the Portland cement and limestone gravel with water, stirring that thick paste, readying to pour and shape the mixture into the concrete that would form Adam's arms and Eve's legs.

4.

It began with the grape arbor, a covered walkway made of concrete, stretching from the back porch to the road, an invitation for passersby to visit. Carved into the stony, hardened arches was a snake, barely noticeable until one saw its head protruding out the end of the arbor, dangling above the sculpture of Eve, dropping an apple into her bloated hand. Exactitude was difficult—he'd get better, but his initial figures were balloon-like avatars of some strange biblical comic book. Dinsmoor modeled Adam on himself, from the thick beard and jut chin down to the slight right-curve of his penis, which when enlarged to scale from his five-foot-five frame to Adam's eight-foot took on magnificent proportions. Later, when people would come to see what he was up to, he was cowed into covering that wonderful cock, not with a fig leaf but with a Masonic apron, which confused them nearly as much.

5.

There'd been that decade of committed political struggle, the 1890s, before Dinsmoor became the genius of concrete. When the Republican Party he'd fought for during the war proved to be the party of plutocracy, of trusts and monopolies, of corporations and big business, he became known as one of the worst Populist howlers in Russell County. He stumped and organized, swam upstream against the Republican current in Lucas, electioneering, running for township clerk in 1892 (which he lost), founding the United Order of Anti-Monopolies in 1893 (which was called "anarchistic" by the Lucas papers despite its call for the expansion of government), serving as a delegate to several People's Party state conventions, even attending the 1896 national convention in St. Louis (having to look on as his party, deciding to back William Jennings Bryan and the Democrats, committed suicide), hosting rallies on his farm (for as many as three hundred people), including one for the "colored people of Lucas" (all eight attended), and finally—*finally*—he experienced his lone political victory when he was elected justice of the peace of Fairview Township, a successful tenure for which he was credited, by friends and opponents alike, for keeping the number of loose horses on the streets to a minimum.

All the while he farmed and collected his military pension, staying afloat in the depression, but by the end of the decade, which was the end of the century, nearing sixty, he was exhausted and discouraged. In 1898 he lost a bid for state representative and, though urged by his Populist and Populist-turned-Socialist friends, he decided he would not run for office again. That work was best left to younger bodies and abler minds. He still howled in private, writing letters to J. A. Wayland, editor of the *Appeal to Reason*. For example:

> The handwriting is on the wall . . . when they learn they cannot stop the onward march of education. They might as well lay their mortal frames across the mouth of the Mississippi—and try to flood the US signal station on the top of Pike's Peak as to stop the onward

march of socialism. The more they oppose, the more opposition they will meet.

But he was already scouting lots for his move into town and plotting retirement. He was already having visions of his garden of concrete.

6.

Next he went to work on the "trees," forty-foot slabs shooting high into the air, developing the tableau, adding impish personal touches like the small figure positioned in the arbor, smiling and waving, so that Frances would see it from the kitchen. There was the Tree of Life, a cloven devil figure, storks, angels, Cain slaying Abel with a hoe, Cain fleeing to the Land of Nod, and perched above everything was the all-seeing Eye of God, which he'd managed to electrify—quite the novelty then—so that it would blink throughout the day and night.

By 1914, Dinsmoor began offering tours—a quarter apiece— some visitors having heard of, some just stumbling upon, his strange Garden of Eden. While Frances led the tours, he sat inside the cabin, speaking into a pipe he'd rigged from the master bedroom to the Tree of Life, which amplified his voice, allowing him to animate the static sculptures.

God: "Cain, you son-of-a-gun, where's Abel?"

Cain: "Darned if I know. Am I my brother's keeper?"

Only afterward would he appear, greeting the confused faces as he collected their quarters.

7.

Why?

Because he'd read the Bible front to back at least two dozen times.

Because it scratched a creative itch.

Because he relished getting a rise out of others.

Because he was a Freemason and loved their love of symbolism.

Because Jesus was a radical.

Because it made money.

Because he craved attention.

Because he could.

Because what is to be done when your dreams have died?

8.

The vision changed the year the rest of the world went to war. News from Colorado about the massacre of striking miners in Ludlow sparked something of the old fire inside Dinsmoor. He went to work on new sculptures, planning a Modern Civilization tableau on the north side of the lot as a counterpoint to the Garden in the west. He sequestered himself in his workshop with his trowel and mixing bins and periodically a new piece would appear on the tour. There was the Chain of Life, showing a soldier aiming his rifle at an Indian, who shot his bow and arrow at a fox that was chasing a cat that spied a bird that was swooping down upon a worm eating a leaf. Nearby a large octopus named "Trust" loomed over a massive cement globe, with tentacles wrapped around the Panama Canal as well as a young woman and her baby. The trust monster appeared again elsewhere, later in the form of a spider being speared by the Goddess of Liberty. Draped in the American flag, she protected a man and woman who held a saw labeled "Ballot" to the spider's "Chartered Rights" platform.

Now his sculptures had a new purpose. When the people were educated, they would vote away the monopolies, they would put people before business, need before profit. He'd become a teacher again, his Garden his classroom.

9.

And still they came, more baffled than ever, almost one hundred a week by 1916, awakening in him a hucksterism that had lain dormant since his campaigning days. Dinsmoor would wait at the train station—an old man in a three-piece suit, foot thumping the platform—and round up as many people as he could convince, herding them the short distance, talking the whole way about righting God's expulsion, promising that a return to their "original home" was imminent. He sold photo-postcards of the sculptures at five cents per. The new-to-town manager of the motion picture house showed interest, made inquiries, and together he and Dinsmoor created a slideshow-cum-speaking-tour of the Garden—"pictorial views and a snappy lecture by Samuel P. Dinsmoor, the Cement Wizard of the World"—screening it in theaters as far off as Illinois. At most stops on the brief tour, people listened politely as Dinsmoor spoke of the dangers of monopoly and preached the Social Gospel. He asserted violent revolution was unnecessary; an educated citizenry would naturally vote socialism into office. And when Dinsmoor finished speaking, most often their inclination was not to applaud but to continue staring at him as he moved away from the lectern and smiled into the dark before the house lights came on and the silence became awkward enough to prompt a few claps that sometimes spurred a majority and sometimes remained isolated reports in an echoey theater. Mostly people just looked. Word spread. Newspapers sent reporters. The New York Sun ran a two-part article, "Garden of Eden in His Front Yard" and "Garden of Eden in Cement: The Work of a Kansas Heretic."

Others:

Salina Journal: "Dinsmoor's Quaint Garden of Eden at Lucas Is Mecca for Thousands of Tourists and Visitors."

Kansas City Post: "Garden of Eden in Cement Makes Kansas Home Weird."

Cement World: "Old Man's Fancies Worked Out in Concrete."

Dinsmoor knew the mainstream papers would see it as nothing more than novelty, the innocuous avocation of a self-serving would-be sculptor. They had to; it was too dangerous to report the truth. But the *Appeal to Reason* would see the glory of the Garden's mission. Though the longtime editor J. A. Wayland had died a few years before, Dinsmoor had continued writing letters and editorials to Wayland's successor. When he wrote to encourage them to send a reporter to Lucas to do a story on the Garden, however, he was rebuffed. *The Appeal* was an atheist rag and took a hard line on religion. He wrote back, explaining his radical reinterpretation of the Bible, the revolutionary potential of his Garden, but this time there would be no response. Dinsmoor would walk through the desert alone.

10.

When Frances died in 1917, she was interred in the Lucas cemetery, but only for as long as it took for Dinsmoor to construct a limestone mausoleum. It was a pyramid-shaped crypt, at the top of which he fashioned a cement angel, and was incorporated into the tour. Inside he sculpted a concrete tomb, in which he secreted Frances's body, having dug her up in the middle of the night and sealed her in with cement. Atop hers he made a second tomb and left it uncovered. Sometimes, without warning,

Dinsmoor, seventy-five now, would climb in and lie down before a group of visitors—a morbid stab at humor, which usually
sparked at least one face-covered dash for the exit. "Heartsick
needn't cloak itself in the macabre, Samuel," said a minister,
aghast after one such incident. Two months later a new post-
card appeared on the merchandise table in the living room of
the stone cabin: a double-exposed photograph that showed
Dinsmoor lying in the coffin as a second—spectral—Dinsmoor
stood nearby, looking at the body.

II.

To scandalize into your eighties is itself an art form. When
Dinsmoor remarried in 1924, he wed his twenty-year-old
Czech immigrant housekeeper, Emilie, who was four months
pregnant. Their sixty-year gap bridged by weeks of feral love-
making, he returned to work just as his eyes were beginning
to fail, causing him to wonder whether the old saw was true:
Could one, in fact, screw oneself blind? But what was taken in
vision was returned in inspiration; he had plans for one final
piece, his grandest yet.

He hired a local black man named Henry and his wife to
help out at the house, and they moved into the stone cabin, just
down the hall. The couple exchanged worried glances the first
few times they heard that ecstatic howling coming from the
master bedroom—Henry even calling out, "You okay in there,
Mrs. Dinsmoor?"—but soon they grew accustomed and their
concern gave way to head-shaking grins. Emilie would give
birth to a second child a few years later. While his young bride
gave tours of the Garden, Dinsmoor and Henry set to work
on the untouched eastern side of the property. It was to be the
meeting point of the two tableaux, the point at which the ancient and modern collided.

By far the largest sculpture, Labor Crucified (the idea taken from a column called "The Crucifixion of Labor" that he had followed regularly in the *Appeal to Reason*), was incomplete at the time of his death. In the scene, Labor, in Christlike human form, is being crucified by the surrounding sculptural figures of a doctor, lawyer, banker, and preacher. The construction required scaffolding and heavy support beams to steady the cross. For a few years, when he still had some sight left, Dinsmoor worked on the sculptures from his stool and directed Henry as his assistant moved up and down the ladder, gingerly sidling across the makeshift scaffolding to secure the figures in place, but by 1929 he was fully blind and could only listen to Henry carry out the plans they'd discussed.

"Where are you now, Henry? Make sure Doctor is parallel with Preacher?"

He followed it all in his mind's eye.

"And Lawyer, he's smiling at us, ain't he, Henry? He's proud of what he's done."

It had been his last joke to model the Lawyer's face on his own. Dinsmoor had extended the end points of the three vertical concrete poles so that they curved back down into overhead streetlights, illuminating the scene. Sometimes at night, unable to sleep, he would remember his way outside and stand before it, feeling the electric light on his face.

12.

He spent his last year, 1932, bedridden, complaining about feckless Hoover, holding out hopes that Roosevelt, primed to become the Democratic nominee, might have the sense to do something if elected. Often Henry read to him. Dinsmoor's favorite book that year was a newly released biography of the radical newspaperman J. A. Wayland, with whom Dinsmoor had carried on a correspondence many years before when the former was the editor of the *Appeal to Reason*. They'd debated politics and current affairs through the post, and occasionally one of Dinsmoor's letters appeared in the back pages of the paper. He had developed a certain fondness and respect for Wayland, a friendliness that never quite grew to friendship, but Dinsmoor realized now how little of the man he'd known.

Though Wayland was twenty years dead and the *Appeal* was no longer printing, Dinsmoor found himself moved by Wayland's life and political commitment to the end. Inspired, he amended his will so that the Garden would be maintained purely for educational purposes in the future. Like a cathedral builder in the Middle Ages, he knew he wouldn't live to see the Garden completed or the socialist society it would lead to, but he could die peacefully, knowing that eventually it would be, and that with it would come change. His thoughts often turned toward the end, and he did not fear death. He wondered if Wayland had. Dinsmoor reckoned that heaven was a place where he would not only be reunited with Frances, but where he'd meet both Jesus and atheists like Wayland, whose principled disbelief would be forgiven, for God knew their hearts were pure, their morals sound, their causes just. Men like Wayland were simply Christians who went by another name.

One afternoon in late July, during the week he would die, he shuddered awake, his empty eyes opening wide, from a nap. "My tools," he said. Emilie told him to rest, but he insisted: "Bring me my tools. Bring me gravel and cement." Such moments had become frequent. He'd wake from the dreamy fog demanding to see the president, telling Henry to bring his gun, asking Emilie to send in Frances.

He listened as she stood and walked around, the swishing sound of her feet on the limestone floors. She returned holding a small concrete figurine of an angel he had made for one of the children. She took his hand and wrapped it around the miniature, but he was weak and dropped it onto the bed. Emilie held his hand, guiding it over the rough grit of the figurine.

"Yes," he said. "Bring it closer."

"Closer, Papa," she said, holding his hand holding the angel, and moved his arm to his side.

"Closer," he said, and she moved their hands to his stomach. "Closer," he commanded again—and then to his chest. "I want to see it."

"Papa, it is on your chest."

"Yes, closer."

"Closer, Papa," she said, moving it into the hollow of his neck and up through the tangle of his beard, curving over his chin. The friction from the figure against his skin, like an unlathered shave from his war days, dragging over creases eighty-nine years in the making. "Papa, the angel is on your face." He told her to keep going, so she inched it toward his lips and he opened his mouth, extending his tongue, ready to accept the figure.

Part II: Wayland

LETTER I

1/29/31

Dear Mr. Bronstein,

How your letter of the 20th surprised me! Pleasantly, I should add, lest I give you the wrong impression. It has been a long time since I've thought of Girard. Fifteen years since my husband and I moved to Kansas City and we've not once returned. The two-hour drive seems worthy of an ocean liner for the remove I feel from little old Girard. Oh listen to me! Such are the vagaries of sentiment for which women can curse middle age. I shall content myself to answering your queries forthwith.

Yes, I knew Mr. Wayland, though I was not involved with <u>Appeal to Reason</u>. We were neighbors. His second wife, Pearl, was my dearest friend in those years.

I would be happy to be of service to you in any way you might find useful. I suspect from the fine prose of your letter that you shall write an excellent book. (I must here correct one small factual error, if you'll forgive my bumptiousness: Mr. Wayland did not take his life on election night. It was three days afterward. I remember this for certain. He passed on November 10th, 1912.)

Please do not hesitate to further inquire. They were, on the whole, happy years I should be glad to remember.

Sincerely,

Mrs. Edward Shaw

p.s. May I ask who put you in touch with me? I have lost touch with most of the old gang.

LETTER 2

2/18/31

Dear Mr. Bronstein,

Oh, it was Fred who gave you my name. Dear Fred, how is he? We corresponded for a few years after I left Girard, but not in the many since. He is a kind man and I'll tell you this, because not many people realize it: Fred Warren was the secret behind the <u>Appeal to Reason</u>'s success. Don't misunderstand me. J.A. (forgive me, but that's what everyone called Mr. Wayland) started the paper and under him it was successful, but it was when Fred came on board as an editor, around 1904 or so if I recall correctly, that the paper really took off. I remember Pearl telling me how Fred and J.A. would argue late into the night in J.A.'s study, shouting about some matter or other at the paper. They were great friends though, and J.A. could not have regretted Fred's influence on the _Appeal_. Circulation rose quickly. J.A. always said he wanted a million readers, but I suspect he contented himself with the half million he received. It is hard to imagine even now. Six hundred thousand subscriptions for a red newspaper. Surely more than a few "papers of the plutes," as J.A. used to say, would have envied such figures. Fred can tell you more of the specifics than I. As you'll recall, I wasn't involved with the paper, nor was I of their political persuasion. I was a friend and most of my memories are of long walks with Pearl or of the spectacular dinners she and J.A. would host. They were generous with everyone. How I miss them both.

Sincerely,

Mrs. Edward Shaw

LETTER 3

3/2/31

Dear Mr. Bronstein,

Forgive me for not answering the questions raised in your last letter. It was not intentional, I assure you. I got to thinking about the past and my mind wandered off as it is wont do. I shall set right to the list you've been kind enough to include to keep me on task.

1. As I recall, Pearl told me that J.A. had come up with the idea for the newspaper here in Kansas City around 1895 and moved with his first wife, Etta (whom I did not know), and children to Girard sometime in 1897 or 1898. I'm not sure why he chose Girard—possibly cheaper printing costs than the city. You might

ask his son, Walter, who took over the newspaper after his father's death.

2. As I say, I did not know Etta. She was sickly when they arrived in Girard and passed shortly afterward. It was not until J.A. and Pearl married in 1901 that I began to know the couple.

3. Pearl worked in the printing office at the _Appeal_ and for a time was a housekeeper for J.A. He courted her fiercely and after seeing a fortune-teller, who bespoke coming happiness, so the story went, he proposed and she was quick to accept.

4. I could only describe them as happy. He was older than she, and she adored him in the manner of daughter and wife. In many ways they were suitably opposite. She was excitable, boisterous, quick to smile, and he was quiet and pensive, often seeking solitude in his office. Their temperaments tamed the other's excesses in these areas.

I hope I have responded to your liking, Mr. Bronstein. I shall be happy to oblige any further inquiries to the best of my capabilities. I must say, however, that while I am flattered you have taken the time to contact me there are others, like Fred or members of J.A.'s family, who are far more knowledgeable than I on these matters and specifics.

Sincerely,

Mrs. Edward Shaw

LETTER 4

3/21/31

Dear Mr. Bronstein,

I suppose I understand why you should want an "outsider's" perspective on things. However, this designation feels inaccurate. I was a friend, neighbor, and fellow townsperson. I was an outsider only to the political aspirations and inner workings of "the Appeal army," to use a phrase J.A. loved. I was not taking communion at their church, one might say, but we got on splendidly. That was one of the interesting things about Girard. J.A. was welcomed upon arrival. Though solidly Republican, Girard had been no stranger to political debate—after all, we counted a fair number of Populists on our rolls in the 1890s. It mattered less what he was preaching than that he was an entrepreneur bringing business to town.

That is what you must realize: he was an interesting breed of socialist because he was one shrewd businessman. The contradictions didn't seem to nettle him in the least. He had made a considerable amount of money with prudent speculation on land in Colorado and Texas, and he continued to do so till the end of his life. He used the profits to support the paper, in part, but he also used them to support his lifestyle, which can only be described fairly as a small step shy of lavish. The notion that a red newspaper could or should turn a profit seems confused, but it didn't stop him. He ran advertisements alongside articles about "wage slavery" and thought nothing of it. He fought the unionization of his own newspaper when his employees complained about working conditions. Now, I seem to recall that some of this changed when Fred became editor, but Pearl always said that J.A. believed these were the necessary compromises to fighting capitalism on its own battlefield. Myself, I believe he was in a financial position amenable to believing such a thing.

I remember one evening Edward came home from the office (he sold, and continues to sell, insurance) and remarked that he had seen J.A. driving through town center in a brand new Ford. There were few automobiles in town then. "If that is socialism, I reckon we better sign on for the revolution," he said, and we had a good laugh. It was, of course, precisely that he did not advocate revolution, which allowed us to laugh. Whatever his rhetoric, he was no Bolshevik; he believed education would hasten the end he desired.

Sincerely,

Mrs. Edward Shaw

4/8/31

Dear Mr. Bronstein,

As you have surely surmised, Girard was a small town, as it still is no doubt. That southeastern part of the state is unordinary for its coal and zinc mines, and surrounding the town in nearly every direction were encampments of the most wretched lot you ever saw. Catholics, most able to summon only a word or two of English. In town proper, however, there was a bevy of respectable families and establishments and it was this quality that likely attracted the Waylands.

Their house was beautiful, you are certainly correct. It was on the outskirts of town on a healthy parcel of land that allowed J.A. to keep a small farm and pasture. Etta was by all accounts serious about her gardening, and after she passed that was a duty J.A. made sure the household staff upheld, because the good Lord knows that's a talent for which Pearl was unblessed. There were trees, stands of fruit and catalpa, that kept their yard shaded, and it seemed there wasn't an hour of the day you couldn't see a pack of neighborhood children there frolicking.

He did employ servants to cook, and launder, as well as to look after the children, especially after Etta died. Even a stranger could have noticed the pall that fell over the house afterward. But as I mentioned previously it wasn't long before his heart had rekindled, aflame for Pearl, and soon it was the warmest home one could hope for.

J.A. and Pearl hosted parties, big affairs for prominent political visitors, but they never failed to open their door to any soul who knocked. There mustn't have existed a tramp in seven states who didn't have their address memorized and who wouldn't receive a hot meal if he could suffer receiving a little socialism in turn. I remember hearing Pearl cater to these men, pitiful-looking as any you have ever seen, while J.A. was at the printing office or away on a trip

*checking on his properties. I will leave it to you to imagine sweet
little Pearl lecturing transients about the "ruling class" as they ate
on china and drank from crystal.*

    *Perhaps the only occasions they'd not celebrate were holidays.
As atheists, J.A. and Pearl passed these days by taking food and
presents to the unfortunate. I just remarked on that fact last week to
Edward at Easter dinner. If they had lived to see the predicament
we find ourselves in today, there would be a line formed at their
door stretching all the way to Missouri. I remember stopping by their
house one Christmas afternoon to drop some gifts off and J.A. answered the door, which surprised me. Pearl was unavailable for some
reason or other, I don't recall, and he invited me in. He had just
come back from visiting the needy and I presented the gifts to him.
He looked down at the brightly wrapped packages for what seemed a
long time and finally he thanked me with that familiar look of his:
a pained smile that to some must have seemed nothing more than a
grimace. He said he had something for me and asked me to follow
him. I said I should be getting home, but he insisted, so I followed
him to his library, which was a magnificent room that doubled as
his office. There was shelf upon shelf of titles that stretched to the
ceiling. He was always lending books to anyone who showed a modicum of interest and a substantial number who showed none at all.
I stopped at the door and watched him remove a book from a high
shelf. He stood on his tiptoes, reaching. I saw the hem of his blouse
stretching tautly in the gap between his vest and trousers so I brought
over a stool, which he dismissed. He pulled down a book, The
Theory of the Leisure Class, and handed it to me. I accepted it and
could tolerate only a few pages, but it was a kind gesture, and something I have always remembered. I recall standing in that library and
for some reason neither of us making a move to leave until I heard
the front door open and close followed by Pearl's voice calling out for
J.A. Quickly I turned, leaving him there, and rushed into the other*

room to wish Pearl a Merry Christmas, as I now wish you a belated
happy Easter, Mr. Bronstein.

Sincerely,
Jane Shaw

LETTER 6

4/12/31

Dear Mr. Bronstein,

Forgive my eagerness in writing so soon. I don't suspect my last letter
has half traversed the distance between Kansas City and New York,
but I realized that in all these letters I've yet to tell you how Pearl
and I became friends.

I won't ever forget that day for it was sweltering, the hottest day
of the year. Though I didn't like the prospect of leaving the paltry
relief of the parlor fan, I went into town to pick up a few items that
I needed to prepare supper. Quickly I rushed to the dairy and mercantile, and my last stop was the butchery. I never have cared for the
aroma, which accompanies that vocation and you can imagine the
stench on that day. I could barely tolerate it and intended to leave as
quickly as possible, but when I entered I saw Pearl facing the counter
ahead of me. We'd never had occasion to speak before, though I knew
quite well who she was. She and J.A. had just married—it had been
the talk of the town for a spell—and I thought it rude not to congratulate her on her nuptials. So I greeted her and she turned around.
You should have seen her—she looked harried and flummoxed. The
poor girl was trying to learn how to cook, I would find out. She didn't
see the need for the servants J.A. had kept since Etta's death. In any
case, we spoke, and she said they had just returned from their honeymoon. Though the heat and the stench were awful, I couldn't help
the curiosity I felt for knowing where the rich socialist would take his
young bride. When I asked, she was silent, and then I saw the runnel

that I momentarily mistook for perspiration fall down her cheek.
Quickly I handed her a kerchief, looking away, and then I removed
the package from her arms, telling Lou to put it back on ice, we would
return shortly, and I led Pearl outside to a nearby stand of trees away
from the road.

Not wanting to embarrass her more than she already was, I
looked away as she struggled to compose herself. "I don't think any-
one noticed," I said. She said she didn't care who saw and sobbed
a few minutes more. I asked her what on earth was the matter,
what should sour such a joyful time in her new life? Then she told
me of her honeymoon: to Kentucky to see Mammoth Cave, taking
in theater every night in Chicago, dining in the finest restaurants
of St. Louis—three weeks in all they were away. I said I felt not
a drop of pity for her in the least, which made her smile. She said
that when they returned home, just a few days prior to our conver-
sation, she was describing the trip to J.A.'s children over dinner and
Walter said, "That's the same trip Father took with Mother." And
so it was, down to the very hotels in which they'd stayed and the
establishments in which they dined. She said she didn't know which
was worse: J.A.'s longing for his first wife or the thought of a ghost
following their every step.

We talked for a long time in that heat, nearly an hour I'd say,
and then walked back to the butchery before returning to our respec-
tive homes. The next morning I found a basket of flowers on my
doorstep that she had picked from her garden. Later, when I ventured
the quarter-mile walk down the road to show my thanks, she invited
me in and we passed another afternoon, more pleasant with the heat
having broken, conversing, which was to become a regular occurrence.
How I miss those conversations, Mr. Bronstein. All should cherish the
pleasant commiseration of a dear friend.

Sincerely,
Jane Shaw

LETTER 7

5/01/31

Dear Mr. Bronstein,

I apologize for the haste with which I now write. In the prolonged tumult in which our country finds itself, Edward's company has suddenly ceased operations, which has rendered his health poor. The circumstances, you'll understand, require my full attention. Perhaps soon they shall allow me to be more charitable to the needs of your work.

Sincerely,
Jane Shaw

LETTER 8

8/17/31

Dear Mr. Bronstein,

Thank you for your kind note. I'm pleased to say Edward's health has improved. A rest much overdue has eased some of the burden and he is slowly regaining the vigor of his old self. Given his recent experience, I understand fully the pressures one's business can exert. As such, I do not find your queries "insensitive." In fact, I've quite missed our correspondence of late and should be pleased to help as your deadline nears.

[1] Of course I knew Debs. He and J.A. were good friends, and after many years of asking, J.A. was finally able to convince him to move to Girard to write for the <u>Appeal</u>. This must have been 1908 or so. He announced his run for the presidency on the front steps of the newspaper's offices. Gene was a sweet man. The children in town loved him because he always seemed to have an ice cream cone to give away. He must have lived in Girard about five years, writing his column, often

leaving to campaign on speaking tours. I would rather not comment on the speculation you mention. I will say he loved his wife, that was apparent. To suggest otherwise on account of salacious rumor is not only unpleasant but unfair. Let's let him rest in peace, shall we. I prefer to remember him as the man with the slow gait and quick smile, passing out ice-cream cones to children.

[2] Yes, Mother Jones, too. I must say, I interacted with her infrequently and what little I did I didn't care for her. She was imperious, liable to say whatever thought drifted into that head of hers, but J.A. carried a great fondness for her. I do recall the first time I saw her. I hadn't a clue who she was. Edward and I had been invited over to Fred Warren's house for dinner and there was this small old woman. J.A. and Pearl were there, along with some folks we were new to meet. J.A. introduced us to the room and she spoke first. She was sitting in a chair, as if she couldn't be bothered to stand and properly greet us, and called out, asking if we had brought any beer. Edward reminded her of Kansas law (Kansas was dry long before the rest of the country, if you recall) and she began to laugh. Something about this tickled her. She must have gone on a minute or so until Fred, who did not drink, rose and left the room, returning not two minutes later with a fresh bottle of brew for his guest.

[3] Yes, I am aware that J.A. had tried to start a "utopian village" in the years after leaving Pueblo, Colorado, and before coming to Girard, but I know little of it. Ruskin, it was called, and located in Tennessee, if I'm not mistaken. I never heard him speak of it much, though I do recall a picture he had framed in his office of the village. Yes, the picture. It was of a stark cabin room. I remember asking him about it one afternoon when I had come to see Pearl but had forgotten that she was away visiting family. J.A. invited me in and I demurred, but he was insistent I come in for a glass of lemonade. (Why in my memories of the time is the weather always sweltering?) He walked back to his office. I was reluctant to follow. I remarked on the refreshing drink

and asked where the children were. He said they were away for some reason or another. Perhaps they were with Pearl. I don't recall the specifics. In any case, I figured he likely wanted to foist some book or other on me, and this was a proclivity I indulged so as not to hurt his feelings, always feigning delightful curiosity at the unbearable Marx he had placed in my hand. However, in my memory of that day, we are sitting at his desk, conversing a long time. Not about politics, just life. At some point I remarked on the photograph behind him on the wall and that's when he told me it had been his cabin at Ruskin. He seemed to recall it fondly, though I do not remember him saying much more. I know nothing of the fray of which you speak. It is news to me if the other villagers kicked him out of the "socialist experiment" he started in Ruskin. I'd be interested to know more. Perhaps your book will educate me.

Good luck to you, Mr. Bronstein, and, again, thank you for your well wishes. I shall pass them on to Edward.

Sincerely,
Jane

LETTER 9

9/2/31

Dear Mr. Bronstein,

I suppose I have always known where your questions would lead sooner or later, but perhaps I've wishfully hoped otherwise. You must understand, it's not a memory I court.

Pearl and I passed most afternoons in a variety of manner, but our favorite pastimes, aside from our frequent and interminable walks, were watching silent pictures and motoring in her new automobile. The picture house wasn't much of a house at all. It was a roofless area of picnic tables with an accompanying piano in the corner. Most pitiful to think of today, but how we enjoyed it then!

Pearl and I would pay our five cents and see the same picture seven times over. That day, I still recall, it was a jungle picture of some sort, silliest thing we'd ever seen. White men dressed-up colored, carrying spears and fighting animals. "Hard to tell one from the other," I remember Pearl whispering to me, and our laughter was shushed. Afterward, we went for a drive.

The Waylands were one of the few families in town who had an automobile at the time and Pearl liked to drive the ten miles to Pittsburg, where we would shop and spend the afternoon. She had little tolerance for the "inchworms" still in their carriages, and Pearl took the Ford to top speed out on the dirt-dust roads that surrounded Girard. We were gone no longer than an hour before returning home. So, yes, I did drive with her that day, but here I must correct Fred. I was not in the car with Pearl when it happened. She was alone. For all the speed she craved, what an accident of chance, a cruel irony, to be thrown from the car as it circled her own home. I was devastated and you don't need to speculate long to venture a guess as to J.A.'s feelings. This was 1911, in less than a year he would be dead.

It was a bad time all around for J.A. The _Appeal_ was indicted by the government for obscenity. Additionally, there was some intimation in private conversations that he was not well. That final year, how-ever, he gave up his monthly visits to his properties in Texas to collect rents and poured himself into Debs's campaign like a man but half his age. For the first time in years he went on the speaking circuit, stumping for Gene. It was the one aspect to find hopefulness about, I suppose. He'd long since turned over most control at the paper to Fred, but he even began writing paragraphs again. That's what I would find him doing most nights in his office: slumped over his desk, spectacles sliding down his nose, grimacing at the paper before him as he worked over his words.

After Pearl's death, I'd taken to stopping by most evenings, for my sake as much as his. If he was out of town at a rally, I sat with *one of his daughters, playing cards. If he was home, I often brought supper and we would sit a long time, talking or not talking, as the mood suited us. Our heartsick was mutual. It is difficult to explain, except that I needed to be in that house. It wasn't proper behavior, I'll grant, but such behavior can the aggrieved's heart effect. Edward, bless his heart, didn't like it and one evening said so. It was, hand on the Bible, the only time I have disrespected my husband. I mean that. I was furious and let him know so—shameful to think of my inso- lence now—but how could I expect him to understand? How can we ever understand the sadness of others? And yet I think I was close to knowing J.A.'s.*

I remember the night of the election. J.A. had a party at the paper's offices—everyone was welcome. Edward said he didn't care to participate in fueling the fantasies of so deluded a spectacle. (He voted Bull Moose that year—even he couldn't support Taft! I do not keep secrets from my husband, mind you, but I must admit that had I been allowed to I would have made my mark next to Gene's name.) "Wilson has it, I'm sure," he said, folding closed the newspaper. "Even if that socialist were to win, I'd still have to get up and work in the morning. Nothing can change that." I told him I wasn't yet tired and took up the paper. When I heard the bedroom door shut, I slipped out. I just intended to say hello and be on my way, but it was quite a scene to behold. Everyone had gathered with their families and was eating—the office seemed fit to explode. There was a mood of merriment that I realized was buoyed not by hope but belief. Edward was right; they truly had believed they could vote socialism into office, but even with a million votes Gene had placed no better than a distant fourth. When the final announcement of Wilson's victory came across the wire, a silence took hold of the room. A few of the women, myself among them, began picking up plates. Pipes were lit, cups sipped, heads downcast at the floor, shaking. And then J.A. said, "We made great strides

*this year. Socialism may be inevitable, but it won't come easy.
We must work harder! We'll get them in '16." For the first time I
imagined what it must have been like to see him on the stump before
a crowd—the fierce power of a quiet man moved to passion. And
with that, the room started cheering. I continued to clean as people
left to return home. I thought perhaps J.A. might want to chat,
as had become our custom, but he just turned away, telling me to
thank Edward for letting him steal my services for the evening. He
hadn't meant this unkindly, I believe, smiling sadly as he spoke the
words, but how it hurt. I could see how disappointed he was by the
evening's outcome and yet it was only a mask of the true sadness
he felt. There was little one could do to ameliorate that burden, so I
returned home and stayed there for two days.*

*On the third day, November 10th, business required that Edward
spend a few hours at the office, though it was a Sunday. He was
always working too hard. I protested, but he took a certain pride in his
effort. In any case, I ventured over to J.A.'s with some extra helpings
I'd made for supper. His housekeeper had already prepared his meal
and gave me a cold eye at the door. But then I heard J.A.'s voice
call out from his study, asking who it was, and I answered him as I
stepped past her.*

*When I entered the study, I found him in his usual spot behind
his desk. He was playing solitaire and looked up, smiling beneath
his push-broom mustache. His mood had improved and we spoke for
a long time. Out of respect for the dead I'd rather keep the conversation as it was then: private. I'll say this, however. It was pleasant.
So pleasant, in fact, that I lost track of time. Before I knew it, three
hours had passed. I thought of Edward returning home from the office.
In my haste, I'd plumb forgot to leave him a note. When I said I
must leave, he looked surprised and asked me to stay for a final cup
of tea. I explained about my error with the note. "He'll have the
sheriff searching every county in Kansas for his dense wife," I said.
Again J.A. asked if I wouldn't stay a little longer. I turned to look*

at the grandfather clock in the corner and as I did so—this I recall
vividly—he placed his hand on mine. It startled me and I retracted
my hand. We stared at each other. He took off his glasses. How can I
explain that one small act such as removing a pair of glasses conveyed
more clearly his anguish than had he collapsed into tears right before
me if you never knew the man? He apologized. I said not to—he'd
only surprised me—but he shook his head and said two or three more
times that he was sorry. I thought of the late hour. Now we were sim-
ply staring at each other and both moved to speak at the same time.
He relented, allowing my voice to take priority—an inane attempt
at humor to lighten the mood. "We'll continue this discussion tomor-
row?" he asked. He put on his glasses and walked me to the door.
"Of course," I said. I looked back once as I hurried home, but J.A.
was no longer in the doorway.

That was the night. He'd been unconscious for some time before
the housekeeper found him upstairs on the floor of his bedroom. She
hadn't heard the noise because he'd wrapped the gun in bed sheets.
To recount it now still vexes my mood. They were such dear friends.
While it's fitting they were unable to continue on without each other,
their deaths, far too soon, were difficult to endure.

Ah, well. I've said enough. Good luck to you, Mr. Bronstein, as
you work to complete what has undoubtedly been a long journey for
you. I much look forward to reading your book.

Sincerely,
Jane

LETTER 10

7/8/1932

Dear Mr. Bronstein,

For weeks since your package arrived I have wondered how to re-
spond. It has been a trying time since we last corresponded. Edward's

health worsened unexpectedly, I'm sad to relate. He passed in January. I say this now because over the course of the past year I had come to think of you as something of a friend, or, at the very least, as a kindly presence in my life despite the fact that we'd never met. I have always tried to be honest with you in my recollections, and I wish you had returned the favor in kind.

To say the least, your "biography" is not what I expected. I was greatly disappointed to see the manner in which you conveyed Mr. Wayland's life and history, perhaps only because it was a history that I, for a short time, shared. Your accompanying note needn't have spelled out for me what is obvious to anyone from the first page. You say that our current economic situation "lays bare the inherent contradictions of capitalism and thus the inevitability of socialism" and I care little to quibble with you. I am not one for political arguments. But to turn J.A. into a martyr—a man dead twenty years, whose name is as familiar now as James Baird Weaver's—for the purposes of furthering your politics seems misguided, and not a little dishonest. You see opportunity in our shared misfortune, but what gives you the right to shape a man's life in any manner you see fit?

At times, paging through your book, I felt as though you'd never read my letters. Pearl merits a few paragraphs in three hundred pages? And what of the other women who worked at the _Appeal_? J.A. a paragon of socialist virtue? The truth of the matter is, J.A. was the best capitalist socialism ever produced. He may have said otherwise, but if you had spent time in his home you might question his commitment to overthrow a system in which he had so prospered. You place his death at the doorstep of Gene's defeat in '12. Perhaps. But had you looked into a man's eyes and seen his heart empty right before you, as I did that night he touched my hand and removed his glasses, you would know it was love, not politics, that killed him, no matter what his note said. He wasn't a victim of capitalism; he was a victim of grief, of love.

What is to be done to rectify this matter, Mr. Bronstein? I must say that for a time I considered legal recourse, but it is done and I am tired. You have used the past for the ends your present requires. The last year has been difficult and with Edward gone I wish only to weather the welter of our current troubles, so that we might come out intact on the other end. I ask only that you remove my name from your acknowledgments in any future printings. You used little of my input, and in any case I would prefer no association with your work.

Despite my objections, I wish you good luck. With Jewsevelt in office, you just might get your wish.

Sincerely,

Mrs. Edward Shaw

I WAS A REVOLUTIONARY

On the first day I tell them:

"When searching for the Seven Cities of Cibola, Coronado was so disappointed by what he found in the land that would one day become Kansas that he strangled the guide who'd brought him here and turned around."

No one laughs. Their blank stares communicate only this: It's the first day of class. Don't get cute. Hand out the syllabus and we'll see you on Tuesday. I ask them to find a partner, thinking I'll have them introduce one another to the group, but cave when I see their eyes roll, hear the groans from the back of the room. "Actually, let's start from here next time," I say, and pass out the syllabus. A modicum of relief enters the classroom as they pack their bags and leave, suctioned from their desks to the door as if by pneumatic tubing.

Afterward I head to the office I share with an emeritus professor who rarely comes around. I check e-mail and find my wife has written. We used to speak openly and directly. Now we e-mail, and hers arrive with all the formality of a communiqué. *Paul, I would like to get some more of my things this evening. Please leave the house from 7–8. —Linda.* Strange to think of her across campus, over in Sociology, composing this terse missive. Stranger still to think that when the divorce papers arrive, we could, if so inclined, settle the whole matter via intracampus mail.

I'm debating whether to reply when Brad, the chair of the History Department, pops in to say hello.

"Welcome back, partner. How was break?"

"Cold," I say.

He laughs and asks if my eleven thirty went okay.

Brad toes a fine line between administrator and concerned colleague, a fact that seems to color any conversation I have with him. I shouldn't complain; he's always been pretty good to me. When the university hired Linda, almost twenty-five years ago, he took me on as an instructor. I was all-but-dissertation with a focus on the post–Civil War period in the South, but those first several years I taught whatever they could scrounge up for me: general history surveys, even the occasional comp class. Brad had pushed me to teach a class on Kansas history, wanting me to be the department's "Kansas guy." And so I put aside my dissertation, telling Linda it was temporary, and educated myself as quickly as I could about a state I'd never given much thought. I understood, of course, that he hired me because the university wanted Linda, and, further, that without the dissertation I would never earn tenure. Even so, I've never forgotten his kindness.

"Are you going to watch the inauguration?" he says now. "Ever think you'd actually see this back in the sixties?"

"I teach Tuesday," I say, and turn back to my computer screen. I can feel him lingering there, the heavy breathing of a big man. "Well, I should let you get back to work," he says. "Say hello to Linda for me."

That night I walk downtown along Massachusetts Street while Linda loots our home. Lawrence is freezing, and everyone is inside watching the basketball game. I like having the streets to myself. Most of the stores have closed, but occasionally I stop to look in a window before I head to Louise's for a schooner of Boulevard Wheat. Surrounded by folks fixated on the game, I wonder how many still remember that our innocuously smiling mascot, an imaginary blue bird, got its name from the militant abolitionists, the Jayhawkers, who fought bloodily to make Kansas a free state. During a time-out the mascot runs around the court, entreating the crowd to clap to the beat of the band's brassy pomp. I watch the game clock, imagining Linda moving quietly through our house alone, taking things. When the game ends, I pay my tab and walk home in the cold January night.

By the time I arrive, she's gone. She left the day after New Year's, informing me when she came downstairs with matching blue luggage as I dozed through the final minutes of a bowl game blowout. She said if she didn't do it that second, she'd lose her nerve, and before I could even rise she was turning the doorknob. She says it's too difficult to see me, that we need some time apart to get used to the separation. So far I have respected her wishes, resisting the fleeting temptation to stop by her office unannounced, or, in my lowest moments, to sneak over and watch her teach from the hallway. I haven't made much of a fuss because I realized soon after she walked out the door that it was the right thing. Despite this, the last time I called her I made a halfhearted attempt to reconcile. When she resisted, I pressed her. "I'm not going to lie in bed next to someone who doesn't love me anymore," she said. "The amazing thing is that *you* could. You could do that, Paul, and you'd never say a word." I was hurt and started to yell, but Linda cut me off—"This is why I don't want to talk"—and hung up. And though I know she's right—we haven't been in love for a long time—it's hard to watch her undo a life together we spent nearly forty years creating. It's awful, these nights she asks me to leave the house. Her incremental disappearance from my world. Each time I return home and walk slowly from room to room, opening drawers and closets, trying to find what she's taken, trying to sense what she's touched.

•   •   •

We talk Louisiana Purchase and Kansas Territory. We talk about Andrew Jackson and Indian Removal. We talk about the Kansas-Nebraska Act of 1854, which left the question of whether Kansas would be a free state or slave state to be decided by its inhabitants. We talk about the New England Immigrant Aid Society shipping abolitionist and profit-seeking easterners to Kansas—how they settled in and established this town, named after their founder Amos Adams Lawrence. We cover Kansas becoming the thirty-fourth star on the flag. We talk Border War and Bleeding Kansas. John Brown and Jim Lane, Quantrill and George Todd. Do they know Quantrill led a raid on Lawrence in 1863, that he and his men rode right down Massachusetts Street and murdered some hundred and fifty unarmed men and boys? Some do. We unpack terms like *Jayhawker* and *border ruffian*. We learn about Clarina Nichols and the failed attempts to gain voting rights for women and blacks. We talk broken treaties, Indian resettlement, and the Dog Soldiers who fought back against white aggression.

Through the first few weeks, the class is slow to come together. They yawn and rub their eyes, nurse their hangovers. They text-message and I pretend not to notice, but it eats at me. It's tough to fail at the one thing you believe you do well, the thing you've come to depend upon. I want them to be as fascinated by the history as I was all those years ago in the library when I should have been doing research for my dissertation on the limits of Radical Reconstruction of the South but was unable to pull my nose out of a volume on Kansas. But they seem largely uninterested. Finally, I ask, "Why did you take this class?" My tone betrays my frustration, and they look alarmed, sitting up a little. There are mutterings of "For my major." No one says it, but I'm afraid a reputation as an easy grader has preceded me. Then a girl in row two says, "Because I'm from here." Truth be told, my memory is poor and I still haven't learned names, but she has stood out as one of the few willing contributors and attentive listeners. "That's a good reason to care," I say. "The history of one's home matters. We should understand where we come from, the legacies we inherit." The thing they need to understand, I tell them, is that the history of a state, like anything, is a history of change. What makes Kansas interesting is that here these changes tend toward social and political extremes. I soapbox like this for another minute, ending emphatically with: "Kansas is and always was a radical state!" I'm staring hard, half expecting the class to rise slowly from their chairs one by one and slow-clap my *Stand and Deliver* moment. But of course they just sit there. There is some nodding of heads, a few grins and smiles at the old prof getting animated. I tell them they can leave early.

A few days later, the girl in row two approaches me after class. Lauren, I've learned her name. She is petite, with a short black bob that accentuates the pallor of her skin. She's holding a book against her chest as she approaches and without a word flips it around. The book's cover announces it as an exposé of the most "dangerous" professors in the country, academics who indoctrinate students with anti-American values. She opens to a spot she has bookmarked near the back. Side-by-side pictures: one, a mug shot from 1968, and the other, a recent photo from the department website. Underneath is a list of "crimes and exploits."

I look away from the book and meet her stare, but she says nothing. There is a long moment of silence that seems to confuse the nature of this encounter.

"Do you want me to sign it?" I say.

"It's why I took your class," she says.

"There are a few things you should know about that book."

"I think what you all did was brave."

"I wasn't that much a part of it."

"Sure seems like it," she says, looking at the book.

I'm trying to think of how best to respond and can only offer: "That was a long time ago." I excuse myself to head to a meeting but turn back to her. "I would appreciate if you didn't go around showing that to everyone."

The book isn't a surprise. Brad approached me about it early in the fall semester. He's familiar with my past and it's never been an issue. This was a matter of PR. "We've had some calls," he said, scratching at his bald head. "From parents and groups. With all the Ayers stuff in the campaign . . . they're concerned about students taking your class."

"You make it sound like I'm a pedophile."

"You know I think you're a great teacher, Paul," he said, placing a hand on my shoulder. "We wouldn't have renewed your appointment all these years if you weren't." He took his hand away, but the weight of his implied threat remained. Brad is big in ways I am not: he's tall and thick, and I'm short and lean. I ran my hands through my thinning hair, sighing, and said from rote: "Like thousands of others who are today valued and contributing members of society, I protested the war and went to jail for it." As I finished saying this, however, I opened the book and read my entry for the first time. "Half of this is bullshit," I said suddenly. "I wasn't involved in any of the bombings."

Brad removed a pair of glasses from the breast pocket of his oxford, rereading the passage. "Technically he doesn't say you perpetrated any of them."

"He sure as hell implies it! Christ, I mean, I wasn't even underground. Linda and I left before everyone disappeared."

"You've been very honest with me about your involvement," he said, closing the book and removing his glasses. What hung in the air between us was the obvious: truth, and its airy abstractions, carried less weight than the physical existence of the book. We thought it would die down, but in the final month of the campaign things got worse. The calls and letters continued, people demanding the university fire a "domestic terrorist." I was really worried for a while. Without tenure, I knew, I was vulnerable. They could have easily let me go, but Brad went to bat for me, attesting to my years of excellent teaching. He dropped my spring semester teaching load from my usual three classes to one. "Just till all the election fuss blows over. By next fall it won't be an issue." For a time I considered legal recourse of some sort, but when I talked it over with Linda she said it wouldn't do any good. "This has nothing to do with you. This is about people who believe we're going to have a black Muslim socialist as president." We were drinking Pinot as we stood at the island in our recently remodeled kitchen. After a moment of silence, she said, "A girl can dream, can't she?" and we both laughed.

We talk about post–Civil War growth and the Industrial Revolution. We talk about railroads and unregulated monopolies. We talk about exodusters and Pap Singleton's black colonies in Hodgeman County. We look at then-and-now photographs of Nicodemus, the oldest, still-surviving, all-black town west of the Mississippi. We discuss the People's Party and the achievements of the Populists. We cover the Legislative War and the first female elected to political office in the country, Susanna Salter, mayor of Argonia. We look at the devastation of tribes confined to reservations. We talk prohibition and Carrie Nation raiding bars, smashing whiskey bottles. We talk Progressive Era. We decode the political and social commentary in the strange concrete sculptures of S. P. Dinsmoor's Garden of Eden. Do they know that *Appeal to Reason*, the largest-circulated radical newspaper in the country, was published in Girard, Kansas?

They do not. We discuss the granting of suffrage eight years
before the federal government passed the amendment. We talk
strikes and oil fields, the IWW and WWI.

One Thursday, at the end of class, as everyone is shoving note-
books into their backpacks, Lauren stands and announces that
there will be a war protest the following Tuesday near the
union. "You all should come," she says to her classmates. "It's
important we make our voices heard." Everyone looks at me.
The class has started to turn a corner since my outburst. They
engage more readily, the discussion is more lively. I repeat the
homework assignment and tell them to have a good day.

After the others leave, Lauren says, "What'd you do that
for?"

I ask her to come to my office. We walk down the hallway
in silence, but when I shut the door it comes out unbidden. I
tell her about dropping out and moving from Boulder to Chicago to join the collective. I tell her about the Days of Rage
and trying to organize revolutionary working-class youth. I
tell her about false IDs and training ourselves to fight. I tell her
about getting beaten by police and jailed.

"What's the point?" she asks.

"I'm trying to explain why I couldn't just say 'extra credit
for anyone who goes to the protest.'"

"Doesn't mean you have to pretend you're someone you're
not," she says.

I try to explain about being a spousal hire and the uneasy
state of my employment after the attention from the book. "It's
why they gave me only one class this semester." To everything
she asks why, and I try to rationalize and explain until all I can
see in her expression is disappointment, the slight accusation of
cowardice.

Next class, I arrive to find a flyer for the protest taped to the dry erase board of my room. Lauren doesn't show. I leave the handbill where it is, writing dates and names from the Kansas past around it. Finally, someone asks what it is. I take it down and read it aloud. They are silent. I set it on my desk and continue lecturing until our time is finished.

Afterward I walk to the union, where the rally is under way. There's a young black man standing on a stone bench. He's wearing a heavy peacoat and a black knit hat that keeps inching higher off his forehead because he's shaking from cold or anger. Suddenly he shouts: "We are at war, and we are the citizens of an empire. The crimes of our government are being committed in our names and we ain't gonna stand for it any longer!" He goes on another minute, and the crowd echoes back, chanting, "Not in our names." Then I see Lauren. Booming forth from the crowd, she joins the guy on the bench. She looks around, taking in the sizable gathering. She opens her mouth but hesitates. I think maybe the moment has gotten to her, but she steadies herself and begins reading the casualty figures—military and civilian, American and Iraqi—the Pentagon tries to keep secret. The crowd shouts its frozen approval, fists raised here and there. She is electric in her nervousness, gaining confidence with each response from the crowd. She tells us that on the count of three we will fall to the ground and lie silent for five minutes in recognition of the war dead.

I'm standing on the periphery with the other interlopers taking in the spectacle, but when she begins to count I move closer and lower myself to the snow-covered brick. Lying silently with the others, I look at the gray, sunless sky, and wonder what Linda's doing. We never went in for something as static as a die-in. We were always marching somewhere, or trying to occupy some building. Looking for confrontation. I think of the March on the Pentagon and trying to break the line of police and National Guardsmen. I see Linda spitting in a marshal's face and feel the old wounds from the clubs in my back when they countered. We were begging to be arrested, and when we finally were, cuffed and put on buses that took us to separate detention facilities, I thought of her then, too, as I stretched out on the holding-cell floor. I wanted only to pay my fine so that I could return to her. I feel no such desire now, just the curiosity of what it would take for her to dirty her winter coat here in the snow.

When the five minutes are over, we all rise and dust off our jackets. I hang around, watching Lauren talk to a group of people who have surrounded her. I look away when she glances in my direction, but turn back to find her smiling.

"You came," she says as she approaches.

"Of course."

The other speaker walks over and joins us. He's thinner than, and not as tall as, he looked standing on top of the bench. She introduces him, Kwame, and we shake hands.

"Lauren's told me about you," he says.

"Don't believe everything you hear."

The shortest month of the year, February won't end just to spite us. We're all runny noses and shivering, Lauren's fair skin almost translucent in the cold.

"What'd you think?" Kwame says, blowing into his hand. I tell them they're doing the right thing, that the pressure will build. He nods as he looks around. "What should we do now?" he asks. I start talking about how it's not just one rally, the commitment has to be sustained, that power concedes nothing without demand, and suddenly I'm twenty years old and standing on a Chicago street corner haranguing some poor guy on his way to work to stop slaving for the Man and come to a fucking meeting. "Nah, I know all that, man," says Kwame. "I just meant what should we do *now*? You wanna grab a drink or something?"

And so I follow them downtown to the Taproom. It's off campus, and we're the only people there, which I like. The bartender wears thick black glasses and a pearl-snap cowboy shirt over a white thermal. He's just opened. As we lean on the bar considering the various taps on draft, he turns and kneels, slowly flipping through a crate of LPs on the floor behind the extra liquor bottles. He picks one and sets the needle before finally turning to serve us. There's the old familiar crackle of stylus threading groove and then Dylan's strange country croon fills the bar as *Nashville Skyline* begins. We take our pints to a corner booth by the window and discuss school. They are studying poli-sci and thinking about grad programs. They don't say so, but I can tell Lauren and Kwame are together. The occasional touch on the other's arm as they work to articulate a point, the hopeful expectancy that undercuts the seriousness with which they look at one another.

"So, Lauren says you were in it deep back in the day," says Kwame.

"Sort of."

"Come on, man," he says, scanning over the empty bar. "What was it like?"

"What, the movement?"

"Being underground."

I think a long moment before responding and when I do I meet their eyes and say, "How do you *think*?"

When I say nothing else, it seems he might let it lie, but Kwame probes further: "What made you do it? How did you know you needed to go under?"

I tell him I knew the exact moment.

"I was in Chicago, walking past Fred Hampton's casket after the police assassinated him and Mark Clark."

"You knew them?" Kwame says.

"The Panthers' offices were close to ours. They used to

come over, sometimes to plan joint actions, and other times, just to fuck with us, they'd take stuff to test how truly anti-racist we were."

"Am I supposed to be impressed you hung out with Panthers or offended you calling brothers thieves?"

"I'm just answering your question, Kwame."

The look in his eyes betrays the edge in his voice. "Go on, then," he says. So I share some of the old stories, confiding how one of the last times I heard Fred speak he seemed to auger his own death: *I might be gone tomorrow. I might be in jail. But when I leave, remember the last words on my lips: I am a revolutionary.* "They killed him in December '69," I say. "By January we were moving underground."

The ease with which I relate this story is familiar. The Hampton-Clark murders had a big impact on Linda and me. Over the years they became part of our personal mythology, a way in which to understand our past and to account for what had become of us since. However, usually when I tell it—now and again it will come up at a cocktail party or university function—it's a cautionary tale meant to explain not why we went underground but why we left the movement altogether.

"Who's 'we'?" Lauren asks.

"My wife. We were there together." There's a pause as they nod, and then I ask: "How'd you two meet?" The look they exchange tells me my hunch was correct. I learn they had a public policy class last fall.

She says: "Even today people sometimes look confused when they see us walking together."

"It's all good, though," Kwame says, a cold smile on his face. "A black man's in the White House. It's like they say: We're 'post-racial' now, right?"

One night in early March, I receive an e-mail from Linda ask-

ing if I'll leave the house so she can gather more of her things.
With the first hints of spring in the air, I decide to walk downtown. As I pass an Italian restaurant we used to go to on special occasions, however, I catch sight of her out of the corner
of my eye, having dinner with a man. I haven't seen her since
she left the house after New Year's and can only stare. She's
straightened the curl of her long black hair, and she's wearing
an outfit I can't recall. I don't recognize the guy. They're eating
and smiling, and then she turns away from him and looks out
the window near where I'm standing. Instinctively, I raise my
hand, meaning, *Why aren't you at the house like you said you'd be?*
and *Who's this asshole you're having dinner with?* But she doesn't
acknowledge me. She turns her attention back to the man and
raises her fork to her mouth. I leave, heading home, thinking
maybe she didn't see me after all. Must have been one of those
tricks of the light where, inside the illuminated restaurant, she
couldn't see anything outside in the dark.

We talk about the pressure to move from agriculture to indus-
try. We talk about the development of the urban centers of the
state. We discuss John Brinkley, the Goat Gland Doctor, who
injected goat glands into men to improve virility. We mar-
vel at how he manipulated early radio to nearly steal the 1930
gubernatorial race. We talk Depression and Dust Bowl. We
read excerpts from the *WPA Guide to 1930s Kansas* and look at
murals. We cover the war years, how Wichita doubled in population overnight after receiving bomber contracts from the
government, how German POWs were relocated to Kansas to
relieve the shortage of agricultural workers. We talk NAACP
and *Brown vs. Board of Education.* Do they know that the sit-
ins at Dockum's Drugstore in Wichita preceded the famous
Greensboro sit-ins by two years? They do not. The sixties get
their own unit, culminating here in Lawrence with the 1970

riots after police shot two students, one black and one white.

On the last day before spring break, Lauren stops by my office. She's been doing this more and more, sometimes to talk about class, but usually just to talk. She says she's going to D.C. for a rally on the Mall to bring the troops home. "Me and Kwame chartered a bus and we've been organizing people to come. It's almost full," she says. "You have any plans?"

"In this economy?" I say. "Thought I might stay home and listen to some fireside chats on the gramophone."

It feels nice to have developed a rapport with her, one of the small pleasures of teaching.

"You should come with us," she says, setting a hand on my arm, which is what I'm looking at when I hear Brad's loud voice from the hallway, asking if I have a second. "Sorry to interrupt," he says. "Didn't realize you were holding office hours."

"It's okay." I wave him in. "Lauren was just leaving."

She shoulders her bag and heads for the door. I wish her good luck in Washington.

"What's in Washington?" asks Brad affably. "Family?"

"A protest against the wars," she answers.

"Ah," he says, looking from Lauren to me and back again. After Lauren leaves, Brad closes the door and pulls a chair close like he's going to give me a real talking-to. He leans forward. "I heard about you and Linda."

"Oh, yeah," I say. "What'd you hear?"

"I bumped into her earlier today. She said you two were separated."

"Yeah."

We let that silence just hang there awkwardly for a few seconds.

"I'm sorry," he says, putting a big paw on my shoulder. "I wasn't aware. Are you doing okay?"

I tell him I'm fine, that we'd been growing apart for years. "Really," I say, "it's the best thing for both of us." He takes this in with a series of hurried nods. He seems to want to say more, but I tell him I need to go.

"I've been through it myself," he says. "I'm here for you if you want to talk."

When Linda left, it felt strange to have time to myself again. Between teaching and our life together, my attention was always directed by the concerns of one or the other. Since January it seems all I've had is time, and without marriage, teaching has rushed in to fill the void. And so over spring break I'm not on vacation or visiting family. I stay home and tinker with my syllabus and course schedule, reading a new book I want to incorporate into class next fall. The Friday before returning to school I get an e-mail from Lauren. For a brief second I misread the name, mistaking it for another please-leave-the-house note from Linda, and feel relieved when I realize the error. Lauren's message is brief. She says the D.C. trip fell through and asks if we can meet. I type: *Come by my office Monday.* My cursor hovers over SEND, then I delete and type: *Walk tomorrow?* giving her my home address and the time.

The following afternoon I'm grading papers when Lauren knocks, forty-five minutes late. She's wearing jeans and a red sweatshirt too big for her. Kwame's, I imagine. "Sorry, I lost track of time." I pull on my jacket and step onto the porch. A cold front has come through and a heavy gust of wind kicks up over the railing. She lowers the hood of the sweatshirt and says she needs to make a phone call before we head out. "Forgot my cell," she says. "Would you mind if I used your landline? It won't take a second."

"Of course," I say, pointing toward the kitchen. She takes the handset from the cradle on the wall, looking at me over her shoulder before dialing. I walk upstairs to my study to give her some privacy. A minute later she calls out my name and I tell her to come here. I've taken off my jacket and slung it over the back of my chair. Linda and I used to work here together, our desks at opposite walls, surrounded by bookshelves. But for a few stray paper clips, hers is cleared out and the bookshelves stand half full. The wooden stairs creak from Lauren's languid ascension. When she appears in the doorway, she's looking all around her like a thief casing the joint. "Last throes of winter out there," I say. "I thought we could talk here." She agrees. "So tell me what happened with Washington."

She explains that the donors who fronted most of the money pulled out two days before, an unforeseen result of the ongoing financial collapse. She's looking across the hallway where I've left the bedroom door open. I imagine what she's seeing. The built-in bookshelves we put in ten years ago that span an entire wall. The green leather ergonomic reading chair by the window imported from Sweden. The attached bath we added with a whirlpool and a dual-head standing shower. "Look at this place," she says, unzipping her sweatshirt. "This could be my parents' home."

I feel a rush of embarrassment, followed by anger and disgust. She's right. I'd often found myself wondering what the hell had become of us over the years. When we were young we'd believed in Karl Marx and permanent revolution but in middle age had come to find our faith in Martha Stewart and the permanent renovation of our home. It wasn't always this way. For a number of years after leaving the movement we were still active politically, but slowly, after returning to school, the concerns of the professional began to eclipse the political. We used to spend entire days knocking on doors, and now we write checks to progressive organizations and donate to Democracy Now! before dashing off to the university for a meeting.

"It was my wife," I say. "She wanted all of this."

"Your wife," Lauren says. She takes a step across the hallway to look farther into the bedroom, as if it were a diorama in a natural history museum. She leans against the door frame and I rise from my chair and move to stand behind her. "Where is she?" she says. "Ex-wife," I correct. I touch her shoulder and my hand moves to her nape and down her spine, but her sweatshirt is so baggy, I wonder if she feels anything. "She did this to you?" I say nothing. I follow her eye-line to the California king, where pillows we bought from a hotel while on vacation after claiming the best night of sleep of our lives are stacked neatly at the head of the bed. "Why'd you let her?" I take her hand. "You didn't have a say?" Then I lead her inside.

Afterward, we lie silent. I think maybe she's fallen asleep, but then she rolls away from me and asks, "Do you sleep with many of your students?"

"This is a first."

"Sure it is."

I feel defensive, then strangely flattered by the awful cliché. "And you and Kwame?"

"We have an open relationship."

She pulls on the red sweatshirt, zipping it up over her bare breasts, and drinks from a cup of water I set on the nightstand the previous evening. I tell her how when Linda and I lived in the collective everyone slept with each other and how much I hated it. She asks if that's where we met. I shake my head. "In school. SDS. We'd been active for a few years but dropped out when it felt like protesting wasn't enough."

She stands and the sweatshirt falls past her underwear, hanging mid-thigh.

"How'd you learn to make bombs?"

She looks out the window, glass at her chest.

"Don't get any ideas," I say.

"Oh, please." She turns, a cruel smile on her face. "Do you know how easy it would be to find out? I was just curious how a bunch of college dropouts became underground bomb-makers before the Internet."

"We weren't underground," I say. She has a bemused look on her face. "The book got a few things wrong." I'm explaining, watching the pale of her skin start to rouge, when she cuts me off.

"Were you planning on telling me this after you fucked me, or had it crossed your mind when you were holding court at the bar, talking Fred Hampton and bombs?"

"I did know him," I say. "And I never said anything about bombs."

"You said you'd been underground!"

Her body's tensed, ready to pounce on any answer I might give, when I hear a funny sound I can't quite place. She stoops to the floor, pulls her jeans from under the bed, and removes something from the back pocket. Her cell phone. "Thought you forgot it at home," I say. She looks at the screen, shaking her head. Quickly she pulls on her jeans—"You're a liar and a bad fuck"—and leaves.

In the following days I try to get hold of Lauren, but she has stopped coming to class and won't respond to my e-mails. When Brad calls me at home in mid-April, I'm sure she's gone to the administration, but he only asks how I'm doing with the separation. Often this is his way of priming you for taking on some extra duty—advising an additional thesis, letting a prospective student observe class, filling in for someone on sick leave—and I wish he would cut to the chase.

"We're getting divorced," I say.

"So you're not going to try and work it out," he says. "It's mutual, then?"

"This was my decision," I say, feeling resentful of his prying.

His response, a plaintive *hmm* hanging in the phone's static ethers, makes me furious. This could go on all night. I tell him I have papers to grade. "Hang on there a minute," he says. "I was just flipping through my calendar here and thought we could pick a time for a year-end lunch." Almost a decade ago Brad began the tradition of taking each member of the department out to lunch after finals, a nice gesture that allowed him to "check in," as he likes to say. We set up a time after my last class and I'm thankful to finally get off the phone.

How quickly a semester moves. I struggle to learn their names, and then I have them, and then our time together is over. I feel good that we rebounded from a rocky start. I take pride in what I feel is their genuine interest in the complexity of the state. In the final weeks we're almost at the present. We've covered the rise of cultural conservatism, the growing activism of the right over the last few decades. We've talked about the Summer of Mercy in 1991, when men and women chained themselves to fences outside clinics in Wichita and laid their children down before cars trying to enter the parking lot. We don't know it yet, but in a matter of weeks a member of an increasingly militant antiabortion movement will murder abortion doctor George Tiller in his own church. We've discussed the state Board of Ed banning Darwin from science curriculums. Do they know that it wasn't until 1986 that liquor by the drink was legalized, as well as other "sin amendments" like the lottery and wagering? They do not. We've looked at clips on YouTube of Topeka's own Fred Phelps protesting, with his followers, at the funerals of Iraq War dead, shouting at aggrieved families that their sons and daughters died because God is punishing us for homosexuality. We're reading *What's the Matter with Kansas?*

• • • •

At the last class, I walk the aisles slowly as I collect their final papers. Lauren's chair, a long time empty, has become the spot where a neighboring student places his backpack. I've checked with her other teachers and they report she hasn't been in class for weeks, but it's only when I e-mail Kwame that I find out where she is. *She's taking a break from school*, he writes. *Went to San Francisco to work for a single-payer group on healthcare reform.* I write back asking for more details but he doesn't respond.

When I meet Brad, he's already sitting at the table of the restaurant he suggested, the Italian place downtown where I saw Linda having dinner. "Fancy," I say, taking a seat across from him. Usually we just grab a burger at the union.

"It's the end of the semester," he says. "We should celebrate."

It's late afternoon and the restaurant is nearly empty in these dead hours between lunch and dinner. We reflect on the semester's classes, float plans for the summer. He tells me about his divorce and I listen politely, occasionally commiserating, though I realize my regret at having stayed in the relationship too long is no match for his pain at having been unable to save his. Our plates have been cleared and we're finishing our glasses of wine when he says, "There's something I need to tell you. Something difficult."

"It's only been an hour," I say. "Why cut to the chase now?"

He smiles, but it turns into a grimace. "This isn't easy for me." He looks down at the white tablecloth. "The administration has decided not to renew your teaching appointment."

"What?"

"I'm so sorry, Paul."

"You're serious? Why?"

"They—"

"Did Lauren come to you?"

"Who's Lauren?"

I look around the restaurant. People, like us, doing what they do in restaurants.

"Because I left Linda?"

"No, of course not."

"I'm a good teacher, Brad. You've read my evals."

"I know you are. That's why I'm sure you'll find a good spot at another school."

"I'm sixty-one and never finished my Ph.D.," I say. "*No* one is going to hire me."

He tells me he can make some calls, that he has friends at many colleges. I've had only one glass of wine, but I feel flushed, florid, as though I've had several carafes. Then I put it together. Of course. "This is because of the book."

A look of confusion comes across his face.

"You're scared of having me on staff."

"The book?" he says. "No, we're past that."

"Bullshit."

"The book's history, Paul."

"You're caving to their pressure because I was a revolution-ary."

"Revolutionary? I defended you, remember," he says, exas-perated. He puts his elbows on the table. "Look, I know this is a shock, but this isn't about the book or Linda. This is about the economy. The university is hemorrhaging money—they're trying to figure out how to keep the people they have to pay." He says things like "tuition spike," "massive cuts," "furlough days," but I barely take it in, dazed.

"What about my classes?" I finally say. "Who's going to teach them?"

"Someone with tenure, most likely."

"Who?" I say. "You?"

"Maybe," he says. "I don't know." He leans back in his chair. "Honestly, I'm not sure whether the Kansas course will survive. They want a more global, international focus. They're talking about restructuring the major, combining departments even. It's a real shitstorm." He shrugs. "We have no idea what's going to happen." I'm trying to imagine which is worse, the thought of Brad teaching my class or the idea that it won't be offered at all. All that history, forgotten again. And then I'm standing. And then I'm walking away from the table.

A few weeks into summer vacation Linda asks me to leave the house a final time while she gets the last of her stuff. I e-mail back, saying I will, but I don't. I wait in the study, updating my CV for the first time in years. When I hear the keys in the lock and the groan of the front door, I don't say anything. I listen to the pop of her heels on the wood floor, the rustle of her turning over mail that still comes in her name that I collect in a pile on the kitchen table. Then she's coming upstairs. She goes to the bedroom and I hear her rummage through the closet, the sound of hangers sliding over the metal rod. As she leaves the bedroom, she glances toward the study—"Jesus, you scared me!"—and drops an armful of clothes to the floor. "What the hell are you doing here, Paul?"

"I wanted to see you."

She looks down at the pile of brightly colored summer dresses and skirts. She's wearing jeans and a T-shirt, the way she used to on the weekends when we'd run our errands or spend a few hours knocking around the yard. "You're not supposed to be here. You said you wouldn't." I tell her I didn't mean to scare her, that I was just enjoying the sounds of her being in the house again. The curl in her hair has returned and she's pulled it back in a ponytail. Though Linda's only a year younger than me, she's always looked youthful, and now I'd wager she could pass for late forties. She squints, sharpening the pierce of her brown eyes. "This is exactly why I didn't want you here. We're not getting back together, Paul."

"I know that. I don't want to," I say. "Just talk to me a minute."

She comes into the study with a huff—"One minute"—and leans against her old desk. I used to love working here together, our fingers hammering at our keyboards in a seductive kind of call-and-response. I swivel slowly back and forth in my big chair, staring at the gaps in my book collection, the parts of the alphabet she has boxed somewhere in storage. I point at *Reform or Revolution*. "Remember when I bought that for you, the Luxemburg?" She turns and picks it off the shelf. The spine is heavily creased, like it might break if someone so much as coughed near it. I bought it for her in a used bookstore in Boulder, and the previous owner's ink ran blue all over the margins. She flips through the pages, smiling. "Poor Rosa."

"You forgot to take it."

"You keep it," she says. "I remember well enough."

"Do you?"

"You want to quiz me about the dialectic of spontaneity and organization?" She closes the book but doesn't put it back on the shelf. She holds it in her hand as if maybe she will take it with her after all. She looks at her wrist, but she's not wearing a watch. "I told you I didn't want to do this. I want a clean break."

"There's no such thing. We have a history."

"What do you want from me?"

"Who is he?"

"Who?"

"The guy you're seeing. I saw you having dinner together. That night you said you were coming here but didn't."

She thinks a long moment, trying, I imagine, to conjure

that winter night. "Richard? I'm not seeing him," she says. "He was interviewing for a position."

"There's a hiring freeze," I say.

"He's taking my place," she says quickly.

"What are you talking about?"

She gathers herself and says: "I was going to tell you. I just . . . I was offered a job in New York. At Columbia. I'm taking it."

"You're leaving the university? You're leaving Kansas?"

"I couldn't turn it down, you know that. Ivy League, Paul," she says, smiling now, as if expecting me to congratulate her. "Besides, I need a new start."

I sit there, silent, trying to imagine her strolling along Broadway instead of Massachusetts Street. Impossible. When I finally respond, I don't tell her not to leave or that I've been let go by the university. When I speak, I describe everything I remember from the day we filed past Fred Hampton's coffin in Chicago. I ask if she remembers.

"Of course," she says. "That's when we left."

"What happened to us?"

"What do you mean?" she says. "We grew apart."

"No, what *happened* to us."

"We grew up." She raises the book, its red cover showing a picture of Luxemburg. "Is this what you wanted? She was killed by reactionaries and dumped in a canal. We were training ourselves to shoot guns. The Panthers were storing bombs in the housing projects. What did we think was going to happen? You don't win an arms race against the Pentagon."

"Maybe I wouldn't have gone underground, maybe I wouldn't have set bombs—"

"Do you actually wish you had?"

"—but I never would have ended up like this if it weren't for you."

She pushes herself off the desk, looming large above me in the chair.

"You're fooling yourself. Even then you didn't have it in you. You want to know why we didn't go underground? Why we lived in this house? Because you wanted this too, you just didn't have the guts to take responsibility for making it happen."

"That's not true."

"You let me be your excuse to leave the movement, just as you let me getting hired here be your excuse to not finish your dissertation. You've used me to not be accountable for decisions you couldn't make and now you're blaming me for it."

"You're wrong, Linda."

"You couldn't even leave me when you were miserable."

"I would have."

"Because you're a coward."

"I am not."

"You're craven and you always were."

It's the small laugh after she says this that sends me out of the chair, my hand reaching back as I rise. The force of the slap sends her to a crouch, holding her face. I'm saying her name, touching her shoulder—"Linda, are you okay? Linda, I'm so sorry"—when she springs from the floor, her arm flailing wildly. The book strikes me across the side of the head and sends me backward a few steps. We are looking at each other, silent, stunned, and below us the book lies open on the floor, pages sticking out ajar, half torn from the binding.

ACKNOWLEDGMENTS

Over the course of nine years working on this book, I've amassed a Tolstoyan-length catalogue of debts to people and institutions that deserve to be thanked, and this is just a fraction of that roll.

First and foremost, thank you to my family, which I mean in the broadest sense of the word, without whom I'd simply be lost and lonesome.

Thank you to the Iowa Writers' Workshop, the Wisconsin Institute of Creative Writing, and the Steinbeck Center at San Jose State University, all of which supported this project in its colicky infancy.

I'm supremely grateful to the Corporation of Yaddo, the Lighthouse Works Foundation, the Joshua Tree Highlands Artist Residency, the Sewanee Writers' Conference, and the Jentel Artist Residency Program for giving me time and support and community. I am particularly indebted to the Lannan Foundation, which gave me a long residency in Marfa, Texas, at a moment of acute pecuniary and existential distress.

Thank you to my agent, Renée Zuckerbrot, who told me that if I never wrote another book she wanted to represent this one and worked indefatigably to ensure a short story collection about radical Kansans found a nice home.

Thank you to my incredible editor, Cal Morgan, who is always right but gracious and kind enough to engage in patient, thoughtful debate so that I can come to that realization myself. Thank you to everyone on the HarperCollins team, who worked so hard to bring the best possible version of this book into the world.

I am very grateful to the editors and magazines where some of these stories first appeared: Michael Ray at *Zoetrope*, David Daley at *FiveChapters*, Travis Kurowski at Story, Adeena Reitberger at *American Short Fiction*, Jodee Stanley at *Ninth Letter*, as well as Jon Parrish Peede and W. Ralph Eubanks at *VQR*.

Thank you to friends who read excerpts of this book and who were willing to engage in protracted discussions about it over the years: Hendree Milward, Harriet Clark, Kevin Gonzalez, Nate Brown, Kathleen Sachs, Monika Gehlawat, and Charles Sumner. I am particularly grateful to Ted Thompson and Stuart Nadler, who read the insane Ur-version of this collection and lived to tell the tale (and found ways to help me fix it). Thanks to Chris Brunt for the careful read of "A Defense of History" at a crucial juncture. Thanks to Marilynne Robinson for eviscerating the very first draft of "The Burning of Lawrence" and urging me to give my characters the dignity of human complexity. Thanks to Tim O'Brien for walking me line by line through "I Was a Revolutionary" and reminding me that fiction is for getting at the truth when truth isn't sufficient for the task.

I would like to thank C. Dale and Janet D. Shearer for their generous financial support in helping me to obtain the images contained in the story "A Defense of History." And thank you to the various sources of those images: the *New York Times*, the Kansas State Historical Society, the Nebraska State Historical Society, Wikipedia, and the Library of Congress.

Thank you to the many historians whose sedulous work over the last 150 years informed and inspired the fiction of this book.

I would like to thank Eric Tribunella and the faculty, staff, and students in the English Department at the University of Southern Mississippi, in particular my colleagues in the Center for Writers at USM: Steven Barthelme, Angela Ball, Monika Gehlawat, and Rebecca Morgan Frank, as well as my editorial teams at *Mississippi Review*, currently the wonderfully dynamic duo of Allison Campbell and Caleb Tankersley.

And lastly, thank you, Kansas, for all that is beautiful and ugly in your complex history. Your nobler instincts inspire me.

A CONVERSATION WITH BEN GREENMAN

Ben Greenman is the author of The Slippage, *along with multiple works of short fiction. Greenman and Andrew Malan Milward discussed the stories in* I Was a Revolutionary *in the spring of 2016.*

BEN GREENMAN: Let's start at the beginning, or near it. How did you pick your epigraphs?

ANDREW MALAN MILWARD: Marilynne Robinson is a writing hero of mine, and I was fortunate to study with her in graduate school. *Gilead* came out the year before I attended the Iowa Writers' Workshop, and I was reading it in a hotel room in Madrid while on my way to Serbia for my brother's wedding when I came across that line. I underlined the hell out of it and knew then that I would use it for an epigraph in a book, though I had no idea what that book would be. But it always stuck with me, and as *I Was a Revolutionary* took shape it seemed like a great preface to the book. Most people don't think much about Kansas, don't realize that amazing things have occurred there. I love that her quote acknowledges that as well as the effort it takes to remember.

The Trotsky quote came much later in the process when the book was in varying states of doneness. I was on residency at

Yaddo doing my laundry and reading *Literature and Revolution* when I came across this line, and it made me laugh. There's much I admire about Trotsky (and some I don't), but if "punishment follows immediately upon the crime" of playing with history—something I'm doing throughout this book—then I suspect I'd be trying to make a go of it in the gulags if Trotsky had his way.

GREENMAN: Your stories look frequently at the relationship between the present and the past. How do you see that relationship, in the main? How does the past inform the present?

MILWARD: The past can help to inform the present, and it should, but too often it's not allowed to. It's true that we are a forgetful people by and large. Some of this is the natural result of living in a period of human history where the speed of life and the filtering of information is so fast as to have no analogue. But some of this is highly conscious and carried out by agents of amnesia who don't want us to remember. Whether it's school boards in Texas and Arizona rewriting history books to exclude the contributions and struggles of nonwhite peoples or political leaders who roll out the same boilerplate justifications for another disastrous war or financial leaders who are willing to destroy our economy the way they did in 2008 for personal gain—these are all examples of sectors of concentrated power that don't want the population to remember so they can advance their agendas because it usually comes at the expense of the population. That's why to remember is a profoundly moral act.

GREENMAN: People talk about "historical fiction" as something that's discrete and identifiable, but isn't all history fiction to some degree? Feel free to reject this notion entirely.

MILWARD: Yeah, I think that's true. One of my biggest influences is E. L. Doctorow—I learned so much from him in terms of how to engage history and politics in fiction—and I remember him once saying in an interview that all history is composed and usually for the needs of the present. I think that's one of the meta-conversations going on in *I Was a Revolutionary*. It's not just about dropping the reader into certain historical moments they might not be aware of—a lot of the stories are interested in how history comes to be written, why, and to what end.

GREENMAN: You've visited Kansas before in fiction—in fact, you've visited it in short fiction. How was the trip different this time around?

MILWARD: This was a very different experience from writing the stories in my first book, *The Agriculture Hall of Fame*. For one, given the historical aspect, this one required much more research. So the stories just took a lot longer to write, whereas the stories in the first book came a little quicker since they were mostly looking at contemporary issues and life in Kansas. In *The Agriculture Hall of Fame* I was writing about a Kansas I both knew well and one I didn't know well at all. I grew up in Lawrence, a progressive oasis in an otherwise pretty conservative and rural state. I wanted to understand the parts of the state that were less familiar. With this book, however, I wanted to understand the legacies, good and bad, we inherit when we say we are from somewhere, and perhaps how those concerns speak to the present. So the books had different ambitions for me personally.

GREENMAN: What was the first throb of this collection?

MILWARD: The first throb was Quantrill's Raid. As I said, I grew up in Lawrence, and you can't live there and not feel the lingering presence of the Raid, even more than 150 years later. I wanted to write a story that somehow captured this horrific event that happened in my hometown so long ago. At the time I had never written anything that engaged history. When I put that very different ur-draft of "The Burning of Lawrence" up for discussion in Marilynne Robinson's workshop my first semester in grad school, I half expected her and my classmates to rise slowly from their seats and give me the slow clap, pronouncing the story an un-workshoppable masterpiece. Of course, I had the exact opposite experience, which was difficult at the time but really helped me grow as a writer. Marilynne was trying to show me that I was writing about historical events in a glib and careless manner, and that I needed to give my characters the dignity of human complexity. It took a while to learn these lessons, but eventually I did and was able to reenter the piece and tell a story I really needed to tell.

GREENMAN: What was the last piece completed?

MILWARD: "The Americanist." For years I'd been working on a story about the Goat Gland Doctor, and it just kept getting longer and longer. By the time it grew to 150 pages it was just too big and unwieldy to cram into a story collection that already had a long story like "O Death" in it. So I took it out, which pained me because given the book's overt interests in politics and radical Kansas history it felt like a crime not to include Dr. Brinkley. At the same time, I was also feeling anxious that I hadn't found a way to capture the rise of the militant antiabortion movement in Wichita and the assassination of George Tiller, so I tried to find characters and create a narrative that could touch on both of those things. It seems like a strange pairing on the surface, but I'm pleased with the way it turned out. It was the last story I wrote for the book, and it started as a desperate last-ditch attempt to find any way to get the Goat Gland Doctor into the collection.

GREENMAN: As you moved through the collection, writing, rethinking, revising, how many times did it change shape?

MILWARD: That particular story changed shape a lot. Early and middle versions were very metafictional, which I would tone down and then ultimately remove entirely.

GREENMAN: If you had to pick one moment that gave you fits, which would it be?

MILWARD: After the book had been accepted there were edits that needed to be made, of course. Most were manageable, but the one that induced fits of hair-pulling was the revision of "A Defense of History," which was a substantial revision. It's a complicated story structurally, and my editor Cal Morgan, and I had many conversations about how to make it work more effectively. Eventually we were able to do that, but there were definitely several moments of defeat along the way when I thought I just didn't know how to make this work.

GREENMAN: Cal has edited me, too. How important is it to have a great editor like that? I ask having obtained the same benefits. But I guess it's a broader question, too: how do you deal with adjustment/criticism/revision, whether internal or external?

MILWARD: Cal was a gift from a benevolent god. Absolutely. Even if he knew he was right (and he pretty much always was) he would take the time to engage with me on issues I was having. He's the perfect editor: not only brilliant but also good-hearted and patient. But I should say too that before the book ever went out I had some writer friends read it and give me feedback as well as my agent, Renee Zuckerbrot, who used to be an editor at Doubleday and has a sharp eye and sense for how fiction works. She was so helpful, and I feel spoiled to have an agent who can work with me to edit my books before they ever go out to editors at publishing houses. As far as how I deal with criticism, sometimes poorly, sometimes pretty well. On rare occasions I'll become a petulant child who doesn't want to eat his vegetables. But I like to think that most of the time I'm pretty good at taking advice and criticism with an open mind. Anyone who's reading my unfinished work at this point in my career is someone I trust and whose feedback, good and bad, is coming from a place of kindness and love, so I try to be open to it all and then use what's useful to me. Sometimes I dig my heels in on things, but often I think, Oh, I see what you're saying.

GREENMAN: Is there one particular sentence or passage that warms your heart every time you think of it?

MILWARD: I think the last paragraph of "The Burning of Lawrence" continues to please me, particularly the flourish of metaphor in the final sentence, which describes the rising sun as "a blister, a blemish, a birthmark." Not only was it pleasing rhythmically and lyrically, but also the birthmark image felt like the right way to end a story that was so much about the birth of this complicated state.

GREENMAN: What is your writing method? Do you use a desk? A laptop? Longhand with a quill pen? Dictation into the ear trumpet of an aged stenographer?

MILWARD: I'm a big routine person. It helps me make sense of time and deal with what can feel overwhelming about it. So on weekdays I like to get up around five or six in the morning and read for two hours and then write for four hours at home on a desktop computer before going to the gym to work out and remember that I have a body. Afternoons, evenings, and weekends are for my teaching and editing work. Oh, and life stuff in general. Some days are better than others, but that routine keeps me pretty productive and functional.

GREENMAN: You mentioned earlier that this book was highly research intensive. How did that affect the pace of composition? It took nearly a decade, right?

MILWARD: I'm not a slow writer, but what made this take a long time was just the amount of research required to write about some of these people and events. I had to do a lot of preparatory work before I could put pen to paper. And research can kind of become addictive too, both because it's really interesting and because it's a great way to feel productive without having to do the really hard work of actually writing. One of my challenges while working on the book was to figure out when I had done enough research to be able to write responsibly about something and when was I using research to procrastinate writing. I got better the longer I worked on the book, but still, damn, nine years . . .

GREENMAN: You're doing lots of shape-shifting as a writer, which is always tricky, but also liberating. Which story required the greatest displacement from self?

MILWARD: One of my goals for the book was to write about a wide range of vastly different characters, and that meant writing from the perspectives of people who've had vastly different experiences than me, whether due to material conditions and temporal distance or factors such as race, gender, sexuality, or class. And yes, this was incredibly challenging, and at times it made me very uncomfortable. And I think it should, though that can't be a reason not to try. After all, that's what fiction is about, and it's one of the civilizing effects of literature that it challenges us to make empathic leaps as writers and readers. So to answer your question more directly, I found it all very challenging (and sometimes liberating as you say), but particularly the stories like "The Burning of Lawrence," "O Death," and "What Is to Be Done?" that were more historical, simply because it was harder to imagine my way into the experiential aspects of being a human being, whatever your race or gender, at a time so distant from my own.

GREENMAN: What other art form do you feel is closest to the way you write? Do you feel like a painter? A choreographer? A stand-up comedian? A set designer? A photographer? None? All?

MILWARD: It may sound strange but basketball, which I definitely consider an art form. I grew up loving the game, played for a time in college, and am still obsessed by it. I didn't realize it for a long time, but I think in some ways the experience of writing and playing basketball are very similar. Both require a tremendous amount of discipline and practice, as well as a real sense of preparedness and mindfulness. And yet, in both activities the hope is that at a certain point in the process the improvisational creativity that can't be planned for ahead of time—the Zone in basketball, the Muse in writing—takes over and allows for beautiful and amazing things to happen. I think part of the magic of both playing basketball and writing well involves negotiating these vacillations of types of consciousness.

GREENMAN: Why are people in the book world obsessed with the notion of the novel? Aren't stories better in every measurable way?

MILWARD: Man, I was hoping you could tell me. Yes, I love stories. What bothers me more is the stupid but pervasive notion that story writing in somehow just apprentice work that writers do to learn the craft so they can write a novel. It's not that that's not true for some people, but as a general notion applied to everyone it's so condescending and wrong-headed. Stories can do something that novels can't, and that something is what Poe—who in addition to being a practitioner was also perhaps the earliest theorist of short stories—called "the unity of effect." What he meant by that is that because of their compression and intensity, in addition to the fact that they can be read in a single sitting, stories can make a stronger impression on a reader than a novel, which the reader needs to put down from time to time when life interrupts. You can escape the novel's grasp so much easier than the short story, which grabs you by the collar and stares you down. And think about it: does any sane person really want to make an argument that Borges, Munro, Carver, Saunders, and many others chose to write stories because they didn't know how to write novels?

GREENMAN: Is it true that you're expanding John Brinkley into a novel?

MILWARD: Good timing! Right after my impassioned defense of the story I'm now forced to admit that I am working on a novel—two of them actually. And yes, one of them is about the Goat Gland Doctor, but he's as tricky a fictional character to work with as he was a real human being. I'm plugging away. Some days he wins, some days I do. I should add that I do plan to continue to write stories as well.

GREENMAN: We are in a strange political year. (Maybe every year is a strange political year, but this seems like the rule that proves the rule.) How can fiction help to illuminate politics in ways that nonfiction cannot?

MILWARD: Yes, it's truly bizarre and pretty scary right now. It's the kind of year that John Brinkley helped pave the way for, whether Donald Trump knows it or not. In terms of your question, again I find myself thinking of E. L. Doctorow, who once wrote in an essay that "the fiction writer hopes to lie his way to a greater truth than is possible with factual reportage." The greater truth he's talking about, of course, is the truth of lived human experience. Nonfiction can give us the facts and figures that show what happened, while fiction can get at the human and heart truths that show us how things happened and why.

GREENMAN: People make, correctly or incorrectly, regional suppositions: Southern writer, New England writer. What's your briefest best-guess description of a Kansas writer? What are the materials in the soil, in the air, and in the history of the place that mix most profitably into fiction?

MILWARD: Boy, you got me there. I'm not sure. I haven't lived in Kansas for a long time, and I suspect in some sense I had to leave to be able to write about it, to have perspective on it. I doubt this is any different from every other writer who writes about a specific place, but I think having a certain amount of critical, if not physical, distance is essential so that we can take a colder eye toward that place and see the good and the bad and hopefully try to capture that complexity.

GREENMAN: Name one place not in Kansas that you predict you will eventually set a book of fiction. Here are some options that may or may not apply: Oklahoma, Russia, the moon.

MILWARD: I'm not sure whether I'll ever have Kansas fully out of my system, but I am really interested to write about the states where I've been living most recently, Mississippi and Alabama. I'm in the early idea phase of a novel that takes place in both states. It'll be a while before I can work on it, but I'm excited to write about the places I've been calling home the last five years.

GREENMAN: We spoke about the diversity of character before. Now I want to address the diversity of narrative approach. One thing I like very much about this collection is the belief in various types of storytelling—or rather, the belief that various types of storytelling can exist comfortably under the same roof. What story was the greatest challenge narratively?

MILWARD: I appreciate that because that was important to me. I wanted to have stories that worked in familiar ways but also some that worked in less familiar ways. It's exciting to me as a reader when writers can pull that off. Probably the greatest challenge narratively was "A Defense of History" because I had to figure out a way to make the unusual form of the story be an extension of the content and not overwhelm or outshine the fictional narrative at play. In early versions of the story I failed to do that. In those drafts I let the amazing history of the Populists overshadow the Assistant's story. His story was just a way to get to the history of these radical farmers who so fascinated me. So I had to really work on it and make the Assistant's story line as important as the history he's researching.

GREENMAN: What risks frighten you more, thematic risks or stylistic risks?

MILWARD: Stylistic risks are always interesting and exciting to me, so I'd probably say thematic risks, though I don't think those really bother me either.

GREENMAN: When you are actively writing, do you read other authors, or do you find that you have to avoid them to hear your own writing voice?

MILWARD: No, I definitely read other writers when I'm writing. I know some people are afraid of being overly influenced in a way that affects how they write, but I don't worry about that. I find it helpful to hear other voices, both for inspiration and to have something for my own voice to push back against.

GREENMAN: When you're not actively writing, what kinds of things do you read? Poetry? Theatre? Fiction? Bazooka Joe?

MILWARD: I tend to have three books going at once. Usually there's a work of fiction and there's always a volume of poetry, which is the last thing I read before sitting down to write fiction. The third book is usually something nonfiction for research or self-edification. Sometimes it's historical, sometimes political or economic.

GREENMAN: Without looking, do you remember the last word in your book?

MILWARD: Definitely: binding. It's not a terribly sexy last word, but I love the last line as a whole and it feels like the right way to close the book (if you've read the line, you know what a bad pun I just made).

ABOUT THE AUTHOR

A native of Lawrence, Kansas, and a graduate of the Iowa Writers' Workshop, Andrew Malan Milward is the author of the story collection *The Agriculture Hall of Fame*, which was awarded the Juniper Prize in Fiction by the University of Massachusetts. He has served as the McCreight Fiction Fellow at the University of Wisconsin, a Steinbeck Fellow at San Jose State University, and has received fellowships and awards from the Lannan Foundation, Jentel, and Yaddo. He is an assistant professor of English at Auburn University where he also serves as the fiction editor of *Southern Humanities Review*.